The Unexpected War

The Unexpected War

A Hero's Legend

Jean-Pierre Breton

iUniverse, Inc.
Bloomington

The Unexpected War
A Hero's Legend

iUniverse books may be ordered through booksellers or by contacting:

iUniverse
1663 Liberty Drive
Bloomington, IN 47403
www.iuniverse.com
1-800-Authors (1-800-288-4677)

ISBN: 978-1-4620-7723-6 (sc)
ISBN: 978-1-4620-7724-3 (hc)
ISBN: 978-1-4620-7725-0 (e)

Library of Congress Control Number: 2011962706

Printed in the United States of America

iUniverse rev. date: 01/12/2012

Chapter 1

"Aunty 159, will you tell me a bedtime story?" the little girl asked, looking up at the young lab assistant.

"Sure, anything for you, 2-5," the young woman replied. She tousled the child's hair and then readjusted her own long white lab coat, which had slipped off her shoulder.

2-5 smiled, looking around as they walked down the dimly lit hall. "Aunty 159, how come I have my own room?" she asked curiously as she glanced through window after window at young human boys and young fiend girls.

Both species were segregated into their own sealed-off white rooms in groups of five or six. Before 159 could answer, she felt a tug on her arm as 2-5 came to an abrupt halt. The child knelt down and stared through one of the windows at a young fiend. It walked over to her, placing its tiny paw against the window and tilting its head curiously. 2-5 smiled warmly, placing her hand against the window where the fiend's paw was.

The fiend returned the smile, faintly revealing its tiny, razor-sharp teeth before letting out a muffled growl and scampering away to join a play-fight with its friends. 2-5 giggled to herself, watching the little girl fiends play-fighting with one another. Their black fur flew all over the place. 2-5 got back up to her feet, glancing over at 159, who was waiting patiently for her.

"You're very special, 2-5," the young woman said, taking the little girl's hand again as they walked down the narrow hall. The echo of their footsteps seemed to chase them.

After a moment of walking in silence, the pair stopped in front of a tightly sealed door with metal bars jutting across it, resembling a bank vault. 159 typed a code on the door, and then it opened, revealing 2-5's tidy white room. "Would you like a glass of milk before story time?" 159 asked.

The little girl nodded her head vigorously. 159 smiled and went over to the fridge in 2-5's room. She took out the milk and poured a glass for the little girl. 2-5 flopped sleepily onto her bed. 159 joined her a moment later, placing the glass of milk on 2-5's nightstand before tucking her in. She then sat at the foot of the young girl's bed.

"This story is about a human," 159 began. She paused for a moment to gather her thoughts. "He killed many people while defending his country, but the unexpected war between the two species became a conflict between two souls."

2-5 beamed up at 159, with her sparkly blue eyes radiating from the reflection of the white lighting overhead.

159 studied 2-5's fascinated expression as she stroked the young girl's hair. Then she closed her eyes and began to recite the story. …

Chapter 2

February 24, 2037

My name is Lance. I'm going to be killed in a couple of hours, if not a couple of days, and if God really hates me, a couple of weeks.

The world is not what it once was. It has been invaded by fiends, in the disguise of humans, slowly over the years, until there were so many here that it happened—the war started, and there was no longer any need for them to hide their presence from us. The world we once knew has been lost. Soon, the human race will be enslaved by their laws of Dracona.

I once was a sniper for the People's Liberation Force. My only crime was defending my country against the fiends, but I was to pay the ultimate sacrifice—death. Another soldier and I were awaiting our execution. I don't know why, but it felt good to know I wasn't going to die alone.

"Do you think we will feel it?" he whispered nervously to me.

I glanced over at him for a moment. I shrugged, not wanting to think about it. "What's your name, buddy?" I asked him. It was an attempt to take our minds off our fate by offering some idle conversation.

"Toby," he muttered, gloomily staring at the ground.

"I'm Lance," I told him with a firm nod.

He smiled, perking up a bit due to the idle conversation, while seeming to lose the feeling of defeat that had been gripping both of us for the past few hours. "How long have you been here?" he asked.

3

"About a week and a half. What about you?" I asked him.

"Only three days," he told me, picking up a pebble and tossing it at a flowerbed in boredom.

"Are you American?" I asked him, while amusing myself by fiddling with a small twig I had discovered beside me.

"I was born in America, but when we had that merge between the United States, Mexico, and Canada, forming us into one country, my parents decided to move here to Nova Scotia to flee from the fiends, thinking it was safer," Toby explained. The sun beat down on us, gaining strength, and the afternoon heat intensified.

"I guess you're just a plain old North American now," I muttered.

He laughed with a nod. "Were you ever in America, Lance?" Toby asked.

"Nope, I've been a Canadian my entire life," I told him, while adjusting the chain around my neck, which painfully bound me to the heavy iron gate I was sitting against.

Toby laughed, glancing over at me. "It's funny how even with that merge, we still think of ourselves as—" He was cut off by the abrupt sound of metal against metal.

I lifted my head, startled by the rattling of the main gate as it opened. Three fiends entered the courtyard and made their way toward us.

"Well, I made it to my seventeenth birthday. Didn't think I'd last that long," Toby muttered as the fiends reached us. They hauled us to our feet and placed us against a cement wall.

I stared, defeated, at the female fiend in the group. The one in the middle loaded his handgun. He was flanked on one side by his buddy, who steadily held his assault rifle aimed at our chests. The female looked away, avoiding my stare. That caught me by surprise; she actually looked ashamed as she came over to me. She tied a blindfold around my head, enveloping me in darkness. "Don't be afraid; it will be quick," she whispered in my ear.

Bang!

The sound sent a chill shivering down my spine. Then I heard the thwack of the bullet exiting the back of Toby's head, followed by the dull thud of his falling to the ground, and I could feel a lifeless hand dangling off the side of my foot. Tears began trickling down my face. I tried to hold them back; I wanted to die honorably for my country, but I couldn't stop myself from crying. The reality hit me that my short life was about to come to an end.

The two male fiends must have spotted my tears, because they began chuckling to one another, saying something in their foreign language. I then felt the cold barrel of the handgun carefully placed against my forehead. "Have a nice life in hell, filthy PLF," the fiend snickered.

Click.

I gasped. My knees buckling in fear, I fell to the ground. My eyes snapped shut, but the pain of the fall quickly made me realize I wasn't dead. I could hear the sound of two male fiends laughing in the background. One of them pistol-whipped me across the face, and the other fiend quickly joined in with a kick to the ribs. Both of them beat me like a piñata.

The female shouted at them; their foreign tongue sounded odd to my ears. The guards stopped and left me lying there in a pool of my blood. I felt the female slipping the blindfold off my face. I gingerly opened my eyes.

Everything was blurry. I could feel myself drifting off into unconsciousness as my gaze shifted to the two male fiends. They were dragging away Toby, the dead PLF soldier, leaving a bloody trail of bone fragments and ooze in his wake. The female fiend slapped my face. It wasn't a hard slap, though; it was only to help me regain consciousness. She crouched down, silently taking out a piece of bread and hand-feeding it to me in little pieces.

She then tilted my head and poured some water from her canteen into my mouth. After that, without a word, she got up and quickly jogged after the other two fiends. Her vanishing behind the main gate a moment later was the last thing I remembered before I blacked out.

I regained my consciousness sometime that night. I was still lying in a pool of my blood, which had dried on the ground. Painfully, I grabbed the side of the flower bed beside me, hauling myself up off the concrete courtyard and into the flower bed. I fell asleep a short time later. The next morning, I awoke abruptly as the gate creaked open, and three male fiends stormed in. They tied me to a flagpole in the middle of the courtyard, where they began to beat me senseless.

"*Information!*" the leader of the three screamed, giving me a sharp punch to the stomach.

"I know nothing," I muttered with a cough, spitting out a mouthful of blood onto the ground.

I realized immediately that was not the answer they were looking for. The leader's buddy came from behind him, striking me across the face with the butt of his rifle. "You talk when I tell you to talk," the leader ordered, pulling up a chair in front of me. He sat down and glared up at me. "My name is Commander Domelski, and I will be in charge of your interrogation for the remainder of your pitiful life." He pulled a package of cigarettes out of his pocket, placing one in his mouth. I eyed it longingly as we stared at each other in silence, sizing each other up. "You would like one, yes?" Domelski asked me with a smirk, nodding to the package of cigarettes in his lap.

"Smoking kills," I grunted, ripping my eyes away from him defiantly as he plucked the cigarette from his mouth, offering me a puff of it.

"So will not accepting the commander's gift, you filthy dog," one of his men grunted, giving me a hard punch to my ribs—I felt them crack.

Domelski raised his hand to the soldier, who obediently stepped aside as his leader got up. He placed the cigarette in my mouth, while looking me over carefully before returning to his seat. "I apologize for my men's aggression. They do not realize that we and the humans are similar to one another. We may be from different planets, but that doesn't mean that we can't share this one, does it?" he asked me thoughtfully as we stared at one another.

I remained silent, and he snapped, jumping to his feet, grabbing my neck, and staring into my eyes as his own darkened a bloodshot red. "Speak when spoken to!" he ordered me with an angry shake, sending what was left of the cigarette flying out of my mouth. It landed beside his foot.

"You and I are nothing alike. I'm a human, and you're a monster," I taunted him. A sly smirk spread across my face as I saw his shock at my bold statement.

"I'm a monster, huh?" He took a step back and nodded to his two soldiers as he picked up the cigarette from the ground and took a last puff. "I'll show you what a monster is," he growled angrily. As the other two fiends grabbed my arms, he came up to me and put the cigarette out on my cheek.

I screamed in pain. I was untied and dragged thirty feet or so to a metal table near the main gate. I was forcefully shoved down, with my head held against the cold steel table. My arms were strapped into arm harnesses that were built into the table, and my legs were bound to a wooden chair. "I tried to talk to you, soldier to soldier," Domelski growled at me angrily. "Now I will talk to you, fiend to human." He placed his hand on top of my hand, claws sprouting from his.

My eyes widened in fear. One of the fiends pulled out a map, tossing it onto the table. Domelski turned to me with a threatening smile. "Where is the location of your base?" he asked coldly.

"Up your ass," I muttered defiantly—and then screamed in pain as his dagger-like claws sank into my hand, forming a pool of blood around it on the table. He withdrew them with a laugh.

"We have ourselves a tough guy, hey?" Domelski asked, nodding to one of his men, who obediently pulled out a pair of pliers from his pocket; the other held my hand steady. "Simply point on this map and this will all be over, comrade," Domelski promised me. He folded his arms as I screamed in pain, while the fiend with the pliers ripped off my first fingernail. After they ripped off three more nails, Domelski raised his hand, and the two fiends took a step back, staring at me with a smirk. I sat there, quivering in pain, blood now stained in the cracks of the table. "You wish to speak now? Yes?" he asked me.

I raised my head, staring at the map. I let out a sigh, and tears ran down my cheeks. I shook my head and then recoiled in pain as one of the fiends smashed my head into the table. The skin above my eyebrows split open, spewing blood down my face.

"That is too bad," Domelski informed me. "I will give you some time to think about it with my two friends." He got up to leave and patted my shoulder; a moment later, he was out of sight.

I glanced up at the two left behind, who were staring at me, happy to finally have their way with me. "You no worry, human. We help you remember your friends' location," one of them promised me in his broken English. The two of them shared a devilish look before approaching me. The relentless interrogation continued for the entire day, without rest. I didn't tell them anything, though—I knew they would kill me sooner or later anyway.

They eventually got fed up and untied me from a flagpole I had been hung from for the remainder of my interrogation. I dropped to the cement with a dull thud as they left. While dragging myself back into the flower bed, I spat out a mouthful of blood, promising myself that I would one day get my revenge on them. I found a rock and devoted the rest of my night to sharpening the edge of it into a shank. Once it was completed, I secretly concealed the weapon in my pants. A content feeling from the possibility of revenge seemed to keep me warm as I drifted off to my dreams.

I was awoken the next morning by a hard punch to my stomach. Gasping in pain, I saw Commander Domelski and his gang staring down at me with a smirk. "Good morning, human. We have much to talk about today!" Domelski told me cheerfully. The other two hauled me out of the flower bed and dragged me across the courtyard, back to the flagpole where I'd been tied up the previous day.

Before the interrogation could commence, the main gate opened, and the familiar sound of metal on metal rang out through the courtyard. The female fiend from my failed execution emerged in the distance and quickly made her way toward us. Her long blonde hair flew out behind her.

"*Tana!*" she called to them in their own language. She held up a piece of paper, and as she reached their side, she showed it to Domelski, who looked skeptical as he read it. "*Renekton apray?*" Domelski muttered, glancing up from the sheet of paper.

She nodded, and then there were a few more brief exchanges between the four of them. This resulted in my three captors looking disappointed. "Well, comrade," Domelski called to me, "it appears there are bigger issues in this war that I must attend to. I hope you enjoy the rest of your short and pitiful life." The three of them picked up their gear and quickly made their way toward the main gate.

The female fiend waited for them to leave and then untied me. She motioned toward the flower bed, and I nodded thankfully. I sat down, nursing my ribs, as she took a seat cautiously by my side.

"What is your name?" she asked.

"I don't know," I replied, cringing, expecting her to hit me. I glanced over at her nervously, but she was still sitting calmly next to me.

"My name is Lara," she told me, extending her hand to me. I ignored it. Her beautiful complexion began to darken, and her smile faded as her hand retreated to her lap. She returned my stare without emotion. "I admire that you are willing to fight and die for the freedom of your country, but you giving me your name is not going to win us the war. So I ask you, as a comrade, what is your name?" She paused for my response, which did not come. "If you cannot tell me something as simple as your name, I will be forced to resort to different measures that I may regret and that you definitely will not like," she warned me.

I stared at the ground, watching two ants fight, as I unhappily considered my options. "My name is Lance," I muttered, breaking the tension between us. This was the first piece of information I had given to the fiends since being taken prisoner more than two weeks ago.

"It's nice to meet you, Lance. It's too bad it's like this." She offered me some water from her canteen as a reward, which I accepted gratefully.

The fiends always denied water to prisoners as a form of torture. It had been close to a day and a half since I'd had my last drink. "I'm sorry about your friend," Lara apologized. I assumed she was referring to Toby.

"I didn't know him," I muttered coldly. I finished off what was left of the water, wiped my mouth, and handed her the canteen.

She remained silent. I guess she took the hint that I didn't want to talk about Toby. A short time later, she spotted me cradling my ribs and asked, "Is anything broken, Lance?"

"No," I lied, defiantly not wanting her help.

Lara ignored me, grabbing my arm forcefully so she could inspect it. Her eyes seemed to quickly scan my hand and took note of my broken index finger and the numerous missing fingernails. She touched my hand and whispered something to herself, sending five blue lights from the tip of her fingers. The light crawled across my hand like worms and disappeared into the wounds, healing them instantly.

I glanced down at my hand in surprise. I clenched it into a fist and then flexed it open. The pain was gone. "I didn't know fiends have healing powers," I said, glancing thankfully at her.

"I'm a pure-blood," Lara explained as she lifted my shirt, revealing the purplish bruises on my ribs.

"What's a pure-blood?" I asked. I sighed with relief as she cast the same spell on my ribs and caused the pain to fade away almost immediately.

"I will be the one asking the questions, Lance," she said firmly. She brushed her hair away from her eyes as her attention shifted back to me. "What was your rank in the People's Liberation Force?" Lara asked. She pulled out a notebook and jotted down something.

I immediately knew she was playing nice to get information from me. I ignored the question, but her blue eyes seemed to burn a hole into me as she waited for an answer.

"Did you not hear me, Lance?" she asked impatiently.

"I'm not a part of the PLF. I'm a civilian," I lied.

She snickered and then ordered, "Get up." I did, and she ordered me to take off my shirt, which I did obediently, sighing as I realized what she was doing. "Turn around," she said. I turned my back to her, exposing the PLF letters seared into my lower back. "Busted," she muttered with a small smirk. I turned back to her in embarrassment. I was surprised to see that she didn't seem angry with me. After a pause, she asked, "So tell me, Lance … what is a civilian doing in the clock tower of Dublin Hill with a sniper rifle?"

I offered an innocent shrug. "Uh … I was trying to flee from the fighting, and it seemed like a good hiding spot. I found that sniper lying there."

Lara chuckled to herself, definitely not buying into my story. "Well, at least we know you're funny." She returned her gaze to her notebook, and as she did, I reached into my pants pocket, pulling out the shank I had designed last night.

She began asking me something but stopped halfway through the sentence as she spotted the shank in my hand. I saw her hand moving to her holstered pistol, but I quickly held up my hand, peacefully surrendering the shank to her. She examined it, patting a spot on the flower bed to indicate I was to sit back down beside her. She glanced from the shank to me, clearly knowing that I'd had more than enough time to attack her with it.

"I had no intention of using it on you. It was meant for them," I explained to her, referring to Domelski and his henchmen.

She finished examining it and then tucked it into her pocket. "You know that building a weapon is illegal and punishable, possibly with the death penalty, right, Lance?"

I nodded, staring at the ground, ashamed.

"We all make mistakes. As far as I'm concerned, it didn't happen, okay?" she said.

I nodded, relieved, but I didn't give her any information for the rest of the day, despite her best efforts. By the end of the day, as the sun slowly began to set in the distance, she was becoming understandably frustrated. She had refrained from hitting me all day, though. I watched the stars slowly appearing overhead and listened to the faint sounds of artillery fire rumbling off in the distance. We sat on the edge of the flower bed in silence.

Finally, Lara broke the silence, saying, "I came from there when I was a little girl." She pointed up to the sky between two stars. "It was a small planet known as Fraturna. I was sent here to blend in with your species, as a sleeper, many years ago. It was before this war began, in case we ever lost our world." She sighed and leaned back on her hands while staring up toward the night sky.

"That explains your English. I was wondering how you were so fluent." I smiled, kind of letting my guard down.

She nodded and returned my smile but then looked back up to the stars.

"What was it like up there?" I asked her, following her gaze.

"There was a war going on between fiends and reliks. It was very cold on Fraturna—minus-fifty was a warm day. Fiends all spoke a universal language known as Jural, unlike you humans, who for some reason have decided to use twenty thousand different languages to communicate with one another." She laughed playfully.

I couldn't help chuckling, knowing that her logic was right. "What are reliks?" I asked her, hoping she wouldn't get angry with my nosiness.

Lara snapped her fingers, causing her entire arm to ignite with flames and illuminating the pitch-black garden. I watched in amazement as the flames jumped off her arm and formed a wall of flames in front of us. Her eyes flashed red, and figures of holograms appeared in front of us, playing out a scene in the air.

There was a little fiend girl who was laughing with her friends. They were all on what appeared to be a fiend's version of a playground. Then, without warning, there was a sudden, blinding flash of light. Screams erupted from everywhere, and the image instantly evaporated into the cool night air, plunging the garden back into darkness.

Lara remained silent for a moment, giving me time to let the scene sink in. Then she explained, "The reliks showed my world no mercy. All of my friends were killed in less than a minute. I was the only survivor." Lara stared emotionlessly at the ground.

"Why would you show me this?" I asked her cautiously.

She turned toward me, responding with a shrug. "I guess to try to justify to you why I'm here." She seemed embarrassed.

I remained silent, holding back from saying anything that might set her off. We sat there in the cool night breeze for a little while longer, and then Lara attempted to interrogate me a bit more. When she was unsuccessful, she left the courtyard but returned shortly afterward—to my surprise with some food and water. She placed it on the flower bed beside me.

She then silently attached a chain to my neck and ankles, clipping the other end to a wall, which allowed me to move around the courtyard semi-freely, in about a two-hundred-foot radius. In a normal situation, I probably would have thanked her for her hospitality; instead, I felt an anger rise up within me, realizing that this generosity was probably part of her secret agenda to obtain information from me.

"You're no better than the reliks!" I spat at her angrily as she left. "Just because your world was taken over doesn't justify your coming to my world and wiping out the entire human race!" I swiped the food that she had set down away from me and onto the ground. I don't know why I did it; I suppose her being nice to me somehow triggered me to hate her even more than the fiends who would beat me senseless every day. She paused at the gate, turning around to face me. I could tell she was about to say something, but then she just turned away and silently exited through the gate, vanishing into the darkness.

I was jolted awake the next morning by the sound of a plane's engine. Joy overtook me as a Canadian fighter jet streaked overhead. Cries of excitement from other prisoners around the compounds erupted as the plane began to circle the fort, while the fiends' emergency alarm began blaring throughout the base.

The jet did a somersault in the air, letting out blue smoke before it sped away, which was the signal that it knew we were here. There was a huge explosion off in the distance, followed by a brief barrage of anti-aircraft fire that lit up the morning air. "*Hell yeah!*" I screamed at the top of my lungs. I jumped off the side of the flower bed, onto the edge of the cement wall that encompassed the courtyard.

Huffing and puffing, I hauled myself briefly above the huge wall, catching a glimpse of billowing smoke from a wrecked fiend vehicle, along with a patrol of fiends scattered everywhere. Some were dead; most were struggling back to their feet in a daze. I yelled out happily, as mass pandemonium rang out around the base. I could hear the cheering of other prisoners, followed by the sounds of windows around the fort shattering, as PLF prisoners began to riot. The whole ordeal lasted only about two minutes or so, but it was the greatest two minutes of my life. I was still screaming at the top of my lungs, with my fist pumping in the air, as the airplane vanished unscathed into the distance. It was strange how something so little could have such a dramatic outcome.

I was wrapped around the edge of the wall, watching the chaos outside, when Lara stormed into the courtyard. "Get down from there, and shut up right now!" she ordered me angrily, grasping the chain around my neck and yanking me down.

Without thinking, I whirled around and punched her in the side of the face. It was like hitting a steel door. My hand throbbed with pain as I backed away. My punch sort of knocked Lara back, but that was about it.

She wiped her nose, glancing down in surprise at her hand, which had some purplish blood on it, before glaring at me. Boiling over with rage, she smashed me to the ground. She then unleashed a barrage of brutal punches, one of them connecting with me, square in the face. Pain exploded as I heard my nose crack from the force of her blow. She let out a non-human growl, baring her fangs at me as her eyes glazed over and became completely bloodshot.

"I'm sorry," I gasped, closing my eyes as I awaited the end of the brutal assault. I felt her pause for a second. She was breathing heavily, and I guessed she was deciding if she was going to kill me or not. I let out a sigh of relief as I felt her soft touch as she wiped away the blood from my eyes with a cloth. I was surprised that she hadn't killed me. Lara's appearance had returned to her human form, and she smiled faintly at me. "You should probably get off me, or people may take this the wrong way," I joked, trying to lighten the mood.

She giggled and got off me, lying down beside me. "So what kind of plane was that?" she asked, staring up at the now-clear sky.

"It was an F-35 scout plane," I muttered.

"What does it do, Lance?" she asked.

I hesitated, not wanting to give her information about the plane, but then I decided that the least I could do to repay her for my violent outbursts over the past two days was to tell her something. "It records locations and takes pictures of the area, and that information is sent to our officers." I knew she was smart enough to decipher what I meant.

"The information is used for planning attacks, right?" she asked, turning to face me as we both lay there.

I nodded, knowing I had given her too much information.

"There will be more?" she asked. I remained silent, but I didn't need to say anything—she already knew that the answer was yes. "My superiors are happy with your progress, Lance," she informed me. "I will be in charge of you from now on, not those men who always beat you," she said happily.

"Sweet!" I replied, trying to throw some enthusiasm into my voice.

She smiled as she began to rummage around in the backpack she had brought with her. "I bought you a few presents last night," she told me, taking out a new set of clothes and an apple.

It took everything I had to contain myself from jumping into the air as I happily grabbed the apple, devouring it in seconds. It had been so long since I last tasted anything other than water and bread. Once I was done, I exchanged the old torn pants and shirt that I'd been forced to wear for the outfit she had bought me. It consisted of a white T-shirt and a gray button-up shirt, along with a clean pair of gray pants and a ball cap.

She even gave me a pair of shoes and healed my feet and fingers, inspecting them to make sure they were healing properly. "It looks so cute on you," she told me as she inspected the outfit. She placed a canteen of water into the side pocket, informing me that it was mine to keep.

"Why are you doing this for me?" I asked her skeptically as she headed for the gate to leave.

"Because you're a good person stuck in a bad situation," she told me as she unlocked the gate.

"I'm not a good person, Lara," I said, leaning lazily against the wall.

She shrugged, glancing over at me with a faint smile. "Join the club."

I laughed, and to my surprise, she took a step back toward me. She extended her hand and said, "Friends?"

I stared at her hand for a second and then nervously grasped it. We stared at each other for a split-second. "Friends," I replied hopefully.

Chapter 3

Over the next few weeks, the People's Liberation Force attempted to make a push toward the fiends' base where we were being held captive, but it was to no avail. I once spotted troops outside of the compound in the tree line. Their artillery fire hit so close to the base that it sent heaps of debris over the walls into the courtyard, but within a couple days, the cracking of gunfire and explosions began to retreat deeper and deeper into the forest. My hope of freedom faded with it.

A celebration soon ensued for the fiends' victory. Music blared out through the windows that night as I sat perched on top of the garden's wall. I scanned the wood line for any PLF soldiers but deep down, I knew they were all gone or dead. The fiends had dragged a few bodies out yesterday and had hung one in front of my compound. They threatened me that I would be next if I tried anything.

"Hey, cutie." Lara's voice rang into my ears as I felt a light tug on the chain around my ankle.

"What's up?" I called back, ripping my attention from the tree line down to her.

Over the past few weeks, Lara and I had slowly become attracted to one another. We both denied it to ourselves, though, knowing a fiend and a human could never be together. I was surprised to see that she wasn't dressed in her usual military uniform; instead, she was in a pretty blue dress, and her long dirty-blonde hair was let down, slightly covering her face. She beamed up at me. "How was the party?" I asked her casually, pretending to not be attracted by her presence.

"I don't know. I never went."

"Why? Shouldn't you be celebrating your spectacular victory over the inferior humans?" I nodded toward the hung soldier swaying in the gentle breeze in front of me.

Lara glanced sympathetically from the soldier over to me. "I'll make sure that he is cut down by tomorrow, Lance," she promised, taking a seat on the edge of the flower bed. She motioned for me to sit with her.

I did so, obediently. She unzipped her backpack and set out a bowl of noodles, an apple and cheese, and a piece of bread. I took the meal from her gratefully, and she filled up my canteen with some juice she had brought.

I glanced at her in surprise. Usually, I just got bread and water, and she would sometimes try to sneak in an apple or something as a treat if I gave her some good information. She pulled out some exotic fiend food—it was a kind of greenish slime with red stains all across it—and she then began to eat. It was kind of awkward at first because Lara had never eaten with me, but the silent tension between us soon faded.

"So why didn't you go the party?" I asked as I sipped on the juice.

She shrugged, glancing over at me. "I guess I wasn't in the mood."

I could tell by the way she kept glancing over at me that she wanted to tell me something. I just nodded understandingly, and we both returned to eating. "You look really nice tonight." I complimented her as we finished our supper.

"Thank you, Lance. You like the dress?" She blushed as we sat there in silence.

"It's not just your dress," I said affectionately, trying to earn some brownie points.

She giggled to herself. I guess she didn't know what to say. She remained silent, packing up our garbage into her bag setting it aside into the flower bed. Music continued to drift through the windows of the compounds around us. Lara glanced over at me nervously as a slow song played. "Would you like to dance with me, Lance?" she asked, standing up energetically.

"Huh?" I thought I must have misheard her.

She beamed down at me, grabbing my hand. "Come on; it will be fun!" She coaxed me to my feet.

"I don't know if this is a good idea," I whispered to her.

"I've had a bad day; it would make me feel better," she replied.

I sighed and reluctantly put my arms around her waist, causing her to smile gently and snuggle against my body. We began to sway back and forth, the chain dragging behind me. She rested her head against my chest as I softly stroked her hair. As much as I didn't want to admit it, I enjoyed having her close to me.

I slipped my hand down her waist, expecting her to get mad, but she giggled and then purred gently, like a cat. She tightened her grip, holding me closer. "Thank you, Lance," Lara whispered, beaming up at me as the song ended.

We both sat down, and she wrapped her arms around me, resting her head in my lap. "Aren't you going to get in trouble for this?" I asked her nervously, but she shook her head confidently.

"The only thing my superiors care about is getting information so that they can look good for their superiors," she assured me. "Besides, what they don't know won't hurt them," she added with a devilish smile, stroking my leg.

Rain began to drizzle on us as clouds formed overhead. Within minutes, it had strengthened into a full-out storm. The continuous sound of raindrops beating on the pavement began to blend with the occasional whoosh of the wind through the treetops around the compound. Mud slowly began to trickle down a stream in the flower bed, soaking my clothes. But as if unaware of her surroundings, Lara remained motionless on my lap, purring contently.

"You're going to get your dress dirty," I warned her as the mud began to run along the edges of the flower bed, threatening to spill over onto us.

"I don't care," she muttered. My words seemed to snap Lara out of her trance, and she sat back up, leaning her head against my shoulder. "I just want to be with you, Lance." She smiled affectionately as the rain pounded against us. We sat in silence for a moment, and then she asked, "Would you like to do something with me tomorrow?"

I couldn't help noticing that her blue eyes seemed to glow softly in the cool night air, reflecting the dull light of the moon that peeked through a cluster of clouds overhead. "I can't do much, stuck in these chains," I told her with a laugh, nodding toward the multiple chains attached to my body.

"You can have them off tomorrow, as a treat," she said.

I looked at her in surprise. She smiled and leaned over to give me a gentle peck on the cheek. I blushed, as I seemed gripped by a loss of words. "It kind of sounds like you're asking me out on a date," I joked nervously.

She stared at me, as if trying to read what I was thinking, while smiling mysteriously to herself. "I might be," she said with a smirk, giving me a playful nudge with her elbow.

"Do you think we can get outside of this courtyard?" I asked, glancing around at the maze of bushes my prison contained.

"Sure, Lance." She smiled and gave me another light peck on my cheek. "I'll be right back." She left the courtyard, returning two or three minutes later with one of her military-issue rain jackets. "Sorry; this is the best I could find," she told me, offering it to me as protection from the rain.

"Thanks. I appreciate it," I replied. I took off my button shirt to use as a pillow and threw the rain jacket over my body as a blanket. Lara gave me another kiss and then hurried away, splashing through the puddles.

I looked down at the rain jacket she had given me. I knew we were playing a dangerous game; even worse, I didn't know if she actually had feelings for me or was just playing me for information. These thoughts raced through my mind as I lay there in the relentless rain, serenaded to sleep by the booming thunder overhead.

Chapter 4

I was gently shaken awake the next morning by Lara, who was dressed casually again in a skirt and a tank top. "Wow, you look amazing ," I said, rubbing away the sleep from my eyes.

She crouched down, giving me a good-morning kiss on the cheek. "Wish I could say the same for you," she joked, plopping down beside me. "When I got to my room last night, I read some things about human activities, and I think I found a good one." She paused for a moment and then asked excitedly, "Do you know how to swim?" I nodded. "Well, then we can do that!" she said happily. She pulled out a muffin from her backpack and handed it to me. "I had some spare time last night, so I tried to make some human food."

I nodded thankfully, accepting the muffin. I took one bite but gagged on it instantly. I held the muffin out to look at it.

Lara glared at me. "You don't like it?" she asked me, quickly wiping away the anger that had crossed her face, even though I knew she was still upset.

"It tastes like pure salt and lemon," I muttered, still recovering from the taste as I stared down at the muffin in disgust.

"Well, duh—it's a salt and lemon muffin, silly!" Lara snatched the muffin from my hand and took a bite out of it. "My book said humans like this stuff. Besides," she added, swallowing the bite, "it tastes fine to me."

"Maybe it's just my taste buds," I lied with a shrug.

She handed me a pair of shorts. "Before we go, I must ask you a few questions, Lance," she said. Lara uncuffed my neck, feet, and wrists, staring at the purple bruises as she took off the chains. She gently touched one, making me flinch. "I'm sorry, Lance," she whispered as her hand quickly recoiled from the wound. "I'll never get over how they lock you guys in here like animals. It makes me ashamed to know that I once lived my day-to-day life honoring the pure-blood line of Dracona."

I shook my head. "Don't talk that way. I knew I was going to end up here—or dead—eventually. It's not your fault. I'm proud of the things I did to get here," I reassured her passionately.

Lara took a step back, staring up at me with a faint smile. "I know that, Lance." She paused, placing her hands on her hips and glancing around the courtyard. "So, how does it feel to be free?"

I rotated my stiff shoulder blades and neck. "Surprisingly good. It's true—I guess that you don't appreciate what you have until it's gone," I told her with a laugh.

She rummaged around in her bag until she found an electric collar. She glanced from it to me with an unhappy look. "I have to put it on you, Lance—you know the rules," she said apologetically, gently strapping it on and adjusting it tightly. "When you went out on your missions, how many would come with you?" she asked casually.

"Usually two or three, depending on the length of the mission," I told her, hating this part of the day.

She smiled faintly, but I could tell she wanted a more in-depth answer. "Who were those two or three?" she asked.

"A machine gunner, a rifleman, and me," I explained with a sigh.

She smiled her thanks. She probably knew how much I hated giving up information about my past. "How long had you three been working together?" she asked, sitting me down and typing something into a strange hand-held device. I flinched, feeling a light electric shock pulse through my body as she made sure the collar worked. "Sorry about that," she giggled, glancing up from the device in her hand. "Had to make sure it works. So … how long had you three been working together, Lance?"

"About three and a half years," I told her truthfully.

"So when did you join the resistance?" she asked, still adjusting the collar.

I hesitated before responding. "The day of the invasion," I finally told her.

"That was about four years ago, so you're around seventeen?" she asked.

I nodded, putting on my shorts as she unexpectedly stripped down to a pretty blue sparkling bikini. I couldn't help staring at her.

She handed me a towel, giggling to herself once she realized I was checking her out. "Men are all the same, even from different species, I guess," she called over to me playfully.

"Sorry. I didn't expect the fiends to have such a stylish wardrobe," I joked, slinging the towel over my shoulder.

"I spent many years with your race before the war, so I guess I just picked up on their ways," she said with a shrug, looking down at the bikini. "You like it?"

"Of course I do. You look beautiful," I said as I followed her to the main gate.

My compliment made her blush. "Thank you, Lance. You're so sweet." She unlatched the gate, leading me down a path to a small pond a couple of hundred meters away from the courtyard. It felt so good to be outside of the prison. I knew the water would feel even better. Lara approached the side of the pond, kneeling down beside it, testing it with her hand. "It's so nice today!" she called over to me happily. I threw down my towel and headed toward her. She whirled around instantly, spotting my intentions. She chucked her towel at me defensively. "Don't you dare, Lance!" she cried out with a laugh.

It was too late, though. I lunged at her, sending the two of us spiraling into the water. She laughed as we both broke the surface and began to play-fight with one another in the water. We splashed each other for a while, eventually settling down as we both began to relax. We lazily swam around, occasionally getting out to dive back in. The summer sun was so warm. It beamed down on us from above while dancing off the surface. I was having such a great time with her, but I knew I had to keep my guard up. This could very well be just a way for her to get me comfortable around her, in the hopes that I would accidently spill an important piece of information.

"I think I'm done for now," Lara said, giving me one last playful splash. She pulled herself out of the water, got her towel, and lay down contentedly.

I swam around for a little while longer until I became bored and swam over to the edge of the pond. I glanced over at Lara, who was still basking in the sun. "Hey, are you going to jump back in or what?" I called over to her playfully, but she didn't respond.

I silently pulled myself out of the water and cautiously approached her side. I realized then that she was asleep. I knew this was the chance of a lifetime. I quickly rummaged around in her purse and pulled out a set of keys. I tried each of them in my collar and almost cried out in excitement as I heard the dull click of my collar coming unlocked. Snickering to myself, I quickly took off the collar, threw it on my towel, and bolted toward the tree line—freedom was within my grasp.

The joyful feeling, however, immediately faded away as I glanced back through the shrubs at Lara, who was still sleeping peacefully, unaware of my escape. I knew if I went through with my decision to set myself free, she would be killed—and this really toyed with my emotions for some reason. She didn't seem to be like the others. "Come on, Lance. It's war. People die," I muttered to myself, trying to convince myself to leave.

I tried to walk away, but to my displeasure, I was unable to make myself move. I sighed unhappily and plopped down on the ground, leaning against a tree in an attempt to enjoy what little freedom I had left.

Thunk!

"Ouch! What the hell?" I muttered, rubbing my head as I saw an apple come to a rest at my feet. I glanced up at the small tree I was leaning against, a dull grin spreading across my face as I realized it was a lone apple tree. "Oh, hey there, little guy. How did you manage to survive this?" I said happily. I stood up and collected a handful of apples from it.

I glanced back through the shrubs and spotted Lara as she woke up with a jolt. I saw her gasp and smack her head when she saw my towel and collar lying there. I sighed in disbelief at what I was about to do. I gathered the pile of apples I had picked and walked away from freedom—straight back into the hands of my captor.

"*Lance*!" Lara screamed in panic, still looking around. She hadn't yet spotted me.

"What's up?" I called from behind her, while cradling my stash of apples.

She whirled around in surprise. I guess she was shocked by the fact that I hadn't run away. To be honest, I was probably more shocked than she was that I hadn't. "You … but it can't be … you're here? You … *you* just gave me a heart attack, you friggin' prick!" She angrily stormed toward me, grabbing the collar of my shirt and throwing me to the ground with her fiend strength. It sent my collection of apples flying. "*I thought you ran away*!" she yelled at me with an angry fiend growl in her voice. "How would I have ever explained what just happened to my boss?" She took in a deep breath in an attempt to slow her breathing as she stared down at me, probably debating how she was going to punish me for what I had just done.

"I *was* going to run away," I told her truthfully.

She stared at me in disbelief for a moment. "Then why are you still here?" she asked tersely.

"I decided not to because I knew you would be killed, so I had to settle for the next best option." I smiled nervously and held up one of the apples for her to see.

Lara stared at me in disbelief, and then, to my surprise, she began to laugh and helped me collect the apples that had scattered all around on the ground. We brought them over to our towels. "May I?" she asked, nodding toward the apples. I nodded, and we both grabbed one and ate happily. "If there's anything about Earth that I love, it's the fruits," she told me, pausing for a moment to inspect her apple. "We never had anything so natural-tasting on my planet."

I laughed, looking over at her nervously as we ate in silence, finishing them off. "So you're not mad at me?" I asked her hopefully.

She laughed and then whispered affectionately, "Of course not. How could I ever be mad at you?" She leaned over to place a light kiss on my cheek. "Would you mind telling me a little bit about the New World Order?" Lara asked me.

"What?" I asked, surprised. Her question had come completely out of the blue, but it was a chilling reminder that even though we were having fun, she was always on duty.

"My superiors feel that the NWO is going to be a threat to us in the near future," she said with a shrug.

"There a radical faction of humans that is our enemy," I told her simply.

"Duh. I'm not stupid, Lance."

"It's a long story," I said.

"We have all day," Lara shot back with a playful smirk.

I sighed, tossing what remained of the apple behind me. "When I was initiated into the PLF there were two men in charge of it: Captain Murphy and Lieutenant Stark. They were both very strong-minded individuals with two completely separate visions for the post-war world," I began. "Eventually, a power struggle developed between them, which finally exploded into a mutiny and an attempt on Captain Murphy's life. The two declared war on each other two years ago, which has been in effect to this very day."

She stared at me; interest spread across her face. "Your loyalty lies in Captain Murphy?" she asked.

"I would die for him. He's basically the father I never had." I couldn't believe how much information I was giving away to her.

"What happened to your father?" she asked.

"Lara ..." I said, not wanting to get into it.

"Fine. I'm sorry. I just have one more question."

"What is that?" I asked her, spotting a playful grin spreading across her face.

"Where is the PLF's base?" she asked with a smirk.

"Um, probably up your ass," I said, giving her a playful push with one hand. We both burst out laughing.

The two of us stayed out until the sun began to set behind the mountains that seemed painted into the background, far off in the distance. As we walked up the path to the gate of the courtyard, I slipped my hand into hers.

"I had a good time today, Lance," she told me.

"Me too, but don't you think, as friends, we're getting a bit too close to one another? Not to mention, aren't we a little too different for each other?" I asked, not wanting to ruin the exceptionally good mood Lara was in.

"How so?" she asked, stopping at the main gate of the courtyard.

I gave a light tug on the electric collar around my neck with a dull smile.

"Huh?" Lara asked, playing dumb.

"Well, for starters, I'm a prisoner; you're my guard. I'm human, and you're not. Did I miss anything?"

"Ha-ha. Those are only minor details, Lance." She playfully ruffled my hair.

"What if we get in a fight and you turn into a ..." I stopped as Lara turned to face me.

"A what?" she asked as a slightly offended expression spread across her face.

"Nothing. It's just ... I don't want to get into a fight and then be killed. But I don't want to mess up what we have going on here either, if you know what I mean."

"A fight? Like this?" she asked, giving me a playful push.

I laughed. "Yeah, something like that." I returned the playful shove, which soon turned into a pushing match and spiraled into a play-fight. After a short scuffle on the ground, I had her pinned. She stopped struggling and beamed up at me affectionately. What was left of the sun seemed to be shining off her as she leaned up to kiss me.

The sounds of guns cocking around us, followed by the cold barrel of a rifle placed forcefully against the back of my neck interrupted us. Lara quickly opened her eyes, glancing around angrily. I got up slowly, with my hands in the air, looking down at her, slightly panicked, for help. Three fiends surrounded us; they seemed a little older than me.

Lara jumped to her feet, scolding them in her native language. I could tell that she was furious that they'd interrupted her moment with me. She pointed into the garden, and they nodded, letting us in.

They followed us, and she sternly motioned for me to sit down on the flower bed, which I did obediently. She reached down into her pile of clothes, pulled out an ID from her skirt, and flashed it at them. She then showed the guards some paperwork and pointed at the electric collar around my neck, still speaking in her language. In the end, the three soldiers nodded apologetically to her, exchanging a couple words with each other before leaving.

"Well, you're lucky they came, or you would have been toast," she said playfully, trying to break the awkward tension.

"Yeah, right, just keep telling yourself that," I shot back playfully.

I tossed over my swimming shorts to her and sat down on the flower bed. She set out two pieces of bread, an apple, and water beside me and then took off my electric collar, replacing it with my shackles. "Sorry for the small meal tonight, Lance," she apologized, looking down at it as she packed up her stuff to leave.

"No worries; I'm used to it. And I got two pieces of bread instead of one! I'm basically living the good life now," I said. I got up and walked her to the gate, stopping at the entrance. "Thank you for letting me out today, Lara," I whispered.

She unlocked the gate and then turned to face me. She seemed to be thinking about something as she glanced around the abandoned courtyard. Without warning, she closed her eyes and leaned forward, giving me my first real kiss on the lips. She took a step back, giggling to herself in embarrassment. We stared at each other in disbelief of what was happening. "We can do it again sometime. Just ask, and I'll talk to my superiors about permission to schedule another outing for us," she told me, still trying to act like a professional guard.

I nodded, folding my arms and going along with it, as if nothing had happened. I could tell she didn't want to leave as she whispered good night, but she stepped through the gate and locked it on the other side with a wink. I watched her head down the path to her dorm. She paused off in the distance, glancing back before vanishing into the base.

Holding onto the gate with one hand, I rested my head against the rusted metal. I let out an unsure sigh, knowing something between us would never be the same.

Chapter 5

Throughout the next few days, Lara needed information to keep her superiors happy, so I would tell her little things, like what units I served with, along with our routine, tours I'd been on, and basic stuff like that. It had been about two months now that I had been held captive by the fiends, and things were beginning to get restless among the prisoners of each compound. Something big was about to happen; I could feel it in the air. Prisoners were circulated from compound to compound in the fiends' attempt to keep us out of contact with each other, to prevent a riot or escape attempt from taking place.

There were now nine other PLF soldiers, all chained in different sections of my compound. We couldn't see anything through the thick foliage of the courtyard garden, but we could hear each other. The hatred for the fiends seemed to be growing stronger as each day passed.

"I think this place is going to explode soon," I whispered to Lara that night as she was wrapping up our daily interrogation session.

"What have you heard?" she asked, quietly leaning closer to me.

"Nothing. I just have this feeling. The prisoner over there is an officer," I told her, nodding toward the right side of the compound. "He has been communicating to us over the past few days in Morse code."

As if on cue, we could hear tapping against the wall in the distance, followed by silence, and then a simple tap, ringing out from each side of the compound.

"What did he ask?" Lara whispered.

"He wants to know if all the interrogators are gone," I replied, staring at the rock on the ground beside me that I had been using to communicate with them. "They all said yes," I added as she stared at me anxiously.

"Say yes," she urged me, but I just stared at her blankly.

"I can't do that, Lara," I told her, refusing to strike my rock against the wall.

She stared at me angrily for a second. I thought she was going to hit me at first, but she soon calmed down, probably realizing that I could have just as easily not given her any information at all. "What have they been planning?" she asked.

I shrugged, knowing if I gave her that information, the rest of them would realize I was a rat and kill me if an uprising took place.

She stood up, moodily grabbing her paperwork and dusting off her pants, which were stained brown from sitting on the ground with me all day.

"I'm sorry; I can't betray my own kind," I whispered to her.

She glanced down at me, placing her hands on her hips. "Why would you tell me this then?" she asked angrily.

"So that you can separate the prisoners before something happens."

"I can't do anything unless you tell me what's going on," Lara insisted impatiently.

"The officer has told us to stay strong. Our day of freedom is coming," I told her hesitantly, not informing her about the upcoming rebellion plan that the soldiers had been devising over the past couple of days.

She shook her head unhappily. "You think my superiors will take the time out of their day to separate you guys based on pointless propaganda that a captured officer is spreading to his troops, just because his ego has been bruised by defeat and he wants revenge?" Lara asked irritably, getting up and slinging her assault rifle across her back.

"People are going to die, Lara. I don't want anything to happen to us," I told her urgently.

"Nothing's going to happen to us, Lance," she promised. She ignored my warning and gave me a kiss good-bye.

"But—"

"Goodnight, Lance," she whispered, firmly cutting me off. "I'll see what I can do."

I looked away unhappily, knowing that she was just telling me what I wanted to hear. She headed toward the entrance. I heard the dull rattle of metal on metal a second later. Her leaving sent the clear reminder that we were not equals. I was the prisoner, and she was my guard.

Lara never came down the following day. Instead, a brunette female fiend with long shiny hair woke me up. I recoiled in shock as I glanced at her, confused, wondering what was going on. The fiend was trying to be nice; I could tell Lara must have told her to be gentle.

She kept a hand on her pistol holster as she placed a bag down in front of me. Then she took a step back to let me grab it.

"Where's Lara?" I asked suspiciously.

"Sick," the fiend said bluntly, the disgust of being in my presence written across her face. "Lara told me to tell you she would be back tomorrow." Then she nodded and walked away, leaving me alone to my thoughts for the rest of the day. Lara came down the next morning, as promised.

"Wow, you're pretty early," I said, surprised to see her. Judging by the sun, I guessed that it was probably around nine in the morning.

"Yeah, well, I missed you!" she told me, smiling as she took her seat on the ground beside me.

"Aw, I missed you, too. How are you feeling?" I asked her, trying to make up for the tense conversation we'd had the last time we'd seen each other.

"Not too bad," she informed me, pausing as she rummaged around in her backpack for my breakfast. "Sorry about the other day. I was a little bit moody. I'm thankful for all the information you gave me," she added sincerely, handing me an apple for breakfast.

"Thanks!" I replied with a nod, accepting her apology.

"So how was Luna? Did she treat you all right?" Lara asked.

"Yeah, she just came down and gave me my food and then left."

Lara smiled in relief. "She's a good friend. I knew she wouldn't let me down." I finished my breakfast and tossed the apple core into the flower bed we were resting against. We sat there in silence for a bit as the morning sun beat on us, listening to the peaceful sounds of the birds chirping in the distance. "You don't understand how hard it is for me to do this job when I have such strong feelings for you, Lance," Lara tried to explain.

I could tell she was in an affectionate mood as she stroked my hair away from my eyes, smiling faintly. "It's okay. I know you have to do it," I told her, paving the way for her to start her interrogation.

She nodded, thankful that I was okay with it, and pulled out her folder, giving me a kiss before she began. "So before the war—"

BANG!

A single gunshot rang out through the compound, breaking the tranquility of the morning air before Lara even finished her first question.

Lara motioned for me to get to the ground. She stood up cautiously, looking around. Her eyes turned red as she peered through the dense foliage surrounding us. I could hear muffled screaming in a corner of the compound, followed by the panicked yelling of fiends, indicating to me that the victim was one of their own. Fully automatic gunfire began to erupt around us, blindly spraying into the compound and ricocheting dangerously everywhere.

"Stay down!" Lara shouted, quickly grabbing her assault rifle and loading a magazine into it.

The gunfire stopped for a second, but panicked screams continued to erupt around us, followed by the cricket chirps of PLF soldiers communicating to one another. The gunfire seemed to strengthen, signaling that more prisoners had been set free. Shots blindly flew back and forth between the humans and the fiends, hissing over our heads. Within five minutes, it appeared that all nine of them were free, and they zeroed in on my corner. I heard the chirping of one of them, asking me where Lara was, but I remained silent. Lara shot blindly through the foliage, which was returned by a barrage of fire ripping through the walls behind us. "Hit me, Lara!" I cried.

"Huh?" Fear and confusion were plastered across her face.

"Just do it!" I yelled.

She obediently smashed the butt of the rifle against my face, and I cringed in pain. I felt my mouth, and saw that my hand was covered in blood.

"Give me your weapon, or you're dead," I told her as shadows began to form in the brush surrounding her.

She glanced at me in fright but obediently set her AK89 on the pavement beside me. I loaded another clip into it and then got up, knocking her over the head with the butt of it. It bloodied her face, and I placed my foot on top of her chest to make it look as though I had just overtaken her. "I got her, boys! It's safe!" I yelled over the roar of gunfire, which instantly stopped. When the fighters emerged through the dense brush, I was standing there, pointing my rifle at Lara's face. She looked around in fright and then up at me, defeated.

"Let's kill this filthy monster," one of them said, followed by a wave of agreement.

"No! Let's keep her as a prisoner. We may need her to get out of here," I suggested. My words were followed by silence.

An older man in his thirties took a step out of the crowd and patted me on the shoulder. "Good thinking, young lad," he said. He bent down and went through Lara's pockets, pulling out maps, folders, pens, keys, two fully loaded pistol magazines, handcuffs, and a 9mm handgun. The man uncuffed the chains attached to me, handing me the 9mm and mags, which I stuffed into my pockets. I put the 9mm in my belt buckle. "She dinged you pretty hard, hey?" he asked me, tapping the side of his face to indicate where I had been hit.

"It's no big deal; just a scratch." I shooed away one of the boys who came over with a rag to wipe some of the blood off my face. "Sir, were you the one sending the Morse code around the compound?" I asked.

He nodded. "Captain Myers. Thirteenth Mountain Infantry." He introduced himself with a firm handshake. "Who are you?" he asked me as he handcuffed Lara.

"Corporal Lance. Tenth Company Light Infantry," I answered proudly.

"Ah, I've heard stories about you. You're that sniper, right?" he asked me.

"Yes, sir," I replied, grabbing one of Lara's arms. We brought her over to where the rest of the fiends were held captive. Twelve were alive and seven dead.

"You have quite a good reputation," Captain Myers said. "I hear you're one of the best snipers in this war."

"I have a decent shot, sir," I told him, embarrassed as he laughed and took a better look at me.

"Don't be so modest, son," he chuckled. "Robinson?" he called out.

"Sir!" a boy about sixteen answered, appearing from behind me.

"Give Lance your sniper."

The boy obediently traded me his L96A1 for Lara's AK89.

"Well, I would love to sit around and chat, but we have a compound to fortify. Lance, try to find yourself a good position. The counterattack is sure to happen soon," Captain Myers ordered me.

"Yes, sir," I replied, saluting him and then strolling away in search of a place to perch myself.

For ten guys, we had ourselves locked down pretty securely. One had to guard the prisoners at all times, while the other nine were spread around the entrances. I found a position behind a cement statue, which allowed me to have a good line of sight to the pathways on my right and left, along with the windows of the base, if I were to peek around it.

I saw Lara watching me, emotionless, as I set up my firing position. I think that she thought I had turned on her, but I knew this plan to hold out until help arrived would never work. I was just playing along with the defense until we were inevitably overrun, so that I didn't seem like a traitor.

Sure enough, the counterattack came, and I began to unload my clip at a group of fiends. I avoided the kill shots and only shot out their legs so they were no longer a threat. The battle raged on all night, with periodic lulls. I had shot about thirty-three fiends by the time Robinson came around, reporting to me that we'd suffered five deaths but managed to kill twenty-three fiends, plus the seven from this morning, and wounded fifty or more.

The fighting ceased for the rest of the night as the fiends realized they were just going to suffer more casualties in trying to take the compound. I went over to the fiends who were prisoner and relieved the sentry. I pulled out my 9mm for protection as they all stared at me menacingly. "Calm down, boys," Lara whispered to them, holding out her hand.

"What are the stats?" Lara asked, wiggling closer to me.

"Twenty-three fiends killed, plus these guys, and fifty or more wounded." I nodded toward the seven dead on the ground.

"And?" I knew she was referring to our casualties.

"Five PLF soldiers killed," I told her, glancing around to make sure no humans were watching me.

"In the morning they're going to storm this place and kill you, Lance," she warned me. Then she asked, "Why did you save me?"

I ignored her question, confused about the answer myself. She knew I loved her; I didn't need to tell her that. Plus, my saving her was kind of an ace up the sleeve, since I knew she was my only hope of surviving this.

"Did you kill anyone?" Lara asked me solemnly.

I shook my head, staring at the ground. "No … well, not today anyway," I began and then paused to glance back over my shoulder, making sure no one was around. "I shot about thirty-three or thirty-four of them though," I admitted.

She nodded, knowing I could have easily killed them.

"I have to go. It was nice knowing you, Lara," I told her, accepting that I was going to die in a few hours.

She tried to whisper something to me, but I left, and she stopped mid-sentence as another PLF soldier took over as sentry. Not surprisingly, they brought in some snipers the next morning, and within the next five hours, as dawn began to creep over the walls, it was only Myers, Robinson, and I left to defend the courtyard.

Bang! Bang! Bang!

I heard the sound of a pistol firing. I jumped to my feet and raced toward the prisoners. Myers was executing them, one by one, with his sidearm.

"What the hell are you doing? Those are prisoners of war!" I yelled at him, slinging the sniper rifle over my shoulder.

He glanced over at me with a careless shrug and pressed the mag release button on his empty pistol. He fumbled around in his pocket for another mag and put it in. I glanced down at Lara, who was staring at him, frozen in fear. She must have realized that she was next in the line. "Come on, Lance. Wake up. Fiends don't follow the Geneva Conventions; why should we?" Myers asked me bitterly.

I tried to reason with him. "We are no better than they are if we start acting like them."

"They're not humans, Lance. They're monsters. We're doing this world a favor." He laughed, waving his pistol in the air before aiming it at Lara's head.

"*Don't you dare!*" I yelled at him, drawing my pistol and aiming it straight at his chest.

"*Drop your weapon,* Lance!" Robinson screamed, quickly taking aim at me to loyally protect his leader.

The three of us stared at each other, and time seemed to come to a screeching halt as we remained locked in our Mexican standoff. Myers was a smart man; he glanced from his weapon to Lara and scanned the rest of the fiends. "Tsk, tsk, Lance. This one's gotten into your head, hasn't she?" Myers called over to me.

"It's over, Myers; we've lost," I called out, trying to reason with him.

"It's over when I say it's over," he growled. His grip tightened around the pistol.

The air lit up with gunfire, and just like that, it was over. My shot had sailed through the air, connecting with Myers's chest just as he fired his shot. It threw him off balance and grazed the fiend beside Lara. Robinson had unleashed a fully automatic barrage at me, just as I dropped to the ground on my back, firing a single shot that sailed right through the bottom of his chin and into his brain, killing him instantly.

Myers gasped for breath, clutching his chest just below his heart. Blood pooled around him, staining his shirt as he fought to cling to what little life he had left.

I ran my hands across my body in shock, realizing that I somehow had not been shot. I glanced over at Myers, and the fiends stared at me in confusion and shock. "You … *ungh* … you son of a bitch," Myers gurgled through a mouth full of blood, letting out his final breath. Silence enveloped the courtyard momentarily. I stared at his body and then up at Lara, who was shivering in fright.

"*Nooooo!*" she screamed.

The pavement around me chipped away as gunshots hissed past me. I felt one rip into my leg, and I cried out in pain. I clumsily lumbered to the nearest flower bed, just as a shot raced past me and hit the wall behind me, an inch from where I just had been. Cheers erupted from the prisoners as the fiends broke through the main gate, setting them free.

I sprayed blindly into the foliage with an assault rifle I had picked up. Its sound was echoed by thirty times the amount of firepower, causing me to laugh to myself as I realized I was about to die. I grabbed my L96 and picked off a few more fiends. "Cease fire!" someone yelled, and the fighting subsided. I looked through my scope, spotting Lara, who was walking slowly toward me with her hands raised non-threateningly.

"Get back, Lara!" I yelled at her, waving my hand for her to go away. I didn't want her to get hit by some trigger-happy fiend. She smiled softly, ignoring my warning and stopped about five meters away, purposely standing in front of me to block any possible shots. "You're so damn stubborn," I called over to her.

She laughed. "Are you okay?" she called over to me.

"I've seen better days," I said, lowering myself onto the flower bed. I was exhausted from the two days of fighting. "Just move aside and let them finish me off. I don't care anymore."

She shook her head unhappily. "I'm not leaving here without you, Lance."

"They're going to hang me for this anyway," I called over to her, but she shook her head again.

"You didn't kill anyone, and the only PLF who did are dead," she debated with me.

"I killed Myers and Robinson," I said as tears trickled down my cheek.

"You saved our lives, though," she said gratefully, advancing a few paces closer. "You're the only one with a weapon that fires 7.62-caliber ammunition." Lara calmly placed her hands in her pockets, as if we were having a casual, everyday conversation. "Ironically, most of the bullets recovered from wounded fiends were the same caliber as your weapon. No one was killed with it." She held her hand out for me to surrender my weapons.

I nodded, handing her my AK89 and L96. She smiled at me, comfortingly shouldering the weapons. "Come with me, please, Lance," she said gently, motioning for me to follow her. She walked toward the fiends who were bunkered down behind cover, off in the distance. Lara waved her hands to them, signaling that I had given up, and I limped a couple of paces behind her. Without thinking, I pulled out the 9mm from my back pocket, unloading the clip and cocking it, causing the chambered round to fall harmlessly to the ground. "*Gun!*" a fiend yelled. His shout was followed by a single shot, which ripped through my upper right shoulder.

The 9mm fell to the ground with a dull clunk, and Lara screamed in panic. I stumbled a step back toward cover and fell behind it in a pool of blood. I cursed to myself, feeling the wound.

"Don't shoot, you idiot! He saved us!" someone called over to the shooter.

"Sorry. Almost got myself my first kill," the shooter called back with an embarrassed laugh.

Lara raced over to me, her familiar gentle touch lifting me up into her lap as she examined the wound. "It's not that bad," she reassured me. I spat out a mouthful of blood. "Why didn't you just give me the 9mm?" she scolded me, running her hand across my leg and shoulder. Her eyes glowed red, and the familiar blue worm-like lights shot out of her fingertips, crawling across my body and into the wounds.

"I don't know. I guess I wasn't thinking. I was just unloading it. I had no intention of hurting anyone," I said defensively.

She nodded understandingly. "It's okay, Lance. Just rest now. Everything will be okay."

My body began to succumb to her spell, and I lost consciousness a moment later. Her soothing touch was the last thing I remembered.

Chapter 6

After the prison riot, I ended up spending a night in the hospital. Lara and a group of heavily armed fiends escorted me back down to the courtyard the following day. I spent another month or so locked up in the courtyard. It was getting pretty nippy out at night, but thankfully, Lara had bought me some winter kit and other warm clothing as a present a couple weeks ago, which I was snuggled into, comforted by the warmth.

My birthday would be tomorrow, and I wondered if Lara even knew. The next day, she didn't come down to interrogate me, which I found unusual. She did, however, to my surprise, come down that night—with a birthday cake—while I was sleeping.

"Happy birthday, Lance!" she whispered warmly, placing the cake down and giving me a kiss.

"Wow, thank you! You remembered?" I asked her, surprised, as I sat up, rubbing the sleep from my eyes.

She beamed down at me, nodding. "Of course I did. How could I forget my man's birthday?" She sat down beside me, wrapped one of her arms around me in a hug, and gave me a light peck on my neck.

I smiled; a satisfied feeling kept me warm as I blew out the eighteen candles on the cake. "How did you know? I don't think I ever told you."

"You told me your date of birth a couple weeks ago, during one of our interrogations. And then, I saw it the other day in your file and thought it would be nice if I did a little something for you tonight. I know how much you must miss your family and friends."

I smiled thankfully but remained silent. I realized her secret agenda was to try to obtain information about my family, which I had never talked to her about. I saw the disappointment fill her eyes as she must have realized that I'd figured out her plan. Surprisingly, she didn't mention my family again for the entire night. I guess she didn't want to ruin the birthday. We only got through about half of the birthday cake before Lara looked at the rest of it. She picked it up with a smirk, glancing over at me.

"What should I do with the rest of this?" she asked me playfully, inching closer.

"Don't you dare," I warned her, standing up.

She laughed, and the next thing I knew, she sprang at me, slamming the cake square into my face. Lara happily cried out victoriously, but I grabbed her by the waist, took the remainder of the cake, and rubbed it in her face. This caused a brief struggle for control over the remnants of the cake until Lara finally called out, "Truce!" I snickered at Lara, who was covered completely with cake frosting.

"Shut up. You're not a pretty sight either," she retorted with a smug expression. We laughed about the play-fight as we slowly eased ourselves down on the edge of the flower bed, fighting an unwinnable battle to clean ourselves off. "So I talked to my boss today, Lance," she began, pausing to making sure I was paying attention. I glanced over at her, and she smiled, continuing on. "Anyway, he told me I could take you to my room for a while, now that it's getting pretty chilly out here." She tried to read my reaction, but I made sure to hide it from her. She pulled out my electric collar from her backpack.

"So we're going to be living together from now on?" I asked her nervously.

She nodded, smiling. "Why do you look so scared? It will be fun!" she told me confidently. She paused. I think she was trying to figure out why I wasn't as excited about the news as she was. "We don't have to do this if you don't want to, Lance," she added in that moody tone girls always get when things aren't going their way.

I knew I had no choice in the matter, so I put on a fake smile. "It sounds like a great idea," I lied.

She happily gave me a kiss and latched the electric collar around my neck, and then we left the courtyard, walking down a path into the main entrance of the base. The only source of light inside the base was a dull red that slowly flashed light, fighting its way through the darkness to light up our path temporarily as we walked down the narrow hall. The smell of decaying bodies forced me to glance down to the ground, confirming my fears—I could make out the dimly lit shapes of dead, half-eaten humans, all scattered along the sides of the narrow hall.

I was filled with panic now as we passed by a pair of half-transformed fiends, gnawing on the remains of a dead body. They snarled at me as I passed, and Lara lashed out at them, baring her fangs threateningly with a low-pitched growl. "I want to go back," I whispered anxiously as we turned a corner and quickly walked down an abandoned hallway.

"You're going to be fine, Lance. I promise, okay? We're almost there," Lara reassured me. She tightened her grip around my hand to prevent me from making a run for it.

I glanced in another room and spotted five dead PLF soldiers, hanging by their necks. They sway back and forth, and the soft, eerie squeaking of the rope echoed around us. "Please let me go," I begged her again, but she ignored me.

I was gripped by fear as we walked across what appeared to be bloodstains on the floor. I suddenly snapped, unable to control myself anymore. I violently ripped myself from her grasp and bolted down the hall.

"Lance!" Lara screamed angrily as she chased after me. She tackled me to the ground with her fiend strength and rolled me over, staring down at me questioningly. "Lance, I'm not going to hurt you. I promise." She helped me back to my feet and resumed dragging my quivering body down the hall. "Just close your eyes. We're almost there," Lara instructed me.

When we finally made it to her room, I forced myself to open my eyes. I expected to be in a slaughterhouse or something, but to my relief, it really was her room. It wasn't like a modern teenage girl's room. I could tell she'd tried to clean it up a little for me.

A light shone dull red, illuminating the room. There were jagged claw marks that ran along the wall, along with a smashed bookcase swept into a pile in the corner of the room. My attention shifted back to huge gashes running along the wall.

I could feel Lara watching me as I ran my hand along the claw marks. They were about half a foot deep in some areas. I wanted to believe that they weren't hers, but I knew deep down that the marks had to be from her, probably after losing her temper at something. I moved along the wall, tearing my attention away from it to the rest of the room.

Lara had a few books about humans on a small table in the middle of the room, and the rest were written in her language. "What language do you speak again? I forgot," I called over to her, picking up a book and flipping it over to the back cover, which was written in her alien language.

"It's called Jural," she told me, approaching my side and examining the book I had in my hand. "That's one of my favorites."

"What is it?" I asked.

"It's a romance about two lovers who are torn apart by the war between the fiends and the reliks," she explained, pausing to glance over at me. "I can read it to you sometime if you would like."

I nodded. "Sounds good." My attention shifted back to the rest of the room, which was covered with fangs, necklaces, and weird prehistoric-looking symbols engraved in the walls. I picked up a picture in a heart-shaped frame on her nightstand. I realized in surprise that it was of me, a couple of months ago, when we had gone down to the pond. "That was a fun day, hey?" Lara's voice said gently.

I turned around to answer, but my voice caught in my throat—Lara had stripped down to her bra and underwear. She giggled, seeing my expression. "I'm going to give you your birthday present now," she told me as she placed her hand against my chest. She pushed me down softly on her bed.

I woke up the next morning with her by my side. She was still sleeping, purring peacefully with each breath. She really was so beautiful. I knew I truly loved her and wanted to be with her, even though she was a fiend.

As she slept, I watched the sun slowly rising in the distance to brave another day. Lara woke up a few minutes later, rolling over sleepily and giving me a kiss. "Did you have a good birthday?" she asked me with a smirk.

"It was average," I joked.

She punched me in the shoulder with a laugh and then snuggled closer to me. She followed my gaze out the window, at the sun slowly peeking over the mountains in the distance. "I love the beauty of your planet; it's so amazing," she whispered.

"Yeah, it's nice to watch," I agreed, rubbing her side affectionately.

She giggled and gave me a kiss. "Well, you must be happy," she said as we cuddled with one another under the blankets.

"Huh?" I asked, confused.

"You're probably one of the first humans to be able to say that he's banged a fiend," Lara told me playfully. She rolled over on top of me, coming to a rest on my chest and staring down at me with an amused expression. "Do you love me, Lance?" she asked nervously.

"Of course. You know I do," I assured her, and her expression instantly washed over with relief.

A moment of silence followed while Lara played with my hair. "Let me hear you say it," she whispered into my ear.

I hesitated, knowing that once I said the words, I was committed to the relationship.

"What? Do you have a girlfriend somewhere in the woods?" she asked. A flash of jealousy seemed to pump through her as she stopped playing with my hair and propped herself up to stare down at me. This was a side of Lara I definitely wanted to avoid.

"It's not that ..." I began.

"Then what is it?" she asked, raising her voice.

"See? Now you're mad." I tried to work my way from underneath her, but she readjusted herself, using her fiend strength to keep me pinned. I realized that I had gotten myself into an unwinnable battle and that I needed to get out of it quickly, or I was going to be in some real trouble.

Her muscles were tense as she glared down at me, disgust written across her face. "I'm not mad, Lance," she seethed. "I'm trying to have a grown-up conversation with you, but you won't."

"Well, yes, I do love you, but what if something happens between us, and you kill me or something?" I told her.

Her clenched muscles relaxed as she slipped back into her loving mood. "Nothing's going to happen between us, Lance," she assured me, kissing me before lying across my chest affectionately.

"You're sure?" I asked her skeptically, placing a hand on her back.

"Of course! We were meant for each other. Sure, we are going to have our ups and downs, but we are two different species, so of course that's going to happen until we can reach a compromise and learn to adapt to our differences," Lara explained thoughtfully.

"Okay," I replied, rubbing her gently. She resumed purring.

"I know I may be moody at times, but I'm a teenage girl. Every girl has those moments," she added with a laugh, trying to get me back in a good mood.

I smiled as well, which seemed to make her happy. She lay her head against my chest, listening to my heartbeat.

"I have a question for you, by the way," I said softly, glancing over at the picture of me that she had on her nightstand.

"What's that?" she asked.

"How do you have a picture of me? I've never seen you with a camera."

"Oh!" She giggled and then explained. "Our minds take in thousands of images every second that we are alive, Lance." She reached into her nightstand and pulled out an empty picture frame. She took out the paper backing behind the glass in the frame, and then glanced out the window at the mountains. She slowly ran her hand along the paper, and I watched in amazement as the dim outline of the mountains began appearing on the blank paper. A few more seconds past, and then the picture was complete. Color spread across the outline of the mountains.

"Wow," I said in amazement.

She smiled, handing me the picture, which looked twenty times better than any picture taken with a camera.

"This puts high definition to shame," I laughed.

She smiled at my amazement. "Would you like to do one?" she offered, taking me completely by surprise.

"Sure!" I flipped the picture over and ran my hand back and forth. "*Voila!*" I said dramatically, showing her the blank back side of the picture.

We both burst out laughing, and she gave me a kiss. "That's amazing," she said playfully. She took the picture from me and flipped it over, running her hand along it and making it vanish without a trace. "Find something you think would make a good picture," she instructed.

I glanced through the window and spotted a bird about fifty meters away in a tree.

"Ready?" she asked. I nodded, and she placed her hand on top of mine on top of the paper. "Okay, I want you to think of nothing but that image," she told me.

I stared down at the blank paper. My eyes widened in amazement as I felt a surge go through my hand, sort of like an electric shock. She ran my hand back and forth, and the picture formed, just like hers. Once it was finished, she let go of my hand, and I felt the light surges of her powers fade away with it.

"There you go! It's beautiful," she said.

I looked down at the picture of the blue jay in amazement. "Thank you so much! That was sick," I said happily. I felt an even stronger bond with her now than I had five minutes ago.

"So what do you want to do today?" she asked.

"I don't care; it's up to you," I told her with a yawn, still trying to shake off my sleepiness.

"Aw, damn," she muttered, hitting her forehead with her hand.

"What?" I asked.

"I almost forgot that I have to do my daily report on you." She pulled out the all-too-familiar folder from under her bed. "I've always wanted to do this without getting dressed in the morning," she teased, trying to lighten the mood of the interrogation. She opened the folder to a new page and snapped her fingers, which sent a pen hurtling across the room and into her hand. "That was cool, hey?" she asked, winking at me.

I nodded and laughed.

"So do you have any family?" she asked, getting right down to business.

"Not really. My mom is dead. I don't know where my father is, and I have two sisters, but I have no clue if they're still alive. Our bases were getting hit pretty hard before I left."

Lara glanced up from her page. "What are their names?"

"Tina and Kate." I pulled a heart-shaped necklace from my shirt—I'd been hiding it from the fiends.

"Wow, how did you ever manage to keep this?" Lara asked me as I opened it up, showing her the picture inside of Tina, Kate, and me when we were younger. We were sitting on the doorstep of our old apartment, before the war.

"I stuck it in my mouth when I was captured and then buried it in the courtyard the first chance I had when I arrived here." I stared down at it fondly. "Before I met you, it was the only thing keeping me going," I whispered passionately, staring at it one last time before snapping it shut and tucking it back around my neck underneath my shirt.

Lara stared at me silently for a moment and then continued her interrogation. "What was your field shift like as a sniper?"

"Seven days on, two days off," I replied.

"How many confirmed kills do you have?" She looked up from her folder to me. I looked away, hoping she would skip the question, but she continued to stare at me persistently. "Come on, Lance. I won't be upset."

"Seven hundred sixty-two," I told her, and her face filled with shock as she stared at me in disbelief.

"You were in the resistance for three and a half years, right?" When I nodded, she asked, "What was the average age for a fighter?"

"They wouldn't let the children or the elderly fight, so it was around sixteen to twenty," I told her.

"Why did you go to Dublin City when you knew that would be a suicide mission?" she asked.

"I guess I wanted it over with. I was tired of hiding in caves, watching my friends die, and listening to the constant barrage of air and artillery strikes," I told her with a shrug. "I had five friends who came with me— they all died." A tear trickled down my cheek as the memories of my previous life flooded back into my brain.

"I'm sorry, Lance," Lara whispered sincerely.

"It's okay. I've always asked myself why they died and I didn't. I still haven't found that answer." I wiped away another tear that was threatening to trickle down my face.

Lara must have felt bad because she put the folder back under her bed and patted my back. She lay her head against my shoulder in an attempt to make me stop crying as we cuddled in silence. "Do you think Lara has nice tits?" she asked with a smile, wiping away a tear from my face.

"They're all right for a sixth grader," I sniffled with a laugh. She punched me playfully and gave me a gentle kiss on the cheek. "Can I ask you a question?" I asked her hopefully.

"Anything," she whispered, snuggling closer with me.

"That day when you guys killed Toby—why did you do it? Why didn't you kill me?" I asked her, finally getting the burning question off of my chest.

"We were in charge of the two of you. It was Domelski that gave us the order. Kill one, and the other will talk, he told us," Lara explained as we relived that day, which seemed so long ago now. We sat there in silence for a few moments as I let her explanation sink into my head. "I'm going to be your lawyer," Lara told me after a few minutes.

"For what?" I asked.

"In a month, you have a court date. You're sentenced to death by firing squad—don't worry; all resistance fighters are. I can prove that you were only fighting to defend your species and that you can adapt to sharing this world with the fiends," she reassured me.

"Gee, that would have been nice to know before," I joked nervously.

She laughed. "Do you know how to read and write?"

I nodded hesitantly. To be completely honest, I had a learning disability growing up, and I had barely used any school-related skills for more than four years, ever since the invasion.

"Good. I signed us up for a class tomorrow," she informed me happily.

"What is it?" I asked, zoning out as I stared at the ceiling fan spinning overhead.

"It's a class on how to solve problems peacefully. You'll learn about fiends a little, and about how to treat us, and stuff like that."

"That sounds like fun," I replied sarcastically.

She rolled her eyes. "I know it's going to be bullshit, but you have to take it in order to be guaranteed that you won't be sentenced to the death penalty."

I sighed unhappily as Lara and I began to get dressed. Once we were ready, she held out her hand to me, which I grasped. I smiled, indicating that I was ready to go. We walked down the hall to the cafeteria, chased by questioning stares of fiends as we passed by.

"Relax; there's no law that says we can't be in a relationship," she whispered to me as we walked down the hall.

I relaxed my grip on her hand but still was nervous. "How can they tell I'm human? We look exactly the same," I asked her as we sat down in the cafeteria with my tray of food.

"Humans have a scent that is released from them. It's different from the scent that comes off us. Humans can't pick up on the scents because their noses are pretty bad, but we can smell about twenty times better than you can." She gestured for me to eat my food. She began to eat some kind of fiend food; it was kind of slimy-looking and bland.

"*Pralango*, Lara!" someone called out in Jural. I turned to see a girl strutting over to us. She sat down beside Lara and stared at me in shock—we recognized each other.

"You remember Luna, right?" Lara asked, trying to break the awkward lull at the table.

I nodded. "Nice to meet you," I told Luna, offering my hand to her across the table.

She looked at it for a second and then glanced over at Lara with a laugh. "If you're going to take your pet on a field trip, you should at least have him trained."

I glanced at the both of them, confused.

"You're not allowed to touch other females when you're in a relationship. It's against the laws of Dracona," Lara told me, looking up from her food but ignoring the comment Luna had just made.

"Oh," I muttered, quickly withdrawing my hand.

"It's fine. Don't worry about it. You know now for next time," Lara told me with a friendly smile. She resumed eating her plate of food.

"So what are you up to today, buddy?" Luna asked Lara when we had all finished our breakfast.

"We're going down to the arcade, if you'd like to come," Lara offered. She stood up and gestured for me to stand up as well.

"*We?*" Luna asked her.

Lara nodded, and Luna whispered something to her in Jural, nodding over to me. Lara answered her, and Luna looked at the two of us, seeming kind of stunned. Without a word, Luna picked up her tray and left.

"I don't think she likes me, hey?" I joked.

Lara smiled, grabbing my hand with a shrug. "She'll come around. Don't worry about it."

The arcade was pretty amazing. I had been disconnected from technology for more than four years, so to see so many flashing lights at once was kind of overwhelming. I felt like a kid in Disneyland at first. Lara and I played a couple of war games to pass the time.

We would strap headbands to ourselves, and then it was as if we no longer were in reality; we were thrown straight into a realistic war scene, fighting with each other to stay alive, which was pretty sick. For the most part, it was an uneventful day, but after being locked up for so long, it felt like the best day of my life.

After the arcade, Lara and I went back to her room. The two of us ate in silence that night, listening to a radio program in Jural. Lara would talk about nothing important, just to spark a conversation. As night finally came around, I grabbed a blanket and lay down on the couch.

"What are you doing, silly?" she asked, patting a spot beside her on the bed.

I obediently got up off the couch and lay down beside her, figuring this sleeping arrangement was permanent. I snuggled next to her warm body, letting sleep overcome me within a few minutes.

"Time to get up, Lance!" Lara chirped happily the next morning, waking me with a gentle shake.

"Mmm, go away," I muttered sleepily into my pillow, rolling away from her.

"Fine. Have it your way," she shot back. She left the room and when she returned a moment later, it was with a bucket of water.

"Unghh, fine … I'm up," I groaned sleepily, sitting up in the bed.

"I got up early and bought you some clothes since you're going to be staying with me from now on," Lara informed me, throwing a black shirt and a black pair of sweatpants over to me.

We quickly ate breakfast and then headed down the hall to an open door. "Ah, you must be Lance and Lara. Welcome." A middle-aged woman greeted us as we entered.

"Yes, we are sorry that we're late," Lara told her as we looked around the classroom.

The first thing I noticed was that unlike the entire base, this was the only room I had seen that was lit with a standard white lightbulb. "Wow, I can actually see," I whispered to Lara, who laughed. The instructor checked us off her list and motioned for us to take our seats.

"Lance, would you mind standing up and reading to the class what is written on the board?" the instructor asked me.

I gulped nervously as Lara prodded me. As I looked around, I saw that everyone in class was staring at me. "The plan … planet Fraturna was a stylish in … um," I began.

"Established," Lara whispered to me, seeming confused by my poor reading skills. Maybe she'd think I was just nervous.

"Established," I corrected myself, glancing at the back of the class, where one fiend was chuckling with another.

"The filthy dog can't even read," I heard one of them say to the other with a laugh.

Rage boiled over me as I angrily turned toward them. "How about you shut the—"

"Lance!" Lara said angrily, stopping me mid-sentence by yanking me down and placing her hand on my lap to prevent my getting up and starting a fight. I glared angrily at the pair of fiends who were laughing at me. I sat there in embarrassment as Lara patted my leg, calming me down.

I found the class, for the most part, to be a waste of time—probably because I was pissed off for most of it. It seemed to me that the instructors tried to make it sound as if the fiends were the peaceful creatures, and the humans were the ones provoking all the violence, when in actual fact, it had been the fiends who'd come hunting for us when we fled into the woods to rebuild our lives.

I somehow managed to make it through it, though, without protesting once. Finally, at three thirty the class ended, and I got a little certificate saying I had successfully completed it. Lara took it from me as we walked down the hall.

"Don't worry; I'm going to put it in your portfolio when we get home," she told me, reading my questioning look.

We arrived at her dorm about five minutes later, where I thankfully flopped down on the couch as she rummaged around under the bed, placing the certificate in my folder, and then going over to the window and opening the curtains, allowing light to come dancing through. "Want to watch some television?" she asked, flopping down beside me with a bag of chips.

"Sure," I muttered grumpily, staring in front of me but seeing nothing that even slightly resembled a TV.

She snapped her fingers, and a bright white light came shooting out of three walls, meeting in the middle of the room and forming holograms of people who began talking in Jural. I realized it was the news. Lara popped open the bag of chips, offering me a handful. "Thanks," I said contentedly, eating them one at a time, savoring each bite.

"So how did you find the class?" Lara asked me casually as we watched the program.

"It was all right," I lied, grabbing a chip and chucking it into my mouth. I kept my attention focused away from her.

She stared at me for a moment, apparently deciding to let the conversation go without arguing. "Thanks for going. I know it was a pretty boring class, and the instructors may have fabricated some of their facts a little, but you needed that certificate," Lara reminded me.

I nodded, and she patted my shoulder happily. She turned up the volume on the television and sauntered over to the kitchen to start cooking supper. I followed her and helped to cook a moment later by cutting up some vegetables for us as a side plate, while she cooked our main course.

It was chicken, which we served to ourselves about twenty minutes later. I quickly realized she was really horrible at cooking human food. The entire thing was black, and each bite tasted like a new brand of charcoal-flavored gum, which took forever to chew into a piece that I could swallow.

Once we were finished eating, she told me to go wash the dishes. I did, obediently, as she went over to the couch to watch more of the news. Finally, Lara flicked off the TV and collected a few plates I hadn't gotten to yet. A few minutes later, I saw her clutching her stomach. "What's wrong?" I asked her.

"I just don't feel good," she muttered moodily, drying the dishes I had just washed.

I could tell she didn't want to talk about it, so we finished in silence, and then she went over to the bed, flopping down on it and looking exhausted. I stripped down to my boxers and flopped into bed. I snuggled beside her, trying to cheer her up. "Thanks for making me supper."

"Shut up," she giggled, knowing that I hated the chicken she had cooked.

"Oh, cool," I said, staring down at her stomach.

"What?"

"You have no belly button." I lifted my shirt, glancing from my stomach to hers.

"Oh, ha-ha. Yeah, fiends don't have umbilical cords. When the mother's pregnant, the baby just absorbs all the nutrients through the skin."

She began purring affectionately and pulled out the book I had been looking at when I first arrived at her place. She lazily perched herself on my chest and read to me in English before we fell asleep.

The next morning, Lara let out a shaky groan, and I woke, startled, when I felt warm liquid spill across my stomach. I yelped in pain—it felt like someone had poured a steaming hot cup of coffee onto me. I jumped out of bed, frantically flicking on the red lamp on her nightstand. Lara was on her hands and knees, clutching her stomach and groaning in pain.

She puked up some purplish blood onto the sheets. Her eyes flashed red as she let out a cry of pain. I looked at the puddle of purplish fiend blood, which was spreading across the sheets and dripping onto the floor. I grabbed some paper towels and started to clean it up, but she motioned for me to stay where I was.

Lara was still on the bed as her muscles began to spasm. She closed her eyes, taking in deep breaths to calm herself. Suddenly, as fast as the pain had come, it was gone. She lay down on the bloodstained sheets, catching her breath, as her chest heaved in and out uncontrollably.

"What's happening?" I asked her.

"My tricnoses is starting," she whispered to me.

"What's that?" I asked.

"Tricnoses," she repeated. "It happens once a month and ranges between a couple hours to a full day. On the days I used to have it, I'd send Luna down to give you your food. You remember that, right?" I nodded. "It usually starts off with weird stomach feelings, and then progresses to puking, mood swings, cramps, stuff like that, until it goes away." She bit her lip nervously.

I could tell there was something else. "But?" I asked.

"But if I get a really bad one, I could transform into a fiend," she mumbled, regaining control of her breathing. This sounded really bad for me, and Lara must have seen my frightened expression. "It will be okay, Lance. We're going to be fine," she promised me.

I came over to her side, helping her up and guiding her into the bathroom, where she wiped the blood off my stomach with a wet rag. Then she shooed me out so she could take a shower. Nervously, I began to make her breakfast. Occasionally, a weird growl would erupt through the door, making me jump, but then her voice would call out to me a minute later that she was fine.

Once I finished making breakfast, I entered the bathroom cautiously, making sure she was still in her human form. I brought two plates of eggs in with me. "At least you're puking up solid stuff now instead of blood," I joked, trying to lighten the mood as she finished throwing up in the toilet.

She glared at me in disgust, and as I set her plate down beside her, she instantly grabbed it and threw it back at me. I luckily dodged it as it sailed by and smashed against the wall behind me. "What the hell is your problem?" she yelled at me angrily. "I'm here in pain, and all you can think about is food?"

I turned to leave, but she grabbed hold of my leg and started crying, begging me not to leave. Her mood swings were so erratic that I didn't know whether to stay or go, but I foolishly sat down, ignoring my better judgment. I hugged her close, reassuring her that I loved her and that everything was going to be okay, even as she had an emotional breakdown beside me.

She held on to her stomach, groaning occasionally.

"Cramps?" I asked. She nodded. "I'm sorry for making you breakfast. I thought it would help you feel better," I told her.

"Don't be sorry. It's my fault. I shouldn't have lashed out at you like that. I just lost control for a second, that's all." She stared at my plate of eggs. We shared it, as her mood swings began to change again. "I love you so much," Lara whispered, placing my hand against her chest. "Wouldn't you like to have little Lances and Laras with me one day?" she asked me with a hiccup, smiling happily as she wiped away a tear from her beautiful face.

I just nodded, agreeing with her, nervously hoping the conversation would pass—I had no other choice. I needed a way out, and to my relief, it came. Lara began to vomit, so I quickly rushed out of the bathroom to the kitchen, getting her another rag to clean up the floor.

"Are there, like, pills for tricnoses or something that you can get?" I asked her as I cleaned up the mess.

"It costs three hundred crome per pill, and from what I've heard from friends who have tried them, you can still feel the pain during your tricnoses; it's just dulled down, making you a bit less moody, with a guarantee that you won't accidently transform." She held onto her stomach as another cramp subsided.

"I wish I could help you in some way," I told her as she stared at the floor.

"You're doing a great job already," she said, looking up at me with a half-hearted smile. She motioned for me to sit back down with her. "Can you massage my back?" she asked, propping herself in between my legs.

I did so, obediently; it was pretty awkward. It felt like there was something bouncing around inside of her. At times, her skin would turn clammy and scaly, making my hands fly away, but she would reassure me she wasn't going to change, and I would continue to massage her. Weird noises periodically erupted from her belly.

She would turn around, giggling at my reactions to the sounds. A couple hours later, Lara asked me to bring her in a bottle of rum. She poured a glass for herself, and I took a tiny sip from it. "If I do change, don't let me bite you," she warned me. "During tricnoses, I crave human blood, so if I even smell it, I lose control. I won't be able to stop myself from attacking you, okay?"

"That's a good piece of information to know," I told her with an uneasy smile.

She laughed. As the day progressed and it got late, Lara had less pain, so I figured that it was almost the end of her tricnoses. But then, my worst fear became a reality.

Chapter 7

Clumsily, I got up to go to the kitchen. I lost my balance and slammed back down to the floor. My hand slid across the heating vent, causing a deep cut across my palm. I cried out in pain as blood instantly seeped from the wound and trickled onto the floor.

Lara turned to see what had happened, and I tried to stop the bleeding out of her sight. "What's wronnnn …" She stared at my bloody hand. Her eyes slit into a star shape and locked onto my palm. She seemed to be in a trance, staring at the blood on my hand while licking her lips. She gasped, and her muscles began to contract, causing her skin to stretch as if it was about to rip apart. "*Run!*" she gasped frantically, crawling away from me into the corner of the bathroom. She let out an anguished, non-human growl, staring at me as I sat frozen in fear.

Her skin began fading away, making way for scaly, dark, fiend skin, with blackish fur sprouting all over her body. Claws similar to a curved dagger burst from her fingers as she screamed uncontrollably in pain, trying to fight the transformation. I got up as fast as I could, stumbling into the living room, but it was too late.

A thunderous roar erupted from behind me, followed by the door smashing into pieces. I was blasted with the debris and was tossed against the wall like a rag doll. I saw the fiend emerge through the rubble. It had bear-like paws, a saber-toothed tiger-like face, with wings, and a long, bladed tail.

Its skin looked as hard as a bulletproof vest, and there was black fur all across its body, with patches of white fur. If I hadn't been scared shitless, I actually would have found it a beautiful creature. Lara snarled at me, batting me to the ground as I tried to run.

I got up and tried to run in the other direction, but she batted me back down to the ground again with ease. I realized she was playing with me, as a cat would do with a mouse before it finishes it off. Grabbing a piece of wood from the broken bookshelf, I swung with all my might and connected with the side of her head.

It stunned the fiend, who buckled for a second from the force of the blow. That gave me enough time to race back into the bathroom. A moment later, Lara regained her senses and let out a gut-wrenching roar before charging in after me, sending what was left of the door into splinters. Her fiend body burst through in a path of destruction, slamming me into the bathtub. I smashed my head against it, crumpling to the ground in defeat.

I was fighting to stay conscious. She opened her enormous jaw, growling at me viciously. I could see the two rows of teeth along her upper and lower jaws grinding dangerously as she prepared to finish me off. "Lara, it's me," I pleaded in a last-ditch effort to save myself.

She heard my plea. Her ears perked up as she approached me. She stopped in her tracks, tilting her head to look at me for a second. Her bloodshot eyes seemed to clear and return to normal as she stared at me, nudging me softly with her paw. And then, as if hit by a Taser, she fell to the ground and started to convulse.

Her fur began to retreat into her skin, followed by everything else. She took on human form, leaving her lying naked on the floor beside me, panting uncontrollably. She stared at her hands in shock and then over at me. Her face instantly filled with concern as she realized what she had done. She crawled toward me, but that's the last thing I remember—the world around me began to spin, and I blacked out.

I woke up the next morning with a warm towel lying across my forehead. Lara came over to my bedside almost immediately. She had soup for me, and she helped me sit up against the backboard. "How are you feeling, cutie?" she asked, softly kissing my forehead.

"Like I just got hit by a pickup truck," I joked, gingerly touching my puffed-up face.

"I'm sorry … I'm so sorry," she whispered apologetically. A tear began trickling down her face.

I quickly wiped it away, soothing her. "It's okay," I reassured her.

She smiled, perking up a little now that I had forgiven her. "I know you don't care much for my cooking, so I went down to the cafeteria and bought you this." She offered me a spoonful of soup. I accepted it gratefully, and she fed me the rest of it. "I don't think we handled last night very well," she said, "so I installed a metal door on the closet. If things get out of hand that way again, you can sit in there until things settle down."

"We would have been fine if it wasn't for that damn slippery floor," I told her.

She smiled, seeing that I was trying to take the blame off her. She ruffled my hair affectionately, letting out a sigh. "We had no backup plan, but now we know what to do for next time." Every bone in my body ached. I could feel swollen areas around my face as well, and there was a throbbing pain in my forehead, which lead me to believe I had a concussion. I tried to get up, but Lara put her hand on my chest, pushing me gently back against my pillow. "Whoa, whoa, whoa—what do you think you're doing, champ?"

"I was going to help you with the dishes," I told her, looking at the empty soup bowl and her plate of food on the kitchen table.

"You have to stay in bed; you have a concussion," she said, fluffing up my pillow and kissing me on the forehead. I could tell that she was feeling guilty, so I decided not to argue with her. She beamed down at me, sliding her hand along my chest, casting a spell that absorbed into my skin and made me feel groggy immediately. "Don't worry; it will make you feel better. I promise," she told me tenderly. She held my hand reassuringly as I mumbled something incomprehensible and drifted off to sleep.

I awoke to the sounds of birds chirping outside the next morning. I got up briefly, sneaking to the bathroom to brush my teeth. Lara instantly noticed my absence and banged on the bathroom door as soon as I turned on the tap.

"Hold on!" I called out to her, putting a silence to the panicked banging.

Her concerned voice came through the door. "Are you all right, Lance?"

"Yes, I just had to go to the bathroom," I replied calmly.

"Okay, go back to bed once you're done. I'll serve you breakfast."

Once I was back in bed, she appeared at the doorway with a bowl of fruit. "I think it's time to try some solid food," she told me, offering me a piece of watermelon and taking one out for herself.

"Mmmmmm," I grunted in satisfaction, eating my piece.

She smiled in agreement. "These are delicious! I've never tasted something natural like this that is so good. What is the name of this?"

"It's called watermelon."

"Watermelon, hey?" she repeated, staring at the fruit.

"Kate use to take me and Tina blueberry hunting all the time when we were younger," I told her, smiling to myself as the memories of the three of us flooded through me.

Lara stared at me for a moment. I let out a disappointed laugh, realizing those days were long gone. "I'm sorry that you're separated from them," Lara said, staring guiltily at the floor.

"It's not your fault," I told her, rubbing her shoulder comfortingly.

She nodded, handing me another piece of watermelon. "Would you like to watch a movie?" she suggested, turning on the television. The lights flashed on, presenting the holographic images of a crucified human nailed to the wooden door of a barn somewhere in Dublin. Fiend soldiers posed triumphantly around him.

"Oh gosh," she muttered, glancing at me as she quickly flipped the channel.

I shook away the image of the dead body, and she flicked on a movie that she had picked out. The movie was fairly good; it was about two fiends who fell in love but were separated by the war. When it was all over—of course ending in the fiends' victory over the humans—they found each other at a spot where they'd first met as children, and they lived happily ever after.

The movie was in Jural, but Lara sat beside me, translating what was going on as the movie played. When it finished, she cast the same spell that she had the previous day, kissing my forehead as I drowsily drifted away. The next morning, I woke up to the sounds of Lara and another female fiend, chatting in the kitchen to one another in Jural.

I pretended to be asleep, eavesdropping on them as they continued talking, trying to pick up bits and pieces of their conversation. They both looked zoned out, sort of like when Lara had seen my bloody finger. I noticed a couple of empty bottles of rum and realized that they were wasted.

"You should drink his blood instead of this stale crap," Lara's friend urged her excitedly in broken English.

I noticed that their rum was mixed with something red, and I pieced together that it must be a mixture of rum and bagged blood. "*Danre de contal Lance I reprudre tamar relation*," Lara muttered in Jural, pausing to take a sip of her drink.

"Besides I love him, and I wouldn't ever want it, unless he gave it to me," she continued in English, wiping the blood from around her mouth.

They continued to talk for a while, but I couldn't make out what they were saying anymore, until Lara's friend brought up marriage in English. "The laws of Dracona state that the male has to propose in order for you to get married. Until then, you will never have a full connection with him. You're never going to see him do that. Men have a hard enough time committing to a normal relationship, let alone a relationship where his wife could kill him just for having her tricnoses," Lara's friend explained to her with a laugh.

"We respect each other enough to talk to each other about our feelings," Lara argued with her.

"Why is he lying in bed with a concussion then? That seems like a real open relationship," her friend replied, provoking a fight.

"I made a mistake, okay? My fiend body didn't recognize him, and I accidently attacked him. There's no law against fiends and humans being together, so if you don't like it, get the hell out of my dorm!" Lara shot back angrily.

I heard the clinking of bottles as they rattled around on the table, some rolling off, smashing on the floor. "You're a disgrace to the pure-blood line, Lara," her friend snarled.

"I've banged him, too!" Lara's voice shouted.

"You have issues, girl, for real. You need your head checked out." The insult came flying back, followed by the slamming of the front door.

Lara let out an angry yell, slamming her hand against the table and chucking an empty bottle at the door, which shattered into a million pieces on the floor. She glanced over at me, embarrassed, realizing that I was awake. "I'm sorry that you had to hear that, Lance," she said, approaching the bed. She gave me a hug and climbed under the sheets with me, getting undressed.

"You're drunk," I whispered to her.

She giggled and put her finger across my lips. "You're cute," she replied with an affectionate twinkle in her eyes.

We silently had sex until she passed out from the mixed blood/rum brew they had been drinking. When I woke up that night, Lara was in the kitchen, cooking. I felt brand new. I no longer had a headache, and the swelling in my eye had gone down, so I decided to get up. "Hey, sexy, I had a good time," I told her, wrapping my hands around her waist and kissing the back of her neck as I came up behind her.

"Oh really? So everything was to my man's satisfaction?" she asked, trying to sound sexy.

"A-plus," I replied, sliding my hand across her waist and down her hips.

She bobbed side to side to the music playing in the background. "Well, I'm glad to hear that." She giggled, turning to hug me, and then leaned back to look up at me.

"Would you like me to give you a hand with that?" I asked, nodding toward the food cooking on the stove.

"Nah, I've got it under control, but thank you." She gave me an affectionate kiss. "You shouldn't be up anyway. You haven't fully recovered yet." She grabbed my hand and a bowl of soup and bustled me back over to our bed, tucking me in like a little kid.

"So what was that whole fight about yesterday?" I asked her casually, trying not to come off as nosey.

"Oh, it was nothing. She just doesn't understand that what we have is something special between us."

"What was that thing about a pure-blood line?" I asked her nervously. This question was either going to pay off very well or blow up in my face.

She paused for a moment, deciding, I think, what to tell me and what to keep to herself. "I'm a pure-blood, Lance, so I'm different from a lot of the other normal fiends. Pure-bloods are rare; we are the blood line of Lord Dracona. We have powers that are much stronger than any normal fiend. We have the ability to heal wounds, and unlike fiends, we are immortal."

"So you're never going to die?" I asked, confused.

She smiled with a sigh, patiently playing with my hair. "I age just like you, but when I die, my body will turn to ash, and I will be reborn out of the ashes, with all my memories still intact, except that physically, I'll be a baby."

"So how old are you, really, right now?" I asked, still confused.

"Two hundred forty-five, but you're over-thinking this. I'm technically nineteen. I just have memories from my previous life, that's all."

"So—" I began.

She cut me off, saying, "That's enough questions for tonight. You need your rest."

"I'm fine, though!" I objected.

She retrieved the bowl of soup she had set aside and sat down on the edge of the bed. "You can get up tomorrow; I promise," Lara told me. She brought the spoon to my mouth to feed it to me. The soup was pretty bitter, but it was really good compared to the stuff that she usually made. "Do you like it? I've been spending the day trying to learn how to cook your human food better."

"Are you kidding me? I love it," I told her.

She smiled happily and continued to feed me, humming to herself. But there was a worrying thought that I just couldn't get off my mind—behind that beautiful smile of hers, which I had fallen in love with, wasn't a fiend. It was a pure-blood.

Chapter 8

Three days later was my court date. I sat anxiously, wearing the suit Lara had brought me. She comforted me as we waited for my escort to arrive. Soon, there was bang on the door, and Lara sprang to her feet to answer it.

"Don't worry; you'll be fine," she promised me while opening the door.

Two guards entered, nodding to Lara and exchanging a few friendly words with her. She laughed and nodded toward me. Their attention shifted to me. One kept an eye on me while the other shackled my hands and feet. "Let's go," one of them ordered, nodding toward the door.

Lara was close to my side as we walked down the hall. We exited the base and headed down a dirt path toward the courthouse. The courtroom went silent as I was led inside. "*Hang* him!" someone called from the bleachers behind us, and a wave of cheers erupted around the courthouse.

I gulped in fear, but Lara gave me a comforting wink. The two guards who had escorted me chained my feet and hands to my surroundings. The courtroom was packed, with about forty fiends watching from the bleachers and five armed guards. The entire thing was spoken in Jural, so I had no clue what was going on.

Lara showed the judge my certificate from the peace class I had attended, followed by a document with some notes that I recognized from her interrogations. When that didn't seem to have much of an effect on him, she began showing him photos of her and me together. Then she turned toward the crowd and gave what appeared to be an emotional speech in Jural. After an hour or so, the judge finally looked content and gave me his verdict in English.

"I feel you and Lara have developed something very special, which proves to me that there can be peace between humans and fiends." He paused to scan the crowd. "You, Lance Andrew Burns, are to stay in Miss Lara Sara Maurinie's residence for the remainder of your twenty-year sentence," he told me firmly. The crowd groaned unhappily as the judge delivered his sentence. I realized joyfully that I wasn't going to be sentenced to another execution. "I would like you two to keep in mind that there is a city being rebuilt for special cases, such as yourselves. I'd advise you both to look into it on your spare time. Maybe you kids would like to apply for a dorm there, in which you have my written permission to live out the rest of your sentence, Lance. I would also like you to keep a mental note of any problems, concerns, or feelings related to the stuff you and Lara do together. This will be monitored by a guidance counselor, to whom you both will be sent to for mandatory periodic checkups," he told us. "You're both free to go now."

The judge slammed down his wooden hammer, and just like that, the trial was over.

"That will be all for today," a dignitary called from beside him. Everyone stood up, and the judge left the courtroom.

I was uncuffed and handed over to Lara's custody. She nodded to them and then happily grabbed my hand and led me out into the warm summer breeze.

I glanced to my left, where noises were coming from. Four PLF soldiers were clearly not as lucky as I was—they were lined up against a wall. "Don't look, Lance," Lara whispered, turning my head away gently with her hand.

"Go to hell, you monsters!" one of them yelled defiantly.

A shout rang out—"Fire!"—followed by four shots simultaneously shattering the afternoon's tranquility.

A group of fiends who had gathered to watch started laughing as the guards dragged the dead PLF soldiers away. I glanced back at the red patch of grass in disgust, just as Lara forcefully led me inside the base. "Executing humans is like your guys' national sport, huh?" I said bitterly, once we were in the privacy of her dorm.

"We don't know what they did, Lance," she told me, trying to justify the killings.

We sat there in silence for a moment. Lara fiddled around with her hair. "I think the judge was pretty fair today," she said.

I nodded unhappily. "Apparently he wasn't as fair before me, though." I couldn't let go of what had just happened outside.

She folded her arms and leaned against the wall, staring at me for a second in silence.

"Don't bother," I muttered, waving my hand for her to forget about it. "So what's the city called that the judge was talking about?"

"Monatello," Lara snapped, still staring off in the distance.

"What's wrong?" I asked her.

"Nothing. I think it's time that you get used to my fiend side, Lance." She stepped away, stripping down to nothing and opening the back door to her dorm.

"No, I don't want to," I told her, hastily backing away.

"This will be good for us. I'm going to do something to you that will hurt, but don't be afraid." She rested her hand on my shoulder consolingly.

I watched her muscles bulge from her arms as she dropped down to all fours. I backed away in fear, accidently knocking over a glass cup and stepping on the shattered pieces. Within a couple seconds, Lara had fully transformed into her fiend form.

Her elegant wings extended as she shook her fur, fluffing it up. Her eyes flashed green, causing the broken glass to fix itself. It floated back up to the table as if it had a mind of its own. Her eyes flashed green again, and my foot healed instantly, relieving the pain.

I cautiously took a step toward her as she bowed to me, lying down on her front paws. I noticed her eyes were bluish, unlike her bloodshot eyes when she had attacked me last week. She was about nine feet tall when she stood up on her hind legs, with about a six-foot wingspan on either side.

She folded her wings up, purring as she came over to me. She rubbed her head against my hip in a friendly way. She gently pinned me to the ground, taking one of her claws and cutting deep into my skin, forming the shape of a fiend on the right side of my chest. I whimpered in pain, but she purred softly and licked the blood off my chest.

Her saliva seemed to heal the wound—the bleeding stopped, and the fiend-shaped symbol turned black, like a tattoo, leaving the imprint of Lara's fiend shape there. She purred again, got off me, and nudged me up with her nose. I patted her back and ran my hand along her soft black fur.

She rolled over like a dog, and I obediently patted her stomach. She purred contentedly, looking lovingly into my eyes. After ten minutes or so, she rolled back over onto her paws and motioned with her head for me to get on her back. "No, thank you!" I exclaimed, holding my hands out in an attempt to push her away. She nudged her body closer and closer to me, pushing me up against a wall, so I had no choice but to go over her.

She growled playfully, finally forcing me onto her back. I could feel her powerful muscles working as she climbed through the open door and into a field, where she began to walk around in circles in an attempt to get me used to her moving. Once I was comfortable with that, she moved onto jogging and eventually developed into a light run.

I held on tightly, wrapping my arms around her neck and trying to get her to stop as she galloped around in the field. I noticed fiends gathering at the windows of the building, looking out at us, pointing and laughing. Lara began to jump while she ran. I realized that she was about to fly.

"No! Bad, Lara!" I yelled at her like I would to a pet. She let out a roar and launched herself into the air. "Let me down!" I screamed at the top of my lungs, which she did obediently, smashing into the ground and sending me rocketing off her back. I slid along the ground fifteen or twenty feet before coming to a rest on something soft.

"Oh shit!" I gasped, looking up into the saber-toothed face of another fiend.

It nudged me with its bear-like paw and bit into the back of my T-shirt to lift me off the ground. It placed me back on top of Lara. "Eat me! Don't let her take me back up there!" I pleaded to the fiend.

Lara and the other fiend both started to make lion-like sounds to each other—talking, I assumed. The fiend bounced into the air, did a circle in the sky, and then landed back down beside Lara, nodding its head toward me. "You're teaching me how to land?" I asked.

They both nodded, and then Lara launched herself back into the air. When she landed, the same thing happened, causing me to skid along the grass another fifteen feet on my back. Lara sauntered over to me, licking my knee, which was bloodied by the fall, and then I got back on, a bit more confidently. I wrapped my hands around her neck as she purred affectionately.

Racing through the air felt sort of like being on the hood of a car. As Lara went to land, I jumped off a foot before she touched the ground. I stumbled a few steps but finally regained my balance and came to a stop. Lara galloped over to me, and I launched myself back up on to her back, excitedly.

She let out a happy roar, rocketing into the air, higher than the last time. We were flying so fast that everything was blurry flashes. I held on tight as she flew around for a few more minutes before plunging, without warning, straight into a lake.

I quickly swam to the surface, gasping for air. Lara broke through the surface a moment later, beside me in her human form. She burst out laughing. I joined in her laughter and splashed her playfully. We swam to the edge of the lake, where we rested on the shore.

"That was fun, eh?" she asked. I nodded enthusiastically. "Do you know what this means?" she asked, poking the black tattoo imbedded in my chest.

"Something good, I assume," I said as she stared at my chest. The warm water gently lapped across our bodies.

She smiled, rubbing her hand along the tattoo. "It's hard to explain in English, but it's basically a form of protection and love, saying we're united as one." She pointed to symbols on the bottom of it. "This is my name. This tattoo represents that we are together. Fiends won't attack you now, since they know they will have to deal with me if they do."

"Fiends are afraid of you?" I asked.

She smiled mysteriously but ignored my question. She glanced up at the darkening sky—the sun was beginning to set behind the trees. "This tattoo will prevent me from harming you during my tricnoses as well, so you will be safe to live with me now." A claw protruded from her finger, forming into a dagger, and she cringed as she engraved a tattoo on herself, next to her breast—it was of me with a heart around it, along with a few symbols at the bottom. She healed it, smiling warmly as she kissed me. "We are officially in a relationship now, under the laws of Dracona," she whispered, beginning to make out with me.

"Well, I should warn you that, unlike those other fiends, I'm not scared of you," I said, hitting her chin gently with my fist.

"You should be," she giggled, snuggling closer to me in the shallows of the lake.

"So today when you transformed and gave me this, how come when you licked the blood off, it didn't like trigger you to attack me?"

"Blood only incites my fiend's wild side during tricnoses," she told me with a laugh. "You still have a lot to learn, my friend." She leaned forward and gave me a peck on my neck.

"Is there a book or something?" I asked her with a playful smirk.

"Why settle for a book when you can have the real thing?" she asked, affectionately starting to cuddle with me.

I chuckled and wrapped my arm around her, affectionately giving her a peck on her cheek. "There's something I think that you should know about me, Lara," I said, becoming a bit nervous as we stared up at the stars.

"What is that?" she asked.

"You've got to promise me you're not going to get mad," I told her.

"I won't, but you're starting to freak me out, so tell me what's on your mind."

"Well, remember a couple of weeks ago when you asked me if I had a girlfriend, and I said no?" I asked her. She nodded, her smile slowly fading. "Well, I lied to you, in a way." I paused nervously as her expression darkened. "I had a girlfriend in the resistance for about two years." I felt her muscles tighten up a bit as she glared at me, grinding her teeth angrily.

"You broke up with this girl, though, right?" she asked.

"She was killed in a raid that the fiends did on our base," I said quietly.

"Did you love her?" Lara asked, clearly trying to control her anger.

"Yes," I said truthfully. "But I love you," I said, brushing her hair off her face affectionately.

She stared at me for a moment. I couldn't tell if she was angry with me but she eventually just nodded her head understandingly. "What was this girl's name?"

"Rachel," I answered.

"That's a pretty name." I nodded in agreement, pausing as she fiddled with her hair thoughtfully. "It's fine, I guess. I haven't always been a hundred percent honest with you, either, Lance," she confessed nervously.

"When we first met, you weren't being nice to me out of the goodness of your heart, were you?" I asked her, already knowing the answer.

"No, Domelski ordered me to put on that little scene in front of you to try to extract information by being the nice guy," she said honestly. I sighed unhappily as she confirmed the suspicions I'd had so long ago. She gently squeezed my hand and whispered, "It started out as an act, Lance, but it turned into something real."

I nodded. I was glad that she wasn't mad and that we had these secrets out in the open. "So what size is the tattoo for marriage?" I asked her, breaking the tension.

"You will find out eventually, I hope." She giggled happily, resting her head against mine.

"I hope so too," I replied sincerely. I gave her a kiss, which seemed to shock her, as I had never really been the first one to show affection in the relationship.

She ran a hand across her body, and tattoos appeared all over her. I guess it was her way to try to open up to me by revealing some of her secrets. "In my culture, every tattoo tells a part of your life. For instance, you get this one when you turn from a child to a teenager," she explained, bringing my hand just below her stomach and giggling affectionately.

She calmly rolled over on her back in the shallows, allowing me to examine her scars and tattoos. I would occasionally ask her what one of them meant, and she would explain it to me. When I was done, she ran her hand across her body, and they all vanished, except the one of me she had recently carved into her skin.

"Why does mine stay?" I asked.

"There is a permanent connection between you and me," she replied simply.

"What do you mean?"

"I can locate you and talk to you now, through my thoughts," she said. *"Like this."* I recoiled in shock as her voice sounded in my head. She giggled at my reaction.

"Hi?" I thought.

Her voice echoed back inside my head. *"Hey, sexy."*

"So you can read my thoughts?" I asked her, not liking the sound of that.

"No. When you or I talk in our heads, the connection opens between us so that the other can talk, but we can only be a certain distance from one another, or we won't be able to hear each other anymore."

"Anything else I should know?" I asked.

"Well, there are other things that I gain out of it, which you can't feel because you're human. But one thing that you can feel is if one of us has a strong emotion run through us—the other can feel it."

"All right," I muttered, going quiet as I stared down at my own scar.

"What's wrong?" she asked.

"I'll never be able to return to the resistance now. I'm a traitor to my own country," I replied. The realization of my actions just dawned on me.

"No, you're not," she comforted me softly. "You're just willing to look past this silly war and accept peace. As far as I'm concerned, you're still a PLF." She smiled, running her hand along my back where the letters were seared into my skin.

"Thanks … I guess. You always know the right thing to say."

She glanced down at her own scar of me. "I know how you feel, buddy," she said softly, placing her hand on my shoulder. "You think people like seeing me walking around with you. But you know what? I don't care, because I know what I'm doing is right."

"Same here," I muttered with a defeated sigh.

"Besides, why would you want to go back to your base, wherever that is, and most likely be killed within a couple months?" she asked, glancing across the lake at the reflection of the moon dancing off the smooth surface of the calm water.

"I don't know. I guess for pride and honor." I shrugged and stared up at the full moon. "I guess we will always be enemies in a way. This war will never end until one species totally dominates the other."

She didn't say anything but rested her hand on top of mine. We lay in the shallows for another hour, watching the stars dancing overhead.

"We should probably go back, or I'll be charged for being AWOL," Lara whispered.

"Sounds good." I felt her human hand change and sprout fur. She left me in the water and took a few paces back.

A moment later, she had transformed, and I crawled up onto her furry back. She let out a gut-wrenching roar and reared up on her hind legs, much like a horse would, and then we soared off into the moonlit sky.

Chapter 9

"Welcome, Lance. Thank you for taking the time to see me." My guidance counselor greeted me the next day as I walked into her office.

It was a small room up on the third floor, with a beautiful view of the surroundings. She flicked off the red light illuminating the room and opened a curtain, allowing the light to flood in.

"Thank you," I muttered gratefully.

She smiled, motioning toward a chair. I sat down obediently while she poured me a glass of water and set it in front of me. She was a pretty fiend in her mid-twenties. She had an athletic build with light green eyes and pale skin.

I could tell just by looking at her that she was very confident about herself. "So how have things been going between you and Lara?" she asked.

"Not bad," I replied. This was the first time I had met with her, so I was kind of hesitant to say anything.

She extended her hand, offering a friendly smile. "My name's Dasha, by the way." I shook her hand with a half-hearted smile. "So how long have you two been together?" Dasha asked, sitting back in her chair.

"About two or three months now."

"What do you and Lara do for fun?" she asked, taking out a notebook and clicking her pen to write something down.

"Shop, talk, go out for walks, or a swim once a week. We sometimes watch a little bit of TV or a movie. Just basic stuff like that." I paused to think about what else to tell her. "I've been teaching her how to play card games, and she collects books, so she's been reading me some of them."

Dasha jotted something down, smiling faintly over her notebook to me, as I waited for her to finish. "So she hasn't hit you or abused you in any way, has she?" Dasha asked.

"No," I replied firmly.

"When I first heard about you two, I was quite surprised to see that you guys had made it this far, so that's why I called you in today for this meeting. To be honest, I thought she would have killed you by now," Dasha told me with a laugh. "So how do you survive during Lara's tricnoses?"

I pulled the collar of my shirt down, showing the scar of the fiend on my chest. Dasha looked at it in shock, her surprise clear on her face. "Lara gave you this?" she asked in disbelief.

"Yes."

"So you guys really are serious about this relationship, huh? I figured Lara was just doing this to attract some attention to herself," Dasha said. "So tell me, Lance … what do you miss the most from your past?" She returned to writing something in her notebook.

"Um … my family and my best friend, Grant, I guess." I did not want to get into my personal life with her.

She nodded understandingly. "I've read about your two sisters. Tell me more about this Grant fellow."

"He was my best friend in the PLF. Anything I needed, he always had my back. I met him about a week or so after I joined the resistance, and I guess we just clicked. We had a lot of the same interests and played a lot of the same sports together, so naturally we became best friends," I said. "Grant and I were also in the same squad. Plus, I could joke around with him about anything."

"You don't joke with Lara?" she asked.

"Yeah, of course I do, but it's not the same. I have to watch what I'm saying when I'm around her so I don't get her in a bad mood or something," I explained defensively. "There are two Laras—the Lara I know and the

Lara that she keeps secret from me." I sat back, melting into my chair as I glanced over at the clock.

"We all have secrets, Lance. I'm sure she feels the same way about you," Dasha debated persuasively.

I laughed, knowing she was probably right. I let out a bored sigh while Dasha sketched the tattoo that Lara had given me onto a piece of paper. "So are we done here?" I asked her.

She sat back, glancing at her notebook with a satisfied look. "Yes," she told me, scribbling down something on a piece of paper. "You can go now; make sure to give Lara this note." She handed me the piece of paper.

I nodded and then exited her office. Once out in the hall, I opened the note to read it, but it was, of course, written in Jural. I let out a defeated sigh, folded it back up, and placed it in my pocket.

Lara was waiting for me outside the office, reading a magazine. "All done?" she asked, looking up from the magazine.

"Yeah," I replied, fiddling around in my pocket to retrieve the note. "Dasha wanted me to give you this."

"Thanks." She opened it up quickly, glanced over it, and put it in her purse. "It was just the date and time for our next appointment." She told me, reading my questioning stare. Lara took my hand, leading me out of the waiting room and to her dorm. She was in a very bouncy, lighthearted mood for some reason, which was rare for her. Once we got in, I flopped on to the bed.

Lara opened up a window, letting in a warm breeze, and then she lay down beside me. "So how did your meeting go with her?" I asked. She had seen Dasha before I had this morning.

"It was all right. Sometimes I wanted to tell her to mind her own business, but I held back. You would have been really proud of me."

Lara glanced over at me. "Was she as nosey with you as she was with me?"

I nodded with a sigh. "That's her job, though, I guess."

Lara nodded in agreement. "She prescribed me some pills," Lara said. She sat up and dug around in her purse, pulling out three bags of pills.

"How? Isn't she a guidance counselor?" I asked.

Lara nodded. "This isn't the nineteenth century, Lance. Counselors can prescribe medication if they feel it's needed for the situation. These two will dull down my tricnoses, and this one is an experimental drug that apparently lets my body adapt so that I can become pregnant by humans."

"*What?* Like, you mean, kids?" I blurted out.

"Chill out. Do you see me taking them?" she asked defensively. "I told Dasha I didn't want them, but she told me to take them anyway." Lara laughed at my reaction.

"All right, that's cool. You scared me for a minute. I thought you actually wanted to have kids," I told her with an uneasy laugh.

She looked at me as if trying to read my mind. "Us having kids? That would be crazy," she told me with a laugh.

It wasn't a very convincing laugh, though. "I don't even understand why she would give you those," I muttered, thinking to myself that there had to be an ulterior motive behind Dasha giving Lara the pills.

"I don't either," Lara said with a shrug. She began talking to me again, but I wasn't paying attention to her anymore. My attention had shifted to the unusual, high-pitched birdcalls outside. I listened to them for a second, suddenly panicking as I realized they were resistance-fighter calls.

"Get down!" I shouted, grabbing Lara and hurling her to the ground. I jumped on top of her to shield her.

"What the hell are you doing?" she asked, pushing me off.

I glanced over the bed, confused. I could have sworn an attack was about to commence. I held her down, regaining my position on top of her as she struggled to get up.

"Lance, let me go, or I'm going to bite you." Her eyes darkened as she bared her fangs at me.

I loosened my grip on her, ready to apologize, but before I could say anything, the building shook violently. Artillery smashed into it, sending shrapnel flying. The room momentarily filled with clouds of dust, and I ducked just in time as the shrapnel dangerously sliced through the air around me.

Lara retreated under me. The windows were smashed; glass sprayed everywhere as the walls began to creak dangerously, threatening to collapse.

I peered through the remains of the window at the tree line. I could see the muzzle flashes of machine gunners opening up on us in the distance. One spotted me, and the hissing sounds of bullets became louder as they flew in our direction. I ducked down just in time as they peppered the wall behind us.

Lara crawled across the floor to a closet, opened it up, and returned to my side a moment later. She was holding some kind of fiend machine gun. It had a scope with a green, glowing liquid in a container on the side of it by the feed tray. "PLF?" she asked me, yelling over the sounds of bullets as she began to set up her tripod.

I peeked over the side again as the machine gunner stopped firing and artillery started to pound the base again. There were two squads running through the tall grass in front of us toward the compounds where I had been held prisoner. They were wearing blue uniforms, not the flashy red ones we always wore on our major attacks.

"They're the NWO—the New World Order," I told her. She cracked open a box of ammunition, fed it into the machine gun's tray, and cocked the weapon. I stared at the silver rounds curiously—it was a unique type of metal.

"Fiend-crafted ammunition goes farther and packs more of a punch," Lara said in answer to my questioning stare.

Gunfire started to erupt from the fiend's compound as the NWO fighters were instantly mowed down. Lara braced herself on her knees, firing through the broken window into the tree line, nailing one of them. He fell limply to the ground, probably dead before he even knew what hit him. I crawled over to the closet where Lara had retrieved the machine gun and brought her a few boxes of ammunition, feeding the belt to her as she fired.

"Over there!" I yelled, pointing toward the right side of the tree line, where fighters were trying to flank the base.

She started firing in that direction, causing them to duck down into the tall grass, narrowly escaping death. She turned back as another soldier ran across the field, but she wasn't fast enough. He hid behind a large boulder, and Lara cursed angrily to herself. The NWO was slowly gaining ground toward the base. The all-too-familiar emergency siren began to blare in the background.

Lara reloaded the machine gun, moving aside. "Use it if you have to!" she told me as the sky began to fill with fiends smashing down helicopters that were barely visible, far off in the distance. "Don't get yourself killed," she ordered, starting to morph into her fiend form. Her clothes began ripping as her muscles and bones bulged from her back. A moment later, she let out a heart-stopping cry as the transformation was complete. She burst through the window and flew out of sight. A loud smash snapped me back to reality as a stray bullet shattered the lamp beside me.

I figured there had to be at least two battalions out there, which shocked me. Usually, both the PLF and NWO used hit-and-run tactics against the fiends, but these guys were digging in for a more conventional battle, which almost never happened anymore. By nightfall, tanks had begun to roll through the woods, firing freely into the now-crippled base.

The war had been raging around me for three or four hours, with the NWO, surprisingly, still gaining ground. They had set up a trench about a hundred meters away from the base, which it appeared they were using to communicate to the tanks and artillery through flares and radio equipment manned by the personnel inside.

The fiends must have really dropped the ball on this one because usually things like that would never happen in the war. I was beginning to get worried about Lara. The ground was littered with dozens of fiends' bodies.

The sound of bullets hissing by kept ringing out around me, and then a stray bullet flew into the room, smashing into my improvised bunker that I had constructed out of the furniture. I hunkered down, trying my best to be as small a target as possible. A round ripped through the bunker, exiting an inch away from my head and coming to a rest in the wall behind me. "That's it," I said angrily to myself. I set the machine gun up inside the bunker and stared through the sights, out into the battlefield. It was strewn with dead figures of humans and fiends.

I mowed down one soldier who was running toward my shattered window with a grenade. He fell, and the grenade blew up harmlessly a couple feet away from my semi-fortified bunker. I reloaded the final belt into the machine gun and fired slow bursts at the trench, trying to conserve what little ammo Lara had left me.

A sharp pain in my chest reminded me of the connection Lara and I shared. I felt an emotion from her. I sent my thoughts to her. *"Can you hear me?"*

"Yes, I'm a bit busy though, Lance," the reply rang back.

"I have no more ammo."

"All right. Hold on, stay low," she told me.

I scanned the sky and saw a fiend smash a fighter jet into pieces with one mighty swing of its paw. I figured it had to be Lara. My worries melted away, and I mowed down another fighter as she raced through the sky toward me. And then as I tried to fire again, I realized that I had wasted what was left of my ammo on the soldier I had just killed.

After a moment of me not firing, heads began to pop up from the trench in front of me. They peered questioningly over at me. "Run out of ammo yet?" one of them called over to me.

"Come find out!" I yelled back threateningly.

Luckily for me, a machine gun opened up on them from the third floor, drawing the attention away from my crippled bunker. Two guys decided to fire into my room, forcing me to hunker back down behind my improvised defense. The bullets were starting to penetrate through the wood, hitting the wall behind me.

There was a sudden flash of bright white light as a flare shot up into the sky, illuminating the entire base. Screams of rage erupted from the fighters as they all charged from behind their cover toward our base. The ones in the trench fifty meters from me jumped out and sprinted toward the base as well. Three of them broke away from their group and headed into my room.

I punched one in the face. He fell over on top of me as the other clumsily shot his rifle at me, killing his partner. I swiftly unbuckled the pistol around his waist and aimed at the soldier's neck, killing him instantly.

A fierce growl of rage erupted behind us as the last guy sprayed wildly, sending bullets flying everywhere. Lara burst in on top of him, biting a chunk out of his chest before violently ripping his head off. She led me into the hall and transformed to her human form as we jogged along corridor after corridor. Luckily, she didn't regain her human form immediately, as one NWO fighter mistakenly ran straight into us.

We both jumped on top of him, and Lara swiftly killed him with her fiend strength. "We're being overrun. I need your help, Lance," she told me as she led me deeper down the hall and into a room. It was an armory, filled with weapons and ammunition. She threw an assault rifle over to me that I had never seen before. She quickly showed me how to load it and turn the safety off and on. She grabbed a backpack, slid her hand along a shelf, and pushed a whole bunch of C4 grenades and magazines into the bag. She tossed it over to me, and then pulled me into a hug, giving me a kiss just before she turned back into a fiend.

Lara took a step back, nodding her head toward a vest that had four rocket-propelled grenades in it, which I used to load the launcher hanging on the wall. I slung the loaded RPG over my right shoulder. Then I grabbed my rifle and peeked out into the hall. A soldier was running down it, yelling out orders. I poked the rifle out the door and killed him as he ran by.

Lara then ran past me into another room. She smashed through the window, and then I jumped through it, clumsily landing on the soft grass. I felt her jaw clamp onto my back, lifting me up, and I then sprinted behind her lumbering fiend body. I jumped on top of her just as she shot into the air. We flew at breakneck speed, and I spotted an artillery gun off in the distance.

The sound of bullets whizzing past my head was shockingly loud. I threw a C4, clicked the remote control to set it off, and was satisfied by the smoke billowing up from the destroyed artillery piece below us. Lara raced over to two more howitzers, and I repeated the process, successfully destroying them.

The fiends were greatly outnumbered. I could see about a dozen fighting in the sky as I began to lose hope. A fighter jet streaked past us, locking onto us. I cringed and tightly wrapped my arms around Lara's neck. The machine gun blared, followed by the sounds of whizzing bullets.

Lara nose-dived, plummeting toward the ground without warning and nearly knocking me off her back. With all her strength, she smashed off the wing of the jet. She caught the pilot in midair as he ejected, and she beheaded him. Lara glanced back, purring to get my attention. I dropped a C4 on the last howitzer, blowing it up. She then raced back to the base, making passes on the trenches below.

I unclipped some grenades, tossed them, and watched in satisfaction as they exploded in and around the trench. Lara was getting tired—I could feel her chest heaving through the heavy coat of fur as she sucked in breath after breath.

Fiends started dragging their wounded comrades from the courtyard, but an American-style helicopter known as an Apache appeared from behind the tall fiend base, mowing them down as the injured fiends attempted to escape; it was like shooting fish in a barrel. I untied the RPG from the side of the backpack. Lara stopped in midair, giving me a split second to aim.

I fired it, and the recoil nearly threw me off her back. I dropped the firing mechanism, which fell to the ground below with a dull clunk. The rocket sailed through the sky, hitting the Apache dead on.

Cheers erupted from the fiends below as we flew by. I took out the rifle, while Lara flew back down to the field. She flew about six feet off the ground, and her claws ripped through NWO soldiers who were retreating into the tree line. I glanced through the sights of my rifle but held my fire. More fiends flew into the air, slaughtering the remaining humans who hadn't retreated yet.

"Please stop, Lara," I told her through our minds' connection.

She flew up from the ground, leaving the rest of them to surrender. Some threw down their weapons, while others sprinted toward the tree line, defeated. Roars of victory began echoing through the moonlit sky as the fiends flew around victoriously.

Lara joined in the cheering and then flew us away to the lake where we had been last night. She landed gently on the ground. I glanced down at the purplish blood oozing out of her massive paw.

"Are you all right?" I asked her.

"It's nothing. I just nicked it, hitting down that jet," she said, bending down to drink the water from the lake. She looked exhausted from the battle.

I knelt beside her, washing the blood from the pilot off me and then gratefully taking a drink from the lake. Fiends started to land on the other side of the lake. Lara's claws retreated inside her massive paws, and she nudged me with her good paw, taking me under her towering body protectively.

I looked around—some fiends across the lake were drinking from it; others were licking their wounds or washing them off in the lake. Some of them were staring at me.

At first, I thought they must want to kill me, but one of them came over and bowed its head, which I returned. Then it shot into the air and flew away. Lara glanced down at me. Pride showed in her eyes, and then she let out her lion-like fiend growl and stood up on all fours, indicating to me that we were leaving. I got on her back, and she shot up into the air. We slowly flew back to the base and landed in the open field a few moments later.

I hopped off her, clinging to her leg like a cub, so as to not be mistaken as a resistance fighter by the other fiends towering overhead. Some fiends were lounging around in the grass, talking to each other in their lion-like growls. Others were eating, maiming, and killing wounded resistance fighters.

A wounded soldier grabbed at my leg as I walked by. I glanced down at him. He was young—only about sixteen—and had a gaping wound in his stomach that was squirting out blood. It was clear that he was never going to make it, even if he got medical attention. "Please, comrade … don't … don't let them take me," he murmured as he slowly started to succumb to his wounds.

Lara was about to kill him, but I forced her to stop, holding out my hand. I unbuckled the pistol from the kid's belts, taking the safety off. "Thank you," he mumbled glancing up at me.

I nodded solemnly, and he closed his eyes, bracing for the shot. I fired, and then I dropped the pistol onto his lifeless body, folding his arms over it. I stood and stared down at him admiringly. He reminded me of myself when I was young. I let out a sigh; the strong emotion of guilt gripped me, making it hard to breathe, as I realized what I had done.

These soldiers might not share my beliefs, but they were still humans. I had sided with the enemy, and there was no way I was ever going to be able to redeem myself from my actions. I could feel Lara staring down at me to see if I was okay.

I nodded, pretending to be fine, and followed her over to a patch of grass where a fiend was lying down. Lara lay down beside the fiend, gesturing with her head for me to do the same. I rested my head against her furry stomach, absorbing the warmth of it, and closed my eyes as Lara and the other fiend talked to each other. I heard a few other fiends walk past. I opened my eyes to see them bowing their gigantic monster heads as they passed. I nodded my head toward them, and they said something to Lara, who replied to them and placed her paw lovingly across me. We got up after Lara had finished her conversation and walked to the main gate, where fiends in human form were handing out pillows and blankets. I grabbed some from them, and then we started walking down the messy hall that was filled with debris and dead soldiers. We tried not to rub up against the bloodstained walls. The hall was so cramped with fiends that I was afraid I was going to be crushed by one of their gigantic paws. I guess Lara sensed the danger as well, because she bit into the back of my shirt, lifting me off the ground as she walked down the hall. I hung helplessly in front of her.

When we entered our war-torn room, she set me down and transformed back to her human form. She put on her bra and underwear as I leaned against the wall with my hands in my pockets, watching her. She let out a playful cry, catching me by surprise as she launched herself at me playfully, sending the two of us tumbling to the floor. There was a brief struggle; I felt her fiend strength surge through her body, and she pinned me to the ground victoriously.

"Hey, you cheated!" I objected.

"Stop lying to yourself. I would have thought that a big, strong PLF sniper would be able to control a poor, little weak girl," she ribbed me.

Then she leaned forward to make out with me. "I'm so proud of what you did today, Lance."

I took her hand in mine. "Let me have a look at that," I told her, seeing purplish blood still seeping from the laceration across her palm. I pulled out a first-aid kit and wrapped the wound with gauze, even though I knew she could just heal it herself.

"Thanks," she whispered softly, lifting her hand up to inspect the bandages. Still on top of me, she reached under the wrecked bed and pulled out a wooden box. She unlatched it and pulled out a bottle of wine that had somehow survived the battle. "Time to celebrate!" she said happily. Her eyes flashed yellow, and the cork went flying.

"Are rum and wine the only types of liquor a fiend drinks?" I asked her as she offered me a sip. I happily took a chug out of it.

"No, I just enjoy them. It's healthy for females."

"How?" I asked with a laugh.

"It calms down my stomach and stops me from eating annoying humans who ask too many questions," she joked, messing up my hair.

I sipped the wine slowly, keeping my thoughts to myself.

"What are you thinking about, buddy?" she asked.

"My sisters," I told her.

"What were their names again? I forgot."

"Tina and Kate," I replied. I smiled at the thought of seeing them again.

"What do they do in the resistance?" Lara asked.

"Kate is the oldest—she's twenty now. She's a doctor. And Tina is my twin—she's a combat medic."

"So you got to see them on a daily basis?" Lara asked.

I nodded.

"I'm sorry; you must miss them," Lara said.

"Don't be; it's my fault. Tina begged me not to go out on so many missions, but I just ignored her. I wanted my revenge, and that's how I ended up here."

"Revenge?" she asked.

"Never mind." I looked away, not wanting to talk about it.

"No, tell me, please, Lance!" she begged.

I shook my head. "I want to keep some things private."

"But I want to know. I barely know anything about you," she whined, staring at me innocently.

I was growing irritated by her persistence. "Why? So you can jot it down in your damn folder?" I snapped, losing my temper.

She stared at me as if I had just slapped her across the face, shocked by my sudden outburst. She growled in her non-human tone. "Where do you get off talking to me like that?" she snarled angrily.

"I'm sorry; it's a touchy subject," I replied, gently pushing her off my chest.

She began to relax, accepting that I didn't want to tell her about it. After a couple tense minutes, she timidly lay her head against my chest and wiggled closer to me. I guess that was her way of apologizing. "Sometimes it's better to let things go, Lance," she whispered, kissing my cheek lovingly.

I sighed, knowing she was right. She began cuddling with me, sharing our one pillow. As we fell asleep, exhausted from the long, hard-fought battle, the ominous sounds of war still could be heard, far off in the distance.

Chapter 10

I woke up the next morning to rays of sunlight dancing through the broken window. The sounds of firefights from the night before had been replaced with the soft chirping of birds as morning revealed itself. If it hadn't been for the hundreds of shell casings strewn across the destroyed room, we wouldn't even have known that one of the biggest battles in the war had just taken place.

"Go back to sleep. I'll make you breakfast in a bit," Lara whispered groggily as she rubbed the sleep from her eyes. She rolled over, staring at me with her innocent, sparkling blue eyes. She smiled warmly.

"Good morning, sexy," I greeted her, resting my hand across her hips and giving her a kiss.

"I see that someone is trying to get lucky," she giggled, returning the kiss.

"Is it working?" I asked playfully.

"It might be."

We finished an hour later.

She lay beside me, purring softly as we basked lazily in the morning sun. "Not that I want to right now," she said, "but would it really be that crazy for us to have a baby, if we ever got settled down?"

"I suppose, when the time is right and we both feel ready, then it would be a good idea," I answered, staring up at the ceiling.

"Really? You're not just saying that to avoid a fight?" she asked, glancing over at me skeptically.

"Nah, for real. I feel that we could do it," I assured her. After a pause, I added, "But … I mean … look around. Would you really want your child growing up in this kind of an environment?"

She sighed, going silent for a moment. "You're so cute. Lance wants a little Lancey," she teased, giving me a light punch on the shoulder.

I think she was trying to lighten the mood in an attempt not to scare me off the subject. I glanced over at her, returning her smile. "Say we were to go through with this. Wouldn't the fiends try to take the baby away or something? I mean, it would probably be one of the firstborn hybrids, wouldn't it?" I asked her.

"We will keep it our little secret," Lara giggled, not taking my question seriously.

"That's kind of impossible since Dasha knows that you have one of the first-ever manufactured pregnancy pills," I debated. "Besides, people aren't stupid. They'd eventually notice that you were putting on weight."

She just smirked, putting her finger on my lips so I would stop making excuses. "I wouldn't worry about our guidance counselor spilling the beans," she told me with a devilish grin.

"Why?"

"She was killed yesterday in the fighting. I saw her room get blasted to pieces by a tank while she was still inside."

"Wouldn't they keep paperwork of what they did with the pills, though?" I asked.

She cursed under her breath. "Yeah, you're probably right."

We were interrupted by a knock at the door. Hastily, Lara threw on my T-shirt and boxers as someone kept banging on the door.

"*Tana!*" Lara yelled, bustling over to it and opening it.

Two men in military uniforms marched in without invitation. One glanced over at me, asking Lara something in Jural. She nodded, and they continued to talk. One guy handed her an envelope, saluted her, and then they both left as quickly as they'd come.

"What was that about?" I asked.

She opened the envelope, glancing over its contents. She looked up at me, smiling happily. "Because of what you did yesterday, the court has decided to lift all restrictions on you." She continued to read to herself, and then said, "Oh, wow!"

"What?" I asked.

"Remember last month, when we filled out our paperwork for Monatello City?" I nodded, already knowing what was coming next. "Well, we have been approved. We can move there any time!" she told me excitedly, tucking the piece of paper back into the envelope and placing it in a drawer.

"That's awesome," I said half-heartedly. I stood up and leaned against the wall.

She was definitely way more excited about this than I was. She happily threw her hands up in the air and jumped into my arms. "You're going to love it there. It's a new city, especially built for humans and fiends to live together in peace. We can finally leave this silly war behind us."

"Where is it?" I asked.

"Far, far away from this place. This is the beginning of our new life together, Lance!" she told me, leaning back in my arms to read my expression.

I smiled, making out with her as I placed her on the counter.

"Get dressed," she ordered me playfully, slapping my butt as we finished. She took off my shirt and boxers and threw them over to me.

I found a pair of pants from one of the tipped-over drawers. "Where are we going?" I asked. Her random moods confused me.

"Operation file folder," she said with a smile.

"What?" I asked.

"We have to go find those papers in the guidance counselor's office to destroy them, silly."

We stepped out into the hall, pausing at a janitor's closet. I glanced around nervously keeping a lookout, while Lara picked the lock. "You almost done?" I whispered anxiously.

"Hold on," she muttered, concentrating on the lock. "There!" she whispered victoriously to the dull click of the door unlocking. She opened it, and we both crammed inside. Lara then dug around in a drawer until she found two janitor suits. We put them on, and she grabbed a mop, while

I filled a bucket with water and soap until the bubbles were threatening to spill over the side.

We then trudged up the stairs to the second floor and into Dasha's waiting room. To our surprise, a secretary was guarding the rooms at the main desk. "Can I help you?" she asked politely as we entered.

"Yes, we were sent to clear out Mrs. Gorald's room," Lara said convincingly.

I kept my head down, avoiding eye contact with the secretary, praying that she wouldn't catch a sniff of my human scent. The secretary nodded us through, and we quickly walked down the hallway to Dasha's office. Inside, there was a tipped-over desk, which Lara instantly began to dig through until she found a key.

She opened a file cabinet and read through it, frowning at some files. I busied myself by mopping the purplish fiend blood from the floor and sweeping debris off the side of the building. I pushed it through the shattered window in an attempt to make it look as though we actually had been up here to clean. "I got it!" Lara called out excitedly. She pulled a piece of paper out of the drawer, locked the file cabinet, and threw the key back in the desk.

She snapped her finger and a flame emitted from it, burning the paper until there was nothing left. "Problem solved," she told me happily, dusting off her hands.

"Isn't there a computer around here that the file is stored on?" I asked, looking around the office.

"Nah, your species are masterminds when it comes to cyber warfare. We lost some very important documents once, so we decided to scrap our computers and resorted to more primitive techniques to secure valuable information."

I nodded understandingly and followed her out of the office, down the hall, and then past the secretary, who didn't appear to suspect a thing.

Once we were on the first floor, we ditched our janitor uniforms back in the closet. I headed back in the direction of our room, but Lara called after me, "Where are you going?"

"Our room?"

"No, no, silly, you obviously haven't been in any battles. We have to go up to my officer's room, where he will give us a speech about how great we did, blah, blah, blah. After that, there will be a dance, which usually takes place for everyone, in celebration of our victory," Lara explained to me patiently.

"Cool. Do you need a date?"

"Nah, I'm going with someone else," she teased, letting me hold her hand as we walked down the hall.

We went up for our debriefing and found Domelski sitting behind a desk. "Well, hello there, Lance," he greeted me.

I remained silent, nervously staring at the floor. The memories of my torture sessions came flooding back to me.

"Keeping out of trouble lately?" he asked, motioning with his hand for Lara to take a step forward.

She obediently stepped up, and he presented her a silver medal in the shape of a star. He hung it around her neck and then motioned me over, hanging a silver medal around my neck. He informed me that it was a lower ranking of Lara's medal, as if I cared about a fiend medal. I silently turned to leave, but Lara quickly grabbed my hand, preventing my escape.

"Why are you in such a rush to leave?" Domelski asked.

I remained silent, staring at the floor.

"I hope that you haven't taken our previous encounters personally, Lance. That was strictly business." He held out his hand, seeming friendly. I glanced away from it and immediately saw anger boiling up in his eyes. "You will not ignore me, human!" he growled threateningly.

"Hey, don't talk to him that way," Lara spoke up.

Domelski looked from me to Lara. "It appears that my experiment went wrong somewhere, huh? I guess it's true—never send a woman to do a man's job." Lara looked away in embarrassment as he turned toward me. "I would like you to work for me, Lance. Not in a combat role, obviously, but we could use someone of your skills on our side to train our snipers."

"I would never work for you," I grunted.

Domelski raised his hand to me, but Lara interrupted. "Don't you dare hit him!"

He stopped, glancing over at her. "I'm going to make both of your lives hell," he promised us with a dull grin.

"You're not in charge of me anymore, Domelski. Lance and I are moving to Monatello. Here is my release paper." She tossed the paper on his desk.

He glanced down at the paper, shock spreading across his face. "Get out of my sight!" he growled angrily.

We departed quickly, not having to be asked twice, as the door slammed behind us.

"What a sexist piece of shit," Lara grunted angrily, as we walked down the hall.

"That probably wasn't the best time to tell him we were leaving." I laughed.

"Whatever. He's always like that." She shrugged and gave me a handful of gold coins.

"What's this?" I asked, curiously looking around as we emerged into what appeared to be a busy shopping district that the fiends had built inside of the base.

"Crome—this is our currency."

"How much is this?" I asked, staring down at the pile of gold coins in my hand.

"Sixty crome. Go get yourself something nice for the dance."

I found this odd—Lara usually picked out everything for me. "You're not coming?" I asked.

"Nah, I trust you," she said, leaning over and giving me a kiss.

I could see in her eyes that it was painful for her to let me go, but she pretended she was cool with it. She walked into a girls' clothing store, giving me freedom for the first time since we'd met. I went into a men's shop and bought a pair of pants and a hoodie, along with a hat, for forty crome. My freedom was short-lived; Lara was waiting for me patiently outside the shop. I handed her the twenty crome I had left, but she just shook her head, letting me keep it.

It was getting dark out, and I could hear the music playing as we walked through the hall toward our room. We entered, and I changed into my new clothes, as did Lara on the other side of the bunker.

"Don't peek; it's a surprise," she called over to me affectionately.

Finally, after ten minutes, she emerged from behind the ruble. "Ta-da!" she called over to me, posing like a model in front of me. She was wearing a skin-tight skirt with a pretty blue tank top. Her hair and makeup were done up nicely. "Do you like it?" she asked.

I could tell that she genuinely cared about my opinion of her. "Of course I do. You look beautiful." I smiled in approval.

She beamed happily, grabbing my hand to lead me down to the party. The dance floor was packed when we got there. A slow song came on, and she wrapped her arms around me, swaying back and forth slowly to the melody. We ignored the threatening stares from other fiends around the dance floor.

"This brings me back to the courtyard days," she whispered into my ear.

"Except it's a lot easier now than it was before," I added.

"It feels more right, huh?" she asked affectionately, drawing me closer. I could feel the warmth of her body as she rested against my chest, peacefully swaying to the song. "I'm glad we were able to see past our differences and make this work, Lance," she whispered.

I stroked her hair affectionately, feeling like the luckiest man alive to have a girl like her. I held her close to me that night, not wanting to let go as she slept. It had been a long time since I'd felt this way for someone and in a way, I think it frightened me.

When Rachel died, a piece of me died with her. I never thought I would feel this way again—not for a normal girl, let alone a fiend. Lara somehow reminded me of the happiness I had once felt with Rachel. I couldn't put my finger on why, but I guess it was just the way she smiled, making me feel like a million bucks every time I was around her. She would purr occasionally in her sleep as I lay there stroking her, realizing that this was the girl I wanted to spend the rest of my life with. I woke up early the next morning, making sure not to wake her up as I slipped out of bed. I silently put on a pair of shorts and then tucked her in affectionately before I left.

I walked down past the food market, taking a left into a jewelry store.

The cashier watched me as I looked at the selection of rings. I finally found one that I knew Lara would love. The small, reddish diamond sparkled as the light from overhead danced off it.

"Is there any way I can work for this ring?" I asked the lady at the counter.

She sniffed the air for a second, picking up on my scent. "We don't serve humans," she shot back.

"Please … I don't have much, but this must be worth something," I begged her, pulling out the twenty crome, my silver medal, and a gold watch that I had found during the battle.

She glanced at my items, and when she saw the medal, she looked at me a bit more warmly. "You must be that human who was riding the fiend around, killing soldiers and blowing up artillery." I nodded. She grabbed my stuff and put it in the pocket of her shorts. "Tell you what," she said. "You clean these windows and counters, and you can have the ring."

I happily accepted her offer, and I finished the job two hours later. As promised, she gave me the ring, wishing me good luck. I put it in my pocket and jogged back up to Lara's room, hoping that she was still asleep. To my surprise, she wasn't lying there anymore. I cautiously opened the bathroom door when I heard sounds coming from there—Lara was puking her guts out. She swiftly turned to me, panting, about to say something, and then turned back to puke in the toilet again.

"Are you all right?" I asked, taking a step closer.

She shook her head, looking up at me again. "Just … just leave me alone. It's my tricnoses. I don't want to hurt you … I'm not safe right now. Go away. I'll come out in a bit."

I nodded and obediently closed the door. I sat down on our pile of blankets, listening to the occasional screams of pain and panting erupting from the bathroom. To my relief, Lara emerged an hour or so later. She sat down beside me and asked grumpily, "So where have you been?"

"I just went out for a walk," I said. "I woke up early and didn't want to wake you up." I looked at the wrapped-up bed sheets behind her. "Is that blood?"

"Yes, I didn't wake up quickly enough. I suppose it's for the best that you weren't here to see me like this." Tears formed in her eyes.

"Did you take those pills for your tricnoses?" I asked, trying to be helpful.

She curled up, leaning forward and holding her stomach in pain. "Don't tell me what to do. I think I can decide for myself if I want to drug myself or not," she snapped.

"I wasn't telling you what to do. I just wanted to know if you did."

"Just sit here and shut up, okay, Lance?" she said bluntly, while leaning her head against my shoulder.

I stroked her hair gently as we sat there for a while. Her pains were becoming worse, and claws would sometimes emerge from her hand and then retreat as she calmed herself down. "Listen, I'm sorry about what I just said," she told me. "Luna had come by this morning and inspected them. She told me that the pills were to aggravate me, so that when I became pregnant, I would kill you." Lara took in a deep breath as a moment of clarity seemed to hit her.

"Why would Dasha want me dead?" I asked, shocked by the news.

"With you out of the picture, she probably figured that I would think it was my fault and would give her the baby, once it was born, for testing. Then they could discover more about mixed breeds between humans and pure-bloods," Lara explained, taking another deep breath.

"So Luna said the pregnancy pills were fine?" I asked.

Lara nodded, shivering violently as a spasm overtook her. I was starting to get a bit nervous, as her symptoms began to get worse and worse. She leaned forward and let out a shrill scream. Her backbone protruded from her back, stretching her skin, which was darkening as black fur sprouted along her back and face. "Oh God, oh God, no!" she yelled in a panic, thrashing around on the floor.

I leaned over her, trying to calm her down a bit. She tried to take off the new clothes she'd bought the day before, but she wasn't quick enough. They ripped as her muscular body protruded, and she viciously swung one of her clawed paws at me. Once fangs began to replace her teeth, I knew she had lost control, so I gently set her down on the ground.

I then hopped over the bunker and dashed behind the metal closet door, locking myself in, like she had instructed me to do in case this ever happened. There was a moment where all I could hear was Lara groaning. She then let out a bloodcurdling scream of pain, and all hell broke loose.

I heard her growl as the transformation completed, followed by the sounds of her stumbling around the room, smashing through everything in her path. The sounds of wood splintering and glass shattering filled the air. I tried to cover my ears, but I could still hear it, along with her enraged fiend cries.

The fiend scar of Lara suddenly started to sear against my chest, causing me to yelp in pain. It burned a bright red, illuminating the inside of the closet, and blood began to leak through it, along with steam rising from the scar. As if responding to my cry of pain, I heard Lara howl and then *bam*! The steel door dented as Lara hurled her body at it, leaving an impression of a claw mark.

She repeated this process a few more times to no avail. The snarling continued, and I could hear her ripping through more stuff in our room. This behavior lasted for at least fifteen minutes, as blood continued to occasionally leak through my scar—it was throbbing painfully, becoming more and more unbearable.

I remembered Lara telling me that her fiend side would never hurt me, and the main job of a female fiend was to protect its male companion. So against my better judgment, I unlocked the door, just as I heard Lara preparing for another attack on it. She instantly stopped rampaging through all the furniture and glanced over at me.

We both stood still, staring each other down for what seemed like a year, although in reality, it probably was only about five seconds. She took a couple steps forward, but I stood my ground, scared stiff, shaking a little as I held out my hand to pet her. She purred, and I scratched the back of her ears.

Without warning, she pounced on me, sending us both to the ground. She licked the blood from my throbbing scar, which immediately relieved the pain and turned the scar from red back to its normal faded black. Her bloodshot eyes stared down at me for a second and then suddenly, her gigantic feet faltered underneath her, and she clumsily fell over on top of me. Her body shrank back to her normal human size, and an unconscious naked Lara was draped across me.

Silence enveloped the room for a split second before she began to moan, regaining consciousness. She looked around, seeming confused for a moment, and then said, "I'm sorry I lost control again. I didn't hurt you, did I?"

"No, I'm fine. Your wild fiend side was actually fairly nice to me this time. I think it's starting to get a crush on me," I joked with her.

She laughed but then stopped. "Aw, shit. I ripped my new clothes already."

"Yeah, you lost control so fast, there wasn't enough time for me to save them," I told her.

"Man … do you know how expensive it is to try to keep good-looking clothes as a female fiend?" she asked with a disappointed laugh. "Oh well, clothes can be replaced. I can't replace you, though," she told me lovingly, with a kiss. "Give me your shorts and T-shirt so I have something to wear. You can wear your pants and hoodie."

"All right."

"We can buy new clothes and stuff once were Monatello," she said. She got dressed and then reached into the pocket of my shorts. "I swear, you're such a guy, Lance," she scolded playfully. "You buy new clothes and not even a day later, you already got it filled with junk."

"Shit!" I exclaimed to myself, whirling around as she reached into the pocket and pulled out gum wrappers from the dance—and the sparkling red engagement ring.

She looked at it for a moment in shock, glancing from it to me. I wanted to say something, but my voice seemed to have abandoned me. At that moment, I would have given anything to just shrink into a microscopic speck and float away.

Lara tried to say something, but it appeared that she was suffering from the same loss of speech as I was. She finally broke the tense silence between us by saying, "Um … I don't think I was supposed to see this yet."

I stared at the floor and kicked some debris away nervously. I took a step forward and took the ring from her. I got down on one knee, and she covered her mouth to stop herself from crying out in excitement. "Um … I was thinking maybe you could be my wife," I said timidly, offering the ring back up to her.

She nodded happily as tears trickled down her beautiful face. I stood as she took the ring and wiped away another tear. "I was thinking maybe you could be my husband," she replied softly in a happy, quivering voice. She tried on the ring and opened up her arms to hug me. She winced as we made out on the floor.

"Are you still having your tricnoses?" I asked after we finished another kiss.

She giggled at my concerned face, whipping her hair away from her eyes to stare up at me. "Watch out, Lance. I'm going to get you!" she joked, baring her fangs, which returned to normal as she kissed me again and held me tightly to her chest. "Don't worry; nothing could ruin this," she whispered in my ear.

I relaxed a bit, and she patted my back, glancing at her hand and then holding it out in front of us. "It's so beautiful. No one's ever gotten me something like this before," she told me affectionately. She gently slid her hand across my cheek. "Thank you so much," she whispered as tears streamed down her face.

We packed our bags that night, after she had said good-bye to Luna and announced that I had proposed to her. A couple hours later, she signed us both out of the base, and I got on top of her as she transformed and took off into the air. It was an amazingly quiet night as we flew along the treetops.

I carried Lara's ring in my pocket—it would have just busted if she'd kept it on while in her fiend form. We arrived at Monatello City around one in the morning. I realized that it was a pretty big city as Lara flew around the fenced-in area and landed gently at the foot of the main gate, where two guards were hanging out.

She transformed to her human form, and I handed her clothes, shielding her from the guards. "I'm missing something, I think." She giggled affectionately, holding out her hand.

I smiled, slipping the ring onto her finger and happily giving her a kiss. Her attention then focused to the guards. She strolled over to them, showing them our approved paperwork. One went inside a booth to check something. When he came out a few minutes later, he nodded us through and handed Lara an envelope. The town was nearly abandoned; streetlights flickered as we walked down the deserted sidewalks to our assigned house.

"This place just opened up a few hours ago. It may be a while before others begin arriving," Lara reassured me.

We came to a stop a moment later, looking at the number on the side of a mailbox and then down at our joining instructions. "Number 365. This is it," I told her, glancing down the pathway that led to our house.

Lara nodded and took two sets of keys out of an envelope. She handed one to me and opened the door with the other. We entered the small house, glancing around as Lara turned on a light. It was a pretty nice little house; it kind of resembled a hotel room.

There was a bed and bedside tables on each side of the bed with lamps on them and alarm clocks. There was also a small six-by-four-foot jail cell in the corner of the room, along with a swinging door that led to the kitchen. By the bedside, there was a round table with four chairs around it, similar to what you would typically see in a hotel room.

There was also a bathroom with a shower and bathtub in it. "If you snore, that's where you're sleeping," I told Lara playfully.

"We'll see about that, smart-ass," she shot back, giving me a light punch on my shoulder.

We set down our bags on the floor beside the door, as the novelty of our new place wore off. "I'm going to take a shower," Lara said. "I'm all sweaty from flying with some fat ass on my back for three hours."

"Hey, don't talk about your mother that way!" I joked.

Lara smirked, flipping me the middle finger. I laughed, flopping onto the bed like a little kid as she went into the bathroom. I let out a sigh, relaxing a little, allowing the mattress to absorb me. I opened a plastic bag on the nightstand that contained a whole bunch of advertisements, magazines, and brochures in it, describing the goals of the community, along with rules to follow while staying in Monatello. There was a list of events for the month, along with a diagram of Monatello City, which showed the locations of restaurants, public washrooms, fields, and entertainment areas, such as the movie theater and bowling alleys. I picked up another brochure, stumbling over the wording of it a little bit. The water in the bathroom stopped running, followed by the sounds of Lara bustling around inside for a few moments.

"Would you mind reading this?" I asked, a bit embarrassed, as she emerged from the bathroom with a towel, drying off her hair.

"Sure," she replied with a warm smile.

That was another thing that I loved about Lara—she knew that I was illiterate, but she never once threw it in my face and always was willing to help me out.

"Welcome to Monatello City," she read. "Thank you for taking the first step toward peace by volunteering to be a resident of our newly developed city. It is our hope that we will be able to integrate our two populations successfully, so that that we can one day live together in peace. The idea was first developed by General Yazika, commander of the Northern Brigade, in charge of all operations in and around the region of the Harush Forest." She paused, glancing over at my smirk. "What's so funny?" she asked.

"I find it ironic that the man who has waged war on me and my people for the past four years is the same man who came up with the bright idea of a peace offering," I told her with a laugh.

She lay down on the bed beside me. "That is pretty funny," she agreed. Then she turned her attention back to the magazine and continued reading. "During your stay here in Monatello City, our staff of highly qualified soldiers will protect you. They have been handpicked to carry out the task of maintaining peace and discipline within the cities limits. Please do not be alarmed by their presence, as they pose no threat to you. Thank you once again on behalf of everyone involved in the creation of this city, for making the smooth transition from war to peace possible and for building a future world that our next generation can enjoy." She handed the brochure back to me and said excitedly, "This sounds like it will be an awesome place for us to start our family!"

I nodded, pretending to be interested in another brochure in order to avoid the conversation. She must have noticed my reluctance because she immediately changed the subject—that was rare for Lara; usually she picked at things forever until they developed into an argument. We talked about all the cool activities we would be able to do over the next month, and eventually she fell asleep, snuggled right up against my chest, purring contentedly.

I was rudely awakened the next morning by Lara nudging my ribs impatiently. "What?" I asked, expecting her to want to talk about something urgent.

"I'm hungry," she said innocently.

"*Ungh* … go to hell," I grunted sleepily, hitting her with my pillow. I placed the pillow over my eyes, trying to fall back to sleep.

"Come on! I want to go eat breakfast with my man," she whined affectionately.

"Too bad. Life's full of disappointments. Get used to it," I shot back sleepily.

"I'll let you say hello to two of my friends when we get back," she bargained with me, a sly grin spreading across her face.

I peeked from under the pillow and saw that she had taken off her shirt. "Urgggh … it's a close call but still no. I see them all the time anyway."

She gasped with mock hurt. "No sex for you tonight!" She gave me a gentle slap as she got up.

I retreated under my pillow, but my victory didn't last long. Lara returned to my bedside for round two—by dousing me with water. "God damn it, Lara!" I shouted as she scampered back to the kitchen with her empty glass. I sighed, chucking my soaked pillow at the door and grumpily putting on my pants and shirt from the day before.

"Aw, now Lance is mad because the mean old Lara made him get up at eleven in the morning," she mocked me in a babyish tone as she came back and sat on the edge of the bed. Her eyes flicked light green, and my shoes suddenly came to life, running across the floor and jumping onto my feet, tying themselves as if they had a mind of their own.

"That was kind of cool," I said, looking at my feet in surprise.

Lara gave me my good-morning kiss before leading me out the front door, where we headed down a long narrow street to a restaurant around the corner from our house. The place was empty, aside from the waitress at the counter. She came over to hand us menus and serve us coffee. Lara ordered some type of fiend food, while I went with the classic bacon, ham, and eggs combo.

Another couple entered the restaurant, and they instantly spotted us and came over to our table. "Mind if we sit here?" the woman asked, motioning to the empty space beside us.

"Not at all; go ahead!" Lara told her pleasantly, eager to make new friends. "I'm Lara, and this is Lance."

"I'm David, and this is Carana," David replied congenially. I couldn't help noticing the scar across the top of Carana's left hand. We all smiled at each other in a friendly manner as the waitress took our orders.

"So where do you guys live?" Lara asked, once all our food had arrived.

"Number 359," Carana said, digging into her plate.

"We're in 365," I told her.

Carana nodded as her eyes flashed green, and a packet of sugar instantly flew across the table, opened itself, and poured its contents into her coffee.

"So David's the fiend, I guess?" I teased. Everyone cracked up at my lame joke.

"So are you guys married?" Carana asked, glancing over at the ring on Lara's finger.

"No," I told her. "Yes," Lara responded at the same time.

David and Carana looked at each other before bursting out in laughter at our response.

I looked away, embarrassed, wondering why Lara thought we were married. I could feel her angry stare burning into the side of my face. I glanced over at her cautiously—she looked like she was ready to strangle me. The four of us sat in silence. Lara seemed to become angrier the longer we sat there.

"I need to go to the bathroom," she said bluntly, getting up and angrily marching down the hall, with her hair flying behind her.

I knew I was in deep trouble—loud noises, followed by the sound of shattering glass, erupted from the bathroom. "Um … I think I'll go to the bathroom as well," Carana told us, rushing down the hall toward the angry sounds.

"Well, I'm dead," I said to David. I folded my hands and twiddled my thumbs, debating how far I'd make it if ran away right now.

"You think she is actually going to kill you?" David asked skeptically.

I shrugged. I was scared stiff. I could actually feel my hands shaking every time a noise erupted from the bathroom. "Does Carana have this kind of temper?" I asked him.

"Worse," he replied with a laugh. "She hung me upside down for half a day in the bathroom, running the shower water on steaming hot because I told her we should wait a couple weeks to get married. But why did you say you weren't married?"

"Because we aren't. We just got engaged yesterday. We never had any of those official 'you may now kiss the bride' words," I explained to him.

"Aw, that's funny. You're going to get yourself killed over a miscommunication."

"So your marriage was forced?" I asked.

He nodded. "Wasn't yours?"

"Nah, I proposed to her," I replied.

"Wow, you're a fool," he grunted.

I laughed nervously, knowing it looked like a stupid decision right now. He didn't know the Lara I knew, though. She wasn't always like this. We were just having a bad day. Every couple has them once in a while. "I don't understand why Carana forced you into a marriage," I said, hoping I didn't seem too nosey.

"Well, from what I've gathered, male fiends apparently treat female fiends like shit, so it's becoming a popular trend for them to shack up with humans," he explained.

I wondered how much credibility this guy had. I had to admit that it made sense in a way.

"You seem like a cool guy," he said. "Here—take this. You'll need it."

He pulled a handgun out of his belt and slid it across the table to me. "The best advice I can give you is to kill her before she kills you. That baby is fully loaded with a fifteen-round clip."

"Nah, I don't need that," I insisted, pushing it back nervously before anyone could see it.

"Take it!" he insisted.

I reluctantly took it and tucked it behind my back, under my shirt, just in time.

Lara stormed out of the bathroom, her eyes flashing yellow in my direction. "Get up right now! We're leaving," she growled at me.

I felt her powers lift me off the seat, forcing me to follow her. She grabbed my arm, letting her power wear off on me, while roughly dragging me outside. She stormed down the street toward our house. Once we reached it, she ripped open the door and threw me in our room. She immediately began to yell as I tumbled across the floor. "Are you *committed* to this relationship or *not*?" she screamed at the top of her lungs. She snatched me by my hair, throwing me angrily against a chair.

"Yes, I'm sorry," I groaned.

"Bullshit!" she shot back, unconvinced.

I saw her claws sprout from her fingertips, and she swiped them across my face in a blind rage, ripping deep into my skin. Blood gushed out the side of my cheek. She picked me up, tossing me like a doll into the wall. I banged my forehead against the side of a table as I fell. I was dizzy; everything was spinning. I reached under my shirt for the 9mm David had given me and pointed it at Lara, just as she took a step forward to finish me off.

"Whoa! What do you think you're going to do with that?" she asked, stopping in her tracks. She raised her hands slightly, gesturing for me not to shoot. "I'm immortal. Did you forget that?" she asked, chuckling to herself.

"I don't want to hurt you, Lara," I said, aiming at her chest. My hand ceased to shake as adrenaline pumped through my veins.

"Me neither," she said sincerely.

I could see the tense muscles in her body were beginning to relax a bit as she came back to reality. "You already have, though, and you were about to kill me," I pointed out, wiping away blood that was trickling down my forehead into my eyes.

"I may have lashed out a bit, but I'm back in control now, Lance," she assured me calmly. She took another step forward but stopped instantly when I clicked off the safety. "Come on—it's me. Your buddy. I'm not going to hurt you. I was just angry. Why would you tell them we're not married? I'm starting to feel like you don't want to be."

"I *do* want to be," I told her, relaxing my grip on the pistol a little.

"A couple days ago, you were talking to me about having a baby. Now you won't talk to me about it. How do you think that makes me feel? I let that slide, and now you're saying we're not married. It was a bit overwhelming." I could tell she was trying to reassure me that she was fine now.

"We aren't married, though. We're engaged. And I do want a baby, just not right now, Lara. We agreed that we would wait until we both felt that the time was right," I replied calmly.

She stared at me, still holding her hands at her side. "What does 'engaged' mean?" she asked, looking suddenly confused.

"It's like being pre-married," I explained to her. "You could be engaged for days, weeks, months, or even years before you decide to have a wedding. Once a preacher says all his stuff, then you're married."

"Well, I apologize then, Lance. I didn't mean to be so pushy. I truly am sorry, but I didn't know there was such a thing. Just put the gun down. It's over now. I'm not mad anymore." She took another step toward me.

"No! Stay away from me!" I ordered her. My hand began shaking again as she ignored me, coming closer. I begged her to back away, but she didn't. Once she reached my side, she slid her hand across my face, instantly healing it and washing the blood away, along with the waves of pain pulsing through my cheek.

The barrel of the 9mm was right against her chest now. She stared at me, not fazed at all by it. "Want to get married tonight, Lance? Under the laws of Dracona?" she whispered into my ear, stroking me comfortingly. Her hand slid along the gun, on to my hand, where my finger was gripping the trigger.

"I want to be with you for the rest of my life, Lance. Just open up a bit to me so I can." She kissed my cheek, the one that had just been healed.

"I do too, Lara," I sniffled, feeling my voice quivering. I knew she could hear how scared I was.

"Do you still love me, Lance?" she asked gently, taking her other hand and running it along my back. "If you don't love me, pull the trigger. You know how to do it. You've done it to seven hundred sixty-two other fiends. How am I any different?" Tears slowly trickled down her face as she told me, "I promise I won't come after you in my next life."

"I love you, Lara. You're not like those other fiends. You saved my life," I told her, returning the kiss. I clicked the safety on the pistol and slowly tilted it into her hand. She took it, placing it in her lap, and plopped down on her butt, reaching back over to me and making out with me. She wiped away her tears and took the magazine out of the pistol, twisting the barrel with her fiend strength as if it were a piece of tin foil.

She took out the ammunition inside the magazine and let it fall harmlessly, one by one, to the floor. "We need to learn how to stop these silly fights, or one day, one of us is going to get killed over something stupid," she sniffled, throwing the magazine aside.

I nodded in agreement. "I feel like I'm in a relationship with a schizophrenic," I joked, pausing for a second to lean across and give her a kiss. "We're fine. Fights are healthy for a relationship," I said, making air quotes with my fingers as I said the word "healthy."

She remained silent for a moment and then nodded in agreement before speaking. "I know they are, Lance, but in our situation, we should try to keep these fights to a minimum level of violence. We've had, like, six fights since we met, and all of them could have been fatal—for you rather than me."

"Two of them you had no control over, though," I reminded her.

"All I'm saying is we should set up some ground rules for our fights, to try to keep them from escalating into something bigger, like today," she suggested.

"All right. I'm down for that." I smiled and leaned over to brush her hair away from her eyes.

"Remember that time by the lake when I first gave you this?" she asked, poking the fiend scar on my chest.

"Of course. And I told you about Rachel."

She nodded. "Well, that should have turned into a physical fight, because under the laws of Dracona, lying is a big no-no, but we didn't fight because we listened openly to each other and worked it out. Am I right?" she asked.

"So basically, you're saying we should try to talk out our problems instead of waiting until the last minute?" I asked.

She nodded in agreement. "And I'll work on controlling my temper," she promised me as we got up. "There is no need to be nervous about our marriage tonight," she added, taking my hand and giving me another light peck on the lips.

"Easy for you to say," I shot back with a laugh.

"No, for real—getting married is not that big of a deal in my culture," she told me, flopping down on top of me as we lay down on our bed. "Where I come from, most girls are married by the age of eighteen."

"You're not like most girls, though, Lara," I told her.

She blushed. "I'll make sure it is a fiend/human-ish wedding," she told me, stripping down to her underwear.

"So you're not mad at me about what just happened?" I asked. I wanted to make sure that everything was cool between us.

"Of course not," she told me with a playful punch. "To tell you the truth, I think it was more jealousy of another female being around you than your saying we weren't married that got me upset."

"Are you going to keep the ring?" I asked.

She looked at the red diamond on her finger. "Of course! It's the most beautiful gift anyone's ever given me. It symbolizes that we love each other, right?"

I nodded, stroking her hair affectionately. "So it's settled then? We're getting married your way tonight?" I asked her.

She rested her head on my chest and nodded. "Our way," she reminded me softly.

Chapter 11

We got married that night, as planned. Lara was on my back, gently cutting the marriage tattoo into it. Once she was finished, she held a mirror for me so I could see it.

It took up my entire back; I smiled and nodded my approval. Her smile reflected back to me in the mirror. She then drew a sketch for me of what her tattoo should look like. She got undressed and handed me the knife to carve it into her skin. It took me about three hours to finish it, stopping for her to heal sections of it periodically.

Once I was finished, she healed the rest of it, making it turn dull black like mine, and then she sat up on the bed with me and looked at me affectionately. She placed her hand against my chest where my heart was and placed my left hand on her chest against her heart. I laughed uneasily as she placed her other hand on top of my free hand, holding onto it firmly.

"Are you ready?" she asked calmly.

I nodded.

"Why are you shaking, then?" she asked. "There's nothing to be afraid of. We're just two friends saying to someone else that we want to be closer friends," she whispered softly.

I took a couple of deep breaths, steadying my hands, and she nodded contentedly as I calmed myself down. I nodded once I was ready, and she closed her eyes. She began to recite a prayer in Jural. I felt shocks from her hands transferring to mine as she continued reciting. Time seemed to stand still as she went farther and farther into the prayer.

Her hair began to float up around her, and she opened her eyes. Silverish-blue light shone from them, illuminating the pitch-black room with a flickering blue glow. Her chest heaved in and out as she strained her voice, reciting what seemed to be the last of the prayer.

I could feel a constant flow of power from her to me now. It felt like it was flowing through my veins. I could feel my pulse in my throat. I wanted to let go, but Lara had such a tight grip on my hand that it did more harm than good to attempt to wriggle it free.

A non-human voice came from her. "Repeat after me. *Tana marana Lara pernado olangi.*"

I repeated the words, and Lara's eyes lit up even brighter. The entire room was now filled with the flashing blue light. She leaned forward, kissing me on the lips.

I kissed her back, and a sudden flash of blinding white light was the last thing I saw before losing consciousness. When I opened my eyes, I was lying down, with white mist gently floating around me. I glanced down and saw the earth hovering below me.

The mist slowly swirled by, making it nearly impossible to make out anything around me. I stood up, glancing around, but felt lost and confused. Lara's outline appeared through the mist a moment later.

I sighed in relief as she held out her hand to me. She was wearing a beautiful white dress. Her hair was tied back, with a rose tucked behind her ear. I grasped her hand, and she smiled reassuringly to me, while I looked nervously around the foggy sky.

"You look beautiful," I told her, focusing my attention on her as she led me through the puffs of mist.

"Thanks. You don't look half-bad yourself."

I looked down at myself and was surprised to see that I was wearing a tuxedo with a tie and dress shoes. We walked along the silent world Lara had thrown us into until the mist began to fade away, and I suddenly could see a man in the distance, standing patiently next to a gazebo. As we approached him I realized that he was the preacher.

He was tall, with aged eyes, but he looked surprisingly young. Fiend wings were visible from his back; he was wearing a white cloth-like material that covered his body from the shoulders all the way down to his feet. Shadowy figures of people appeared around the foot of the gazebo, all looking up at us. Some waved, while others tried to communicate with us, but no sound would escape their mouths. A girl—or what I assumed was a girl—pushed through the crowd of black-misted people and rushed up to me.

I couldn't make out many of her features; I only assumed it was a girl by the long mist protruding from the back of her head. She tilted her head, giving me the peace sign, and I instantly knew who it was.

"Rachel?" I exclaimed in disbelief.

The shadow nodded, bringing its hand up and touching the sides of my face. She accidently shattered her mist hand, but it reformed itself as she took a step back. She glanced over at Lara, who was waiting patiently, and then turned back to give me a thumbs-up in approval. I glanced at Lara pleadingly, and she nodded, knowing what I wanted.

I hugged the mist—and accidently broke it. Once the mist figure of Rachel reformed itself, she wrapped her arms around me and then walked away from the gazebo, waving good-bye before vanishing back into the crowd.

"Lance?" Lara asked softly, taking my hand and nodding toward the preacher.

"Okay … I'm ready." I tried to get a hold of myself as the preacher began to speak.

"We have gathered here today to witness the first-ever mixed-species marriage," he began. "A day to remember. A new page to be written in the laws of Dracona. Lance, do you take Lara to be your lawfully wedded wife, through sickness and health, until death you do part?"

"I do," I replied firmly.

He turned to Lara, said my name and a whole bunch of stuff in Jural, and then Lara confidently said, "I do."

"You may now present each other with your gifts," he told us.

Lara snapped her fingers, and a gold watch appeared out of nowhere, falling from the sky into her hand. I held out my arm to her, and she put it on and then stood back, looking at me, waiting for her gift. I snapped my fingers, half-expecting the ring to fall from the sky, but of course it didn't.

Lara and I both laughed. She nodded to my pocket. I glanced at the preacher; even he had a smile on his face. Embarrassed, I rummaged around in the pocket, pulled out the beautiful diamond ring, and slipped it onto her finger. I stared into her sparkling blue eyes; she smiled, glancing down at the ring and then back up at me.

"I now pronounce you husband and wife. You may now kiss the bride," the preacher told us.

I did, and a shining light seemed to break through the clouds, sending sunlight beaming down on us. I held her, not wanting to let go.

"Through your long and hard journey together, you will face ups and downs, but remember—no words or actions are stronger than love," the preacher told us. He slowly dissolved into the air, completely vanishing a second later.

I blinked, and the next thing I knew, I was back in our house, still holding onto Lara's shoulder. I looked down at my wrist—the gold watch was there. Lara opened her eyes. I was about to say something, but she just placed her finger against my lips and lay down on top of me.

I knew what she wanted.

Chapter 12

"Hey, there's my sexy husband," Lara called to me affectionately the next morning. She had just emerged from the bathroom and was drying herself off from her morning shower.

"There's my sexy wife," I called back. I leaned over to kiss her as she gave me my morning hug. I strapped on the gold watch she had given me for our wedding and looked at her fondly as she finished drying off, briefly naked before putting on a nice outfit. "So was last night real?" I asked her. I wondered if the whole thing was just an illusion she had created to make me feel like it was an actual wedding.

"Of course it was. I know the sex felt a little bit unreal, though," she joked.

I laughed and stared at her. "You know what I mean," I said.

She sighed patiently, placing her hands on her hips and staring at me with a warm smile. "That was as real as it could get, Lance," she reassured me sincerely. "That place that I teleported us to last night is our sacred ground. It is tradition that every couple from Fraturna gets married there. Everything was real, Lance—the preacher, the crowd, even Rachel," she promised me.

I decided that what she was telling me was the truth, and I gave her a grateful nod. "Thank you. I just wanted to make sure."

With an understanding nod, she grabbed my hand and led me out the door and down to our mailbox. Inside, there was a bag with five thousand crome in it.

"Wow! What's that for?" I asked.

She gave me half of it. "The creators of this city are trying to stimulate the economy," she explained.

"How?"

"They give each couple five thousand crome, and then that money circulates from person to person. Plus, the money that people bring in from the outside gets circulated into the economy as well, letting it expand at a gradual rate. Understand?"

I nodded.

"They're creating jobs for people to apply to as well," she said as we walked down the street.

I couldn't help noticing it had come to life with people moving into their new homes. "So you want me to work?" I asked. When she nodded, I said, "I don't know how I'm going to go from what I've been through into flipping burgers for fiends."

"Cheer up. I'm going to get a full-time job as a waitress. I feel the exact same way as you, but it has to be done."

I nodded understandingly. We walked down to the main strip, where there was an outdoor coffee shop up on the hill. It had a basketball court below it, and there was a pool and baseball field on the other end of the strip.

Lara applied for a job at the coffee joint and had an interview a few minutes later. She came out triumphantly—they'd given her the job; she was starting tomorrow. "Your turn, buddy," she told me, sitting down with a coffee and offering me one.

"What? I don't want to serve coffee," I told her, shooing away the offer.

She stared at me, a bit surprised; I guess she figured I was just going to follow her line of work. "Well, I'm not going to be the only one pulling in money," she warned me.

"I know. I'm going to play basketball," I told her.

"Come on. Get real, Lance. There isn't even a basketball league."

"I'm being serious. I used to be the best of the best at basketball. I don't mean playing in an actual game; I'm talking about playing two-on-two for money."

She stared at me; she did not look amused.

"Are those two guys on the court human?" I asked her.

She looked at them for a second and then nodded.

"Watch. I'll show you," I told her. I got up and jogged over to the court.

"Yo, what's up, guys? Want to play some high-stakes basketball?" I assumed they were ex-PLF members.

"Sure, but isn't high stakes two-on-two, not one-on-one?" the shorter player of the pair asked.

"You two versus me. I just got this money in the mail, so I'm cool with losing it. I'm just here to play for fun," I lied.

"All right. How much do you want to lay on the table?" he asked.

"One thousand crome," I suggested. "Does that sound good?"

"So if you win, we pay you one thousand each, and if we win, you pay us one thousand and we split it, five hundred each?"

I nodded. "It's only fair. It's two against one."

"Twenty-one point games?" the taller one asked.

I agreed, and we started the game. I ended up losing, twenty-one to eight. I tossed them the ball with a defeated sigh, cursing under my breath. I glanced over at Lara, who was clearly pissed by my poor performance. "One more game?" I asked them hopefully, pulling out another thousand crome from my pocket.

"Sure, why not?" they both agreed.

This time, I beat them, twenty-one to eighteen. I nailed every shot, intercepting most of their passes and stealing the ball from the taller guy almost every time. "Wow, you got game," the shorter player said.

"I just got lucky," I said, but I was relieved that I wasn't going to walk away empty-handed.

"Want to play another game?" the taller guy asked, eager to earn back the money they had just lost.

"I can't. My girl wants to go shopping. You know how they get if you keep them waiting," I told them with a laugh, nodding over to Lara. I jogged up the hill, and Lara jumped into my arms excitedly, kissing me on the cheek. She bought me a water bottle, and we headed down the street toward the shopping center, although we briefly got lost and had to refer to the map.

"Not bad, hey? Made a thousand crome in half an hour," I bragged.

"That was amazing. How did you turn from bad to good so fast?" she asked.

"It's simple. I used the first game to identify their weaknesses—for instance, the taller guy always faked left, and the short guy always passed instead of shooting. Then I used that against them," I explained as we navigated our way down the busy street.

"I'm sorry I doubted you."

"It's fine," I told her, giving her an extra five hundred crome to shop with as we finally arrived at the shopping district of Monatello.

We bought all the clothes and accessories that we would need, such as toothbrushes, combs, shampoo—stuff like that. We returned home a couple hours later, where Lara spent the rest of the day unpacking our stuff. I flopped onto the bed and flipped through a magazine I had bought at the mall. Lara hung pictures of us on the wall and placed a few on our bedside tables.

"You could help me, you know," she reminded me playfully, flopping down on the bed beside me.

"What would be the purpose of keeping you around then?" I shot back playfully.

"If I were you, I'd sleep with one eye open tonight." She gave me a playful shove as she got back up and busied herself for the rest of the day with decorating the house.

I woke the next morning to the sound of the shower running. After a while of lounging around in bed, waiting for Lara to get out of the shower, I got dressed.

"So are you ready for work?" she asked me as she emerged from the bathroom. She quickly slipped on her waitress uniform; she was in a rush to leave because she was running late for work.

I watched her frantically do up her hair in front of the mirror. "I have to find a partner today, so I probably won't make much money," I explained.

She paused, glancing at me in the mirror. I tried to figure out what she was thinking, but it was always too hard to tell with her. "I don't know anything about this gambling business, but I'm going to assume you know how to make a profit out of it, and I trust you," she told me, handing me a thousand crome.

What I had done yesterday was a very risky move. I knew I probably would never do again, but it was necessary to show Lara that I could succeed at the underground basketball business. "You look nice," I told her as I opened the door for her.

"Aw, thanks, you look like you."

"Ha-ha. Real funny, smart-ass," I grunted, closing the door behind us.

We walked along the sidewalk, holding hands, cutting through some backyards and ending up at the entertainment court where Lara worked. "All right, buddy, good luck. Play hard, or you will be flipping burgers for fiends," she joked with me.

I could see the underlying threat behind her joke, though, and I smiled nervously as she gave me a kiss good-bye before walking up the hill toward the café. I plunked myself down on a rock at the side of the court. People began to show up in pairs, and games started to commence. It turned out that the underground basketball business had already started, which didn't surprise me—it was basically like a religion in the PLF.

If you didn't have your legs blown off, then there was no excuse to not play basketball. I noticed that most of the players weren't top-notch like I was used to playing against. Don't get me wrong; they were all right, but it was hard to watch some of them play. I chuckled to myself, watching one of the players trip over his own feet, face-planting onto the concrete as the ball rolled away.

A chick's voice rang out from behind me. "Yo, you ain't got no partner?" A slim black girl, about five foot eight, was walking over to me. She sat down beside me in the grass.

"Nah. I'm just watching some games, trying to find myself one." I was annoyed by the distraction.

"Well, that's good, because I'm looking for a partner as well." She looked up at me as she fiddled with her hair.

"You're kidding, right?" I laughed. She reached for my water bottle and took a drink from it.

"Yeah, go ahead help yourself," I added, rolling my eyes as she wiped her mouth off and screwed the cap back on.

"Thanks, champ," she shot back, tossing the water bottle on my lap. She held out her hand. "I'm Tracy, by the way."

"Lance," I replied, shaking her hand, half-interested. "Oh, shit," I blurted out as I saw Lara sauntering down the hill toward us.

"What?" Tracy asked, looking confused.

"My wife is a fiend. Touching other females is against the law in her culture."

Lara walked up behind us. "What are you guys up to?" Lara asked innocently as she sat down on the rock with me and wrapped her arm around me in a jealous manner.

I sent her an explanation in my head. *"It's not her fault. She was looking for a partner, and I forgot about the no-touching-other-females rule."*

"You still need a partner to play?" Lara's voice echoed back.

"Yeah, everyone else is taken right now," I told her.

"Give me a second with this human then," she ordered me.

"I need to go to the bathroom. I'll be right back," I said, excusing myself and walking up the hill. I stayed out of sight until Lara called me back in my head.

Once I got back down the hill, Lara kissed me and said her break was over. She walked back up the hill. *"You can be her partner. I'm willing to bend that no-touching rule as long as it's appropriate places. Just make sure to tell me in advance who your female friends are,"* she told me in my head.

"So … would you like to be my partner?" I asked Tracy, pretending to not really be interested in the answer.

She nodded, trying to match my lack of enthusiasm.

"What did Lara say, by the way?" I asked casually as we watched a game going on between two pretty tough-looking teams.

"Oh, your wife's a real angel," she snapped. "She told me she liked my hair and thought you and I should be partners. She also told me to keep in mind that if I made any moves on you, she would make sure that I had a long, painful death."

I snickered. "Yeah, that sounds like my wife."

We got up as one of the games on the court ended. Tracy wasn't as bad as I expected; in fact, she was pretty decent. I sunk a lot more baskets during our games than she did, kind of making her a weak link, but the way I looked at it, it was better to get slow money than no money at all. I ended up making a hundred fifty crome by the end of the day, winning four games to one.

I wasn't very satisfied with the amount we'd made, knowing that Lara made two hundred twenty-five crome a day, but I figured we would make more once Tracy and I adapted to each other's playing styles.

"You want to show up early tomorrow and get some practice hoops in before the games start?" Tracy asked me.

She seemed afraid that I was going to ditch her and find a new partner. "Sure, and thanks again for teaming up with me today," I told her sincerely.

She seemed relieved that I had accepted her as my partner. When I arrived at our house, Lara still hadn't returned home, so I jumped in the shower, cleaning off all the sweat and dirt from running around in the blistering sun all day. A couple minutes later, Lara came home and jumped in the shower with me. She hugged me close, telling me about her first day at work.

"So how much did you make?" she asked.

"A hundred fifty crome," I replied with a shrug.

"That's not bad," she told me, taking the shampoo and redoing my hair.

"Were going to make more as we get better," I promised her.

"You and Tracy?" she asked casually.

I nodded. "You're cool with that, right?"

"Yes, I don't see any harm in your hanging out with her," she told me, but I could tell from her fake smile that she was unsure.

David and Carana came by that night, asking us to play some pool with them, which we did. Lara didn't know how to play, so I had to teach her. It was fun, for the most part. The four of us ended the night by drinking at the bar, sharing love stories of how we met one another.

The next couple of weeks flew by pretty quickly. Tracy and I had become pretty good players together, and she started tagging along with David and me to the bars at night.

"Let's go home, buddy," Lara bugged me as I was finishing a game of poker with David, Tracy, and her new boyfriend, Mike.

"Yeah, are you almost ready to go, David?" Carana asked impatiently.

"Can you at least let us finish our game in peace?" David asked.

They sat beside us and bugged us every five minutes. "David, Lara wants to go home. Just let Lance take his money," Carana suggested impatiently.

"You're only playing for fifty crome. Let's just go. I don't care about the money anyway," Lara added.

Carana agreed, bugging David to just give up as well.

"I'm almost done. What's the rush anyway?" I asked Lara, becoming annoyed by her childish behavior. She unbuttoned her shirt, flashing me her bra in front of David and the rest of the crew.

"I'm no expert, but I'd say tonight might be a good night for you." Tracy's boyfriend laughed.

"All right, I fold. You guys win. See you later." I grabbed Lara's hand and we rushed out the door, chased by the laughter and cheering of the others in the background.

Lara giggled as we rushed down the road like little children after an ice cream truck. "Slow down a bit, buddy," she begged me, stopping in the middle of the street. Her stomach groaned and she gasped for breath, and then, after another groan of pain, she straightened up, grabbed my hand, and playfully bumped into me before running down the street toward our house. I hesitated, a bit freaked by her overly happy mood, especially since it appeared that she was starting her monthly tricnoses. "Are you coming or what?" she called to me playfully.

I shook it off and laughed, chasing her down the street and into our house as she playfully taunted me with insults. "I got to use the bathroom real quick.

Then we can have some fun!" she told me, stripping down to nothing in front of me while pushing me onto the bed and pulling off my pants and shirt. She headed to the bathroom, stopping at the table by the mirror to hunch over as a cramp hit her. She pretended to be reading, as if nothing was happening.

I could hear her groaning as her chest heaved in and out forcefully. Once it stopped, she turned to me and said that she must have eaten some bad seafood at the bar. Then she rushed into the bathroom. She closed the door quickly and turned on the faucets—I could hear water running in the sink. Soon afterward, Lara returned, flopping on top of me.

"You would do anything to make me happy, right?" she asked.

"Of course. Why?"

"No reason. I just want you to know I'd do anything to make you happy as well," she whispered back drunkenly, beginning to kiss my neck as she got on top of me.

"I know you would, but shouldn't we wait until after your tricnoses to do this? Besides, you're a bit drunk," I told her, feeling her backbone jut out a tiny bit but recoiling into her spine a split second later.

"It's only a light one, like last month's, and I'm pretty sure you've had more to drink than me. I'm fine, Lance! Let's do it now."

She was definitely right about one thing—I was drunker than she was, because if I'd been sober, I never would have agreed … but I reluctantly did. And as the night progressed, she became more and more aggressive. I started to get a bit scared when she paused on top of me to let out a non-human growl. She stared up at the ceiling as fangs jutted out of her mouth and her claws ripped from her hands.

"Ugh! Let's stop. I'm not comfortable with this anymore," I told her, my voice shaking as she regained control. Her fangs and claws retracted back into her. I slipped into my boxers.

Lara objected unhappily. "Oh, come on, Lance! I'm having fun. I want this to be a special night for us. Stop being such a buzz-kill," she scolded me gently.

"Why don't you just sleep off the rest of the tricnoses in the cage, and then we can continue tomorrow night?" I bargained with her, trying to escape from underneath her.

She forcefully pushed me back down and adopted a very dangerous tone as she tried to slip off my boxers again. "You want to lock me up in the cage? Ha-ha! I own you, not the other way around." She sounded demented, and then she began to kiss my neck again.

"Please, Lara, you're losing control," I begged her.

She continued to groan from her constant pains now. "I ... will ... never ... be locked up," she told me slowly, through clenched teeth. Her wings suddenly burst out of her back, and she let out a non-human roar.

I stopped struggling as a claw jutted from her finger. She placed it against my neck, laughing, half-insane, as she began to rape me. "Stop ... please!" I kept begging her, but it was useless. After being raped for fifteen minutes, her eyes flashed for a second. I could see her worried expression as she stopped and got off me. She angrily let out a cry of pain, becoming upset by what she had done to me. She hurled herself into the jail, tearing up the walls of it and letting out enraged, lion-like sounds.

I rushed over to lock it and then slumped down a couple feet away. Lara continued to thrash around in it angrily. She fully transformed, briefly biting herself and causing fur to fly everywhere. She seemed to be fighting an invisible enemy. A couple minutes later, she passed out, like usual, on the ground and returned to her naked human form.

I felt a few tears trickle down my face as the fact that I had just been raped by my own wife dawned on me.

"I'm so sorry. Please forgive me," Lara's quivering voice called to me as she regained consciousness.

"Don't be. I can't complain that I got to have sex with my beautiful wife. It doesn't matter." I wiped away tears, turning away from her so that she couldn't see me silently crying.

"I'm sorry, Lance. I'm so, so sorry. Are you all right?" She kept repeating the same words in a very soft, caring voice.

"I'm fine," I lied, trying to act tough as I wiped away the remainder of the tears. I pulled out her pajamas from a drawer and passed them through the bars to her. She thanked me and put her hand out through the bars. "Keep me company?" she whispered. "It's lonely in here." She appeared to be thinking of a way to redeem herself from what had just happened.

I paused for a second, still a bit mad at her, but I hid my anger and nodded. I lay down beside the jail, holding her hand. "Of course I'll keep you company. You're my girl, and you always will be. That pesky tricnoses isn't going to stop me from loving you."

She sniffled, holding back from crying, and nodded. "I knew there was a reason I kept you around," she joked, with a playful poke on my nose. "I'm going to start taking pills for my tricnoses. I can't keep putting you through this. It's not fair for you or me," she whispered.

I felt myself jump for joy at this news. I nodded happily in agreement. "Good night, buddy," I told her, flicking off the light.

We both stared out the window at a single star shining brightly in the sky. I couldn't help but wonder how two species that were so different could be so much alike.

Chapter 13

Two and a half months later, I found myself in the waiting room of a doctor's office. Lara had been sick for the past few weeks. She'd been throwing up periodically and always seemed drained of energy. Her monthly tricnoses had mysteriously disappeared as well, which was even more worrying.

She was reluctant to see a doctor at first, but after a week of my nagging her to get checked out, she finally agreed to see our family doctor.

"This is such a waste of time," she said unhappily after we'd sat there for over two hours, waiting for our turn.

"Making sure you are all right is not a waste of time," I said affectionately.

She smiled gently and gave me a kiss. "I'm fine. I just caught a bug going around at work, that's all." She rested her head on my shoulder and stared gloomily at the floor.

"Lara Marini," the secretary at the front desk called out.

"Finally," Lara muttered under her breath. We both got up and headed down the hall to the examining room. A moment later we took our seats inside, as an older woman in her late forties sorted through some paperwork and pulled out a folder before acknowledging our presence.

"Hello there. What seems to be the trouble today?" Dr. Green asked us warmly, as a gentle smile spread across her face.

"I haven't really been feeling like myself over the past few months," Lara explained.

"I'm sorry to hear that," Dr. Green said. "Let me have a quick look at you." She rolled her chair over to Lara and told her to open her mouth. "Everything seems fine there," Dr. Green said after looking at Lara's throat. She then told Lara to strip down to her underwear.

I felt useless. I stood up and found a spot against the wall. I watched as Dr. Green made Lara do seemingly random things, such as stand on one leg, lift her arms up, and stuff like that. "Your skin is fairly pale and clammy. Have you been drinking your daily ration of blood?" Dr. Green asked.

Lara nodded, and I told the doctor, "Her skin has been that way for about a month now."

Dr. Green and Lara both turned to me, as if just realizing I was still there. "Thank you, Lance," Dr. Green said and then turned her attention back to Lara. "Are you still able to transform?"

Lara shook her head.

"Would you mind leaving us, Lance?" Dr. Green asked. "This may take a while."

"But—" I began to protest.

"Go play some games with Tracy," Lara interrupted. "I'll meet you there." She smiled and gave me a reassuring wink. "I'll be fine."

I glanced at the two of them unhappily but obediently left the room, angrily heading outside and down the street to the basketball court. Tracy was hanging out, relaxing in the sun against a tree, half asleep. "Hey," I muttered, trying to hide my anger. I gave her a light kick against her shoes.

"Oh, hey, Lance! Lara's done already?" she asked, opening up an eye.

"No."

"Why are you here then?" she asked.

"That's what I'm wondering," I said grumpily.

"She'll be fine, Lance. Want to kick someone's ass real quick before she's done?" Tracy asked.

I sighed, knowing she was trying to cheer me up. I took off my shirt, accepting her offer and getting ready for a game. We stood on the sidelines, waiting as another game finished. It was extremely hot out; I didn't even understand how people were able to play in this heat. Tracy and I found a match, but my head wasn't in the game at all.

We walked out to center court where two tough-looking opponents were waiting for us. The stronger looking one of the pair was there, the ball grasped in his hands. He glanced back to his partner ready to start the game by checking me the ball. A player checks by simply passing the ball to his opponent at the start of every point to reinitiate the game.

I was checked the ball, trying a quick fake on the guy but failing miserably and nearly colliding into him. I backed off and heard Tracy clapping her hands to signal she was open. I spotted her and chucked it in her direction, but it was too far to the right and one of our opponents intercepted it.

"God damn it!" I cursed angrily as Tracy ran after it, trying to recover from my mistake.

A strongly built guy knocked her down and snatched it from her. Then he did a beautiful jump shot from the three-point line, which swooshed right through the net. I was checked the ball again, trying to fake my man out instead faking myself out by accident as I fumbled the ball. He jumped on the opportunity, instantly grabbing it and racing toward the net. He threw it up against the backboard as his buddy raced to the net, jumping up and slam-dunking the ball.

"Come on, Lance. You're better than that!" a kid called from the sidelines. I looked away in embarrassment. I was not only letting myself down but also the fans that Tracy and I had attracted over the past few weeks. "Looks like the legend is crumbling," one of them grunted.

I stood there, panting for breath, as our opponents scored two more three-pointers; it was already eleven to zero on us. "Let me take back," Tracy said to me, taking my spot at center court getting checked the ball. She faked left, bolted right, and sprinted in between the pair, laying the ball up into the hoop and nicely bringing the score to eleven to two.

"Lance!" I heard Lara's voice call out.

I glanced over to the bleachers and spotted her waving at me. She took a seat to watch the game. I felt a new hope surge through me, instantly gaining my confidence back. "I got this," I promised Tracy.

"Are you sure, Lance? We're down way too far to let them get any more baskets."

"Give and go," I said.

She nodded, retaking her old position. I was checked the ball instantly and tossed it to Tracy. She faked a shot, and her man fell for it trying to block her. She passed it through to me. I raced to the net, grabbing it with one hand, lunging up, and slam-dunking. "*Wooooo-whooo!*" I heard the crowd cheer from the sidelines.

We nearly lost the game but it ended at twenty-one to nineteen, our favor, probably one of the closest calls we'd had in the last couple of days.

"Nice game, man. Anytime you want to go again, just hit us up," one of our opponents told us as we shook hands.

"For sure," I said, and Tracy and I received our fifty crome each for the win.

"Nice job!" Lara said, but she was interrupted by a few fans who rushed over to Tracy and me, asking for our autographs. We both obliged, and then the three of us rushed away. "Geesh, you guys are like superstars out there," Lara said with a laugh.

"I know. I almost want to lose, just to get them off our backs for a little bit," Tracy told her.

The three of us laughed and then parted ways, as Tracy headed in the opposite direction toward her house. "So?" I asked Lara.

"So what?" Lara said. A dumb grin spread across her face.

"What did Dr. Green have to say?"

"She told me that everything is fine. She thinks that I might be ascending, so I need to drink more blood for the next couple of months in order to prepare my body for the change."

"Ascending?" I asked.

"It's when a fiend makes the transition from being a teenager to adulthood, becoming more powerful," Lara explained.

"Oh, that sounds cool."

We held hands as we walked along the street to our house.

"It's ridiculously hot for mid-September, huh?" Lara said conversationally, once we finally arrived back to our place.

I grabbed us both a drink from the fridge. Lara took a bottle of pills from her pocket and popped one in her mouth; then she chugged down the soda I had offered her.

"What are those?" I asked, pointing to the pills.

"Supplements that Green gave me. She told me it would help me feel better." After a couple of minutes of sitting around in boredom, Lara asked, "So what would you like to do today? It's too hot to get anything done."

"Maybe go for a swim down at the pool?" I suggested hopefully.

"All right, sick idea," Lara agreed. "I'll be right back." She grabbed her bathing suit and went into the bathroom to change.

I rummaged around in my dresser for a second and found my swimming trunks. After putting them on, I went to the bathroom door and peeked through the crack. Lara was standing in front of the mirror in her bikini. She turned sideways, placing her hands underneath her breasts and lifting them up momentarily. Then she lowered her hands to her belly and let out a sigh as a tear trickled down her face. "God, I hate you, Lara," she whispered to herself, wiping away the tear and flicking her beautiful long hair away from her face. She stared at her reflection gloomily.

I felt so bad for her. I didn't know what was wrong, but she had been this way for the past two months now. It felt like the more I tried to help, the more frustrated with herself she became. I knocked on the door, and she quickly straightened up and messed up her hair. "Come in," she said.

I put on a fake smile, pretending I hadn't seen her little breakdown. "You ready to go?" I asked.

She beamed at me and held out her hand, which I accepted, hugging her close as we made out with one another. "Geesh, what's gotten into you today?" she giggled as we finished up and headed out the door toward the pool.

"What do you mean?" I asked as we walked along the busy sidewalk.

"I don't know; you just seem more affectionate than usual," she said, glancing up at me with a shrug.

"That's because I love you," I whispered. I ran my hand along her back and rested it on her waist.

"Tell me, Lance … what do you love about me?" she asked. She stopped in the middle of the baseball field and stared up at me to see if I was telling the truth.

"Everything," I whispered, leaning forward to give her a light peck on her forehead.

"What's everything?" she asked.

"Your hair, your eyes, your beautiful smile—see? There it is." I paused as she smiled genuinely up at me. "That smile is what kept me going when times were hard, back in the prison, Lara. I love your personality; how you never take no for an answer. In a way, you're just like me—a stubborn son of a bitch—and that's the only reason we fight so much. But you know what?"

"What?" She giggled, knowing I was telling the truth.

"I love it, because life without you would not be worth living."

She gasped, my line seeming to have shattered her wall of isolation that she had set up over the past few weeks. "Oh, Lance … I love you so much. Don't you ever forget that!" she cried out happily, hugging me close for what seemed like forever, as tears began streaming down her face. "There's something I need to tell you," she said nervously.

"What is that?" I tried to mentally prepare myself for whatever was coming next, knowing it was going to rock my world.

"I'm pregnant."

We stared at each other for a moment, her words not quite registering in my head. "But … I … I … what?" Her words hit me like a freight train, and I began to panic.

"Shhh … shhh … Lance. Lance, calm down. It's going to be okay." She tried to comfort me by resting her head against my chest and holding onto me tightly.

I tried to calm myself down, convincing myself that it wasn't completely her fault. Yes, she had lied straight to my face not even an hour ago and intentionally had taken that pregnancy pill without my consent. But on the other hand, I had been avoiding the topic completely. She probably didn't bring it up because she didn't want to have another fight with me.

Taking a deep breath, I slowly placed my hand on her belly, confirming her story. It wasn't noticeable, but there really was a tiny bump that could be felt around her stomach as I ran my hand along it. "You can let go now; I'm fine," I whispered, stroking her hair affectionately.

"I'm not falling for that trick," she whispered, holding on to me for dear life, as if I might just take off, hop the two-hundred-foot fence surrounding Monatello, and make a beeline into the woods, never to be seen again.

"I can't … breathe …" I said. I coughed, and then we both broke out laughing. She loosened her grip and looked up at me, love sparkling in her baby-blue eyes. We lay down in the middle of the field, stunned by the realization that we were going to be parents—it seemed to hit both of us.

"Lance, listen to me," she said gently, running her hand across my face. "I would never lie to you to hurt you in anyway. I asked you if you would do anything to make me happy, and you said yes. I, in turn, promised you that I'd do anything to make you happy."

I glanced over from her stomach to her face before responding. "I know," I said. I gently rubbed my hand across her belly and asked, "What is it?"

"A girl," she said. She took my head in her hands and pressed it against her stomach; I rested there, happily. "I've decided to call her Rachel, in memory of your old girlfriend, even though traditionally, most female names end with the letter A," she informed me affectionately.

I knew this was her peace offering for lying to me. I contemplated how to respond and then said, "I like Rashellia."

She beamed at me. "I think that's a beautiful name too." She wrapped her arms around me, giving me a kiss. We lay there in silence, gazing at each other. "You're nothing like your father, Lance. I'm proud of you, and Rashellia will grow up to be proud of you too," she promised me.

"Thank you," I whispered sincerely.

"For what?"

"For everything—saving my life, changing me into a free man, even making me a part of your family. I didn't grow up with an actual family, yet you looked past our differences and made this work. Now look at where we are—a house, kid on the way. We're living the dream. Many aren't fortunate enough to even come close," I said emotionally. I nodded toward her belly while thinking about all my buddies, still stuck in this brutal war.

She shook her head vigorously. "No, I'm not the hero you're making me out to be. I used to kill humans for pure satisfaction. I once ripped a kid's heart out and kept him alive, just so he could watch me eat it, and then I slit his throat, leaving him to bleed out with no heart. You saved me from myself, Lance. I was a monster," she confessed. "I should have asked you before taking the pills. I know that was wrong, and I'm sorry, but I figured once you had the baby in your arms, you wouldn't be scared anymore."

"How did you intend to hide the baby from me at nine months when you're not even three, and you're already starting to bulge? Plus, why, of all days, would you decide to have the baby during your tricnoses?" I snorted.

"I had a hundred percent chance of getting pregnant during my tricnoses, whereas it was only fifty/fifty during a normal day, because during tricnoses, my reproductive system becomes vulnerable. Besides, I didn't want to fully be conscious of what I was doing to you."

"Oh, well. Either way, I'm glad you did what you did, because I never would have been ready. At least now that it's actually happening, I'm ready."

She smiled warmly as we stared at each other affectionately for a while, letting the dull rays of sun bounce off our skin as we lay in the middle of the baseball field in silence.

A patrol of the city's guards walked by and stopped in front of us. "Hey, what are you kids doing here?"

"Ugh ..." we both muttered, glancing at each other before breaking up in laughter.

They seemed confused by our lack of concern for their presence. "We're going to have to ask you to move along if you're not here to play a sport," one of them told us.

We obediently got up and jogged over to the pool entrance. Lara looked nervous as we entered. There were a lot of hot girls in magnificent bikinis. Lara's self-consciousness took over, as she seemed to be comparing herself to them. "I'm not really feeling that good," she said.

"Oh, come on; it will be fun." I wrapped my arm around her waist and gave her a reassuring kiss.

She sighed and then said, "Fine."

I could see in her expression how painful the decision was for her. We found two chairs and laid our towels down on them. Then we jumped into the pool. "Aw, this feels so nice," I said happily, as we swam around for a while.

"Mm-hm. I'm glad you talked me out of leaving," Lara said. She turned over and floated on her back, closing her eyes and relaxing in the sun.

"How do you do that?" I asked, swimming up beside her.

"Do what?"

"Float on your back. I've always wanted to learn, but no one's ever taught me."

"It's magic," she teased.

I laughed, and she flipped back over onto her stomach, swimming over to the shallow end with me. "Roll over," she instructed me. She placed her hand against my back and all my worries evaporated. "All right … take a deep breath." When I did, she said, "I'm going to let go now. Are you ready?"

"Yeah, good to go," I said, feeling her slowly take her hand away from my back so that I was floating on my own.

"Just try to balance all your body evenly, kind of like a star shape," she instructed me. I wavered a little bit but stabilized myself successfully. "There you go, buddy. You're a natural," Lara congratulated me. She lazily flipped back onto her back and floated beside me.

"I'm having such a good time. I don't think anything could happen right now to ruin this day," I whispered to her lovingly, relaxing as the water lapped against our bodies.

"The baby isn't yours, Lance," Lara murmured.

"*What?*" I exclaimed. I splashed around as I flipped back onto my stomach and looked at her in shock.

Lara burst out laughing. "Ha-ha. Got you! You should have seen the look on your face—absolutely priceless."

"That's not funny," I said but then laughed and gave her a playful splash.

We swam around for a little while longer, and when the sun began to set, Lara asked, "You want to go back?"

"Sure," I said. I followed her over to the ladder and helped her out; then I pulled myself out as well.

As we dried off, a girl's voice called from behind us. "Um … excuse me. Are you Lance?" My jaw almost dropped as I turned and saw the girl's stunning figure. She smiled, tilting her head a bit, probably recognizing that it was me. "I'm Ava, a big fan of yours and Tracy's."

I offered a friendly smile as I shook her hand—and then instantly realized I shouldn't have done so. I glanced back at Lara, who was pretending disinterest in Ava's presence.

"Would you mind giving me your autograph?" Ava asked, handing me a piece of paper. "And could I get one for my little cousin too? He's a big fan." She pulled out a ball cap from her backpack and handed it to me. I signed the paper and the cap, and Ava thanked me before saying good-bye.

I then followed Lara out the exit of the pool and back to the road that led to our place. "Well, don't you feel like Mr. Popular today, hey?" she asked me playfully as we reached the sidewalk.

"It won't last. I'm just a fad for now, until a new player emerges," I told her thoughtfully.

She smiled; I could tell she was trying to mask her jealously as she grabbed my hand and swung it back and forth happily. "You're always so modest, Lance. I've seen you play—you have a gift," she said supportively.

I smiled thankfully at her. Our house came into view in the distance, and once we were inside, I helped her with supper. We ate in front of the television and watched a little bit of the local Monatello news. After dinner, we washed the dishes together.

Once we were done with the dishes and relaxing back in our room, Lara said playfully, "Um, excuse me, mister … are you Lance Burns?"

"Yes, it is I, Lance the superstar."

"Could I … um … get your autograph?" she asked, pretending to be nervous.

"I suppose," I sighed, pretending to sign a napkin with an invisible pen and handing it over to her.

"Oh, my gosh, you're so sweet!" she said, looking at the napkin as if it was a million dollars. "Would you mind if I brought my two friends over to meet you?" she asked, casually beginning to slip off her shirt, bra, and underwear.

"I suppose so. It's always nice to meet new fans." I wrapped my arm around her now-naked body as she stared down at me innocently.

We had the most romantic night ever, taking breaks in between the sex by listening to the soft music in the background and talking about our childhood funny stories—and then starting up again. I fell in love with Lara all over again, and by the end of the night, I wished that our little girl was there in our arms. Lara rested my head against her chest and told me to go to sleep as she lay sprawled on the bed, purring affectionately and stroking my hair.

"I love you so much," she panted groggily into my ear. My breathing slowed, and I returned her affectionate gesture with a kiss, just before sleep overtook me.

The next morning Lara had breakfast already done up for us by the time I woke up. She was dressed in a tight skirt and tank top, with her plump belly showing.

"Aw, you look so cute," I told her, sitting up in bed.

"Really? It feels a little tight under my belly." She turned around like a model, showing me the full three-sixty view.

"You could weigh three hundred pounds, and you'd still look beautiful," I said affectionately as she approached the bed with a breakfast tray. I kissed her belly and then her.

She giggled as I kissed her belly again. "I've never seen you so affectionate. What happened to the stone-cold killer I know?" she asked, handing me the plate of sausages and eggs before sitting on the bed beside me.

"He retired," I told her with a laugh as we dug into our breakfast. "Thank you for making this, by the way. I'll hit you up with the good ol' Lance special tomorrow morning."

"I don't think you can call toast and a glass of orange juice a 'special,'" she joked.

"Wow, what a hater," I muttered, pretending to be hurt by her comment.

She laughed. "I had a really good time last night, Lance."

"Me too. It's too bad we won't be able to do that for a while now."

"That's not true. I'm still in business until probably around ten months. Then you'll have to suffer for the next little bit until the big day," she told me with a laugh.

"Ten months?" I asked. "Don't you mean nine?"

She shook her head, probably realizing that I knew nothing about fiend pregnancies. "A fiend pregnancy can last as long as a full year. At ten months, the pregnancy is at full term—that's when I'll probably slip into labor. I'll be so big by then that sex won't be that appealing anyway," she explained to me with a smirk. "It becomes hard to walk and stuff by then. Most girls even crawl for the last bit of their pregnancy until the baby is born because it's that much of a hassle to try to walk." She took her fork and pushed some eggs and a sausage onto her plate from mine. When I protested, she gave me a playful poke with her elbow. "Suck it up, muffin. Survival of the fittest!" she joked as she gobbled it up.

She got up, taking my plate to the kitchen and returning a moment later. "Unfortunately for you, your skirt-watching days are numbered," she giggled, catching me checking her out as she walked back in the room.

"I know. I'm going to miss it, but at least I'll still get to see you in sweatpants!" I retorted.

She smiled at me. "I've already called my boss and Tracy to tell them we're taking the day off, so what would you like to do? It's an exclusive Lance and Lara day."

I shrugged as I got up to run water in the kitchen sink, starting the dishes. "I'll help out more around here, so you don't have to worry about doing this stuff. You can just focus on making our little angel," I told her affectionately. She came over to dry the dishes as I set each plate into the drying rack.

"You're so sweet, buddy, but I'm pregnant, not crippled. So don't smother me, or I'll be bored out of my mind." She laughed as I gave her a playful bump with my hips, insisting that I would dry the dishes.

"I'll go take a shower, and then maybe we can go catch a movie or something," she suggested.

"Sounds good," I agreed. I happily hummed to myself and continued washing the remaining dishes. As I did, I glanced outside at the beautiful day and saw a family walking down the street. I realized that soon enough, that would be us.

Chapter 14

I woke to the sound of Lara's eating of crackers—she tried to quietly eat her morning snack before getting up but failed miserably. She was six months pregnant now, with her tummy openly showing. I listened to her munching for a few minutes, pretending to still be asleep, not wanting to get up.

I was kind of excited—today was Christmas. Lara and the gang had all agreed that we'd celebrate it together. It took a fair bit of persuading Carana and Lara, though, because apparently, the whole idea behind Christmas and worshiping another god was against the laws of Dracona. After explaining the idea behind it and reassuring them that they didn't have to believe in God and that it was a holiday to unite friends and family, Lara and Carana both agreed to celebrate it with David, Tracy, and me.

Once Lara had finished her crackers, she got up and tiptoed into the bathroom. The familiar sounds of the shower running soon filled the room, along with Lara's beautiful voice, singing to herself. I lounged around in bed, peeking out the window at the freshly fallen snow before closing my eyes to go back to sleep.

The sounds of the shower soon pattered away, and a moment later, I heard the door open. Lara tiptoed back into the room and crawled back into bed, giving me a light shake. "Happy Christmas, Lance," she whispered, giving me a gentle kiss.

I beamed up at her, happily returning the kiss. "Thank you, buddy. It's Merry Christmas, not Happy Christmas, by the way."

She giggled, embarrassed, and cuddled under the blankets with me for a little while, doing our usually morning routine of waking up and chatting. "How did you sleep?" she asked.

"Not bad. What about you?"

She patted her belly contentedly. "It was all right."

"Did the baby keep you up?" I asked.

She nodded unhappily. "I'm feeling kind of nauseated this morning, so you better have gotten me something nice for Christmas, or I might just puke all over you," she threatened me playfully. Then she saw my look of guilt and said, "I'm just playing around with you, Lance. I'm fine."

I felt bad about what she was forced to go through by being pregnant, but I nodded, pretending to believe her, knowing she wanted to make today a special one for me. I gently gave her stomach a kiss and then sat up, sleepily wiping the crud out of my eyes. "Looks like we got quite a bit of snow last night," I said.

She nodded in agreement, hopping out of bed to make me something for breakfast. "We're supposed to be getting hit hard tonight," she called to me as she threw four pieces of bread into the toaster.

"Yeah, I heard." I got up and put on a pair of jeans, along with a nice dress shirt for the party. I joined Lara in the kitchen and buttered the toast as it popped out of the toaster. I handed her plate to her, and then we went back to the bedroom and sat on the edge of the bed. "Thanks a lot," I said as she handed me a cup of coffee.

"Anytime," she answered, but she seemed preoccupied with her thoughts.

"What's wrong?" I asked.

"Nothing. Why?" She offered me a faint smile.

"I don't know—you just seem really quiet."

She laughed, returning to her normal self. "It's nothing for you to worry about—just girl issues," she said, giving me a kiss.

"Like what?" I persisted.

"Well, I was wondering what I'm going to wear for this party since my nice clothes don't fit anymore, and I feel like a mess right now. I have to do my hair, my makeup—stuff like that; things you don't want to hear about."

I wrapped my arms around her consolingly. "You look beautiful just the way you are," I reassured her.

She smiled, giving me a light pat on my leg. "I don't think a T-shirt and pink maternity underwear is going to cut it."

I laughed, finishing off my toast and bringing our plates over to the sink. She watched me as she sipped her coffee. I began to rummage around in her closet, looking for something nice. I emerged with a pair of maternity sweatpants and a nice white button-up dress shirt. "How's this?" I asked her.

She laughed unhappily at the outfit I had picked out. She was used to being stylish and beautiful—the kind of girl every guy wishes he had—so I realized this pregnancy must be pretty hard on her. I knew she was self-conscious about how big she was getting, but all I could do to help was keep reassuring her how much I loved her.

"So how are my two beautiful girls this morning?" I asked her.

She tried on the outfit, looking at herself in the mirror before sitting beside me on the bed. "She's pretty active this morning. I think she must have missed her daddy," Lara teased, giving me a kiss. She gently placed my hand on her belly, and Rashellia shifted around inside.

"You're getting pretty big," I said, staring down at her bump.

She smiled in agreement, snuggling up to me. "Tonight should be fun, hey?" she said happily.

I stroked her hair softly in her favorite spot and nodded enthusiastically. "If you start bleeding, though, tell me, and we will come back," I instructed her firmly.

"Don't worry about me. I'm not going to ruin our night together by getting myself worked up, Lance."

The doorbell rang, and we got up to answer it. "Hey!" everyone called to Lara and me as we opened the door, greeting them with smiles, and stepped aside to let Tracy, Carana, and David come in. Lara and I set out some chairs for everyone, and we all sat down to exchange gifts.

"Where's Mike?" I asked Tracy.

"We broke up a few days ago," she informed me unhappily.

"Aw, I'm sorry to hear that, sweetie," Lara said, rubbing Tracy's shoulder.

"Thanks. … You're getting big, by the way."

"Yeah, well, you know, Lance. He just won't stop stuffing my face," Lara joked, patting her belly. She looked at me and winked.

"I still remember a couple months ago, when you had to go to the doctor's—Lance was so worried about you, he looked like he was going to cry," Tracy said.

"Aw, how cute," David and Carana cooed.

I felt my face flush in embarrassment. "Hey, I was worried about my wife, okay? I thought there was something wrong with her," I said defensively.

They all laughed at my embarrassment. I couldn't help laughing along with them, but I gave them the middle finger before returning to my gifts.

"I'll give you your gift tonight," Lara whispered to me in my head.

I nodded to her as David handed me his last gift. "Trust me—you will like this one," he promised.

"Oh, really? Is this what I think it is?" I asked.

Before he could answer, Lara happily called out, "Hey, Lance, is this nice or what?" She held up some maternity clothes that the rest of them had gotten her.

"Yeah, I'm digging the skirt," I said, and I winked at her.

Lara opened another box and exclaimed, "Oh, wow!" She held up a check saying, "This is too much, guys."

"How much is it?" I asked as the others looked on happily.

"Five thousand crome."

My eyes lit up in surprise. "Wow, thanks, guys!" I shook David's hand, and Lara hugged the girls.

Then Lara cleared her throat as she opened the card and read it aloud. "This is from the four of us, from the bottom of our hearts. We hope it helps our two best friends overcome a few of the financial obstacles in the future of taking care of your little one. Always remember that whatever you two need, we will always be there for you."

"Thanks, guys!" we both told them again.

They nodded, telling us it was no problem.

"I'm going to go try this on," Lara told us, excitedly grabbing her new set of maternity clothes. "I'll be right back!"

"Sweet—now's the time to take a quick look," David urged me.

I laughed, opening up my last present.

"Oh, my God, David, you didn't actually get him that, did you?" Carana hissed as I pulled a magazine out of the gift wrapping—it had a nude girl draped across the hood of a car as the cover page.

"Hey, the poor guy has a pregnant wife. He needs something to take his mind off things every once in a while," David said with an innocent shrug.

He and I laughed as I flipped to the first page.

"Men are so disgusting," Tracy grunted.

"What the hell do you think you're doing?" I heard Lara's voice ring out angrily.

I felt a sudden gust of wind around my hands, which ripped the magazine out of my grasp. It flew through the air and into her outstretched hand. She looked down at the magazine in disgust—it was turned to a picture of a half-naked girl on a motorcycle. She growled angrily at me as her rage boiled over. The magazine ignited into flames. "Merry Christmas, you filthy pig," she said, angrily tossing the burning magazine into my lap.

I swiftly brushed it off my lap, crying out in surprise. "What the hell, Lara?" I yelled angrily. "It was just a magazine. I didn't break any of the stupid laws of Dracona."

She glared at David and me, as he sulked about the ruined magazine. "Damn, Lara, that cost me seventy-five crome," David muttered.

At first, I thought she was going to lose it and kick everyone out, but her tough demeanor quickly faded. Her lips quivered and tears ran down her cheeks. She angrily punched the wall with her fiend strength, putting a hole in it. Then she disappeared back into the bathroom, where crying could be heard a short time later.

"Don't worry about it, guys. I'll deal with her," Carana said, as I was about to comfort Lara. Carana got up and knocked gently on bathroom door; then she disappeared behind it.

"Well … um … Merry Christmas," Tracy said with a smirk. The

three of us sat listening to the dull unintelligible sounds coming from the bathroom. We laughed, sipping on our drinks. I felt so bad; I should have known better than to open that gift, but I guess I wasn't thinking.

"I'm sorry about that, man. I should have gotten you a T-shirt or something," David said.

"It's all good, man. At least we know no pornos for next year," I muttered, making the two of them laugh.

"I'm baking cookies next year, so don't worry about it," Tracy joked.

Lara and Carana came back in the room shortly after, and although I was nervous, Lara smiled at me, and I knew she had gotten over it.

She was wearing her new maternity skirt and looked more beautiful than ever. She sat on my lap, and I cried out in mock pain, "Ow! My leg!" Everyone burst out laughing, even Lara. She hit my chest playfully and then gave me a loving kiss on the cheek and whispered in my ear that she was sorry. "It's just … well, you know. I sometimes lose my temper. I'm not mad at you; it just happens. I hate these damn pregnancy hormones."

I nodded and wrapped my hands around her belly as I returned to my conversation with David.

"So are we going to this party or what?" Tracy asked impatiently.

"Yeah, let's do it," Lara agreed. She jumped off my lap and put on her coat. We all hurried along the street, across the basketball court where Tracy and I used to play, and then went into the bar. We sat down at an empty table in the back corner and ordered drinks. Lara was forced to get a Coke—she couldn't drink while pregnant, which was kind of a drag. She seemed to have a good time, though, as the night went on, and that was all that mattered to me.

Tracy eventually ditched us for a guy she met at another table. David and I drank, while Carana and Lara talked to one another in Jural. A few hours later, I was pretty buzzed.

"Hey, check out that one on the pole," David whispered drunkenly as we stood at the bar. I glanced over at the stripper in the middle of the bar. She was wearing a Santa hat, and I quickly nodded in approval. "If we weren't tied down by two girls who could kill us with a blink of an eye," David said, "I'd be all over her."

"I'm sure you would," I laughed, grabbing our drinks and paying the bartender. We returned to our table with the drinks, which David and Carana chugged down. They'd decided to dance for a bit—and by "decided" I mean that Carana told David they were going to dance. I felt bad for him; I knew his case was completely different from mine. He didn't really have feelings for Carana, and from what I'd heard, she usually treated him like dirt. On the other hand Lara treated me as if I was the world.

I was tempted to go mingle at the bar, but I didn't want to leave her alone, so we sat in silence, sipping on our drinks. I could tell that Lara felt guilty for tying me down, as she occasionally glanced up at me without saying anything. Then she'd smile faintly and stare at her Coke. "Would you like another one?" I asked as she finished her drink, hoping to spark a conversation.

"No, thank you, I'm fine," she said, glancing around the bar. "You can go up and dance with those girls if you would like," she finally said. I think guilt overtook her.

I glanced at the group of girls, eighteen or nineteen years old, in the middle of the dance floor. I shook my head unhappily, knowing that was not what she truly wanted. "The only girl I want to dance with is sitting across from me," I told her, leaning across the table to place my hand on top of hers.

She smiled, and I think she was debating whether or not to dance with me. She got up energetically, surprising me as she held out her hand for me to get up. She giggled and grabbed my hand. "Come on … let's party!"

I chugged down the remainder of my beer and followed her onto the dance floor. The rest of the night was kind of a blur to me, as we danced and drank happily. Carana and David found us a little while later, looking surprised to see us dancing.

"We are heading home, if you two want to come with us," Carana offered.

"Nah, we're fine," Lara told her.

I had a feeling it was a horrible idea for us to stay, but we were having such an awesome time together that it didn't seem right for me to interfere with her decision. I couldn't even remember the last time Lara and I had this much fun together.

"Are you sure?" Carana asked. She glared at me, trying to persuade me to get Lara to go home.

"Yes, we are having fun. We'll see you guys later," Lara told her firmly. She wrapped her arms around me tightly, clearly getting annoyed by Carana's persistence.

Carana seemed to pick up on Lara's tone, so she and David said their good-byes.

"God, she can be so annoying sometimes," Lara whispered to me. She rested her head against my chest as we bobbed back and forth to the song that had just begun.

"Mm-hm," I muttered. "I'm pretty drunk, though. We should probably go home in a bit."

"In a little while," Lara said, swaying happily to the music. I accidentally bumped into her belly, and she flinched. "Whoops. Sorry!"

"No problem. Just be careful, please."

"I'm having an awesome time!" I told her happily. "You're the coolest girl ever."

As the song came to an end, I gave her a light kiss on her forehead. She smiled at me happily, comforting me with the warmth of her body. "One more song," she whispered, and I agreed, continuing to dance with her.

I sipped on my twelfth beer as a club song came on. Lara began to jump around ecstatically, waving her arms. Suddenly, she stopped and clutched her stomach.

"Are you okay?" I asked worriedly.

She nodded and straightened up. "I'm a little tired. I think I'm going to sit down," Lara told me. She grabbed my hand and led me over to our table, looking grateful that she could sit down. I finished my beer, and she stroked her stomach, gently calming Rashellia, trying to get her to go back to sleep.

"Let's go home," I said when I realized I had nothing left to drink.

"What? Why? I thought we were having fun!" Lara patted my hand lovingly.

"I'm having an awesome time with you," I told her happily. I accidently knocked over a few cans on our table and cursed under my breath. "I just think maybe I should walk you home, so you and the baby can get some rest. We can do this again some other time." I picked up the empties that had fallen on the floor and put them back on the table. "Besides, I'm out of beer," I laughed.

When Lara looked at me, she seemed unhappy for a second, as she seemed to be debating her options. "Trust me, buddy. I'm fine. Don't worry about me." She got up and left the table momentarily. When she returned, she had a fresh beer for me.

I laughed, thanking her for the beer she handed to me. "You look beautiful tonight," I said as I cracked open the beer.

She smiled and blushed shyly. "Want to go play some pool?" she asked.

"I don't know—I'm kind of drunk," I admitted, not wanting to play poorly—my competitive side took over.

"What? Are you scared?" she challenged me playfully. She helped me up and nodded toward a free pool table near the entrance of the bar.

"Fine, but I don't think you can handle this," I teased, messing up her hair and wrapping my arm around her waist as we slowly waddled over to the pool table. I showed Lara how to hold the pool cue since she had only played once before. "Aw, damn it," I muttered, glancing at the floor and realizing I had just spilled my beer.

"Ha-ha. Don't worry about it. I'll get you another one," Lara said. She momentarily left my side and returned with a new one.

"Thanks. That's just downright depressing," I muttered, staring at the puddle of beer by my feet.

She giggled and took her first shot. I know that I won the game, but that's about all I could remember, as the last beer messed me up pretty badly.

"Where is your friend?" some girl asked me. She was stroking my head as I came to.

I lifted my head off the bar table, realizing I must have passed out. "I'm … I don't know … ungh … my head," I muttered unhappily, plopping it back down on the counter and trying to block out the club's music.

"I think she left you," the girl said, placing her hand on my knee and rubbing my leg affectionately.

"I'm … I'm … so tired, Lara. Take me home," I whispered sleepily, glancing at the girl unhappily.

She smiled and kissed my neck. "I'll take care of you," she promised me as she rubbed my back.

"Get off him!" someone screamed, and I felt myself being hauled away. There were blurry figures, and then the cold night air hit my face.

"Get off me!" I cried in a panic, ripping myself away from the stranger. I stumbled for a few steps before passing out in a snowbank.

I heard Lara crying, which brought me back to my senses, as I realized one blurry figure was her. "Lara!" I cried out in a panic, trying to get up, but it was useless—I could only lie face down in the snow. I rolled over, the world began spinning around me, and I passed out momentarily.

"Lance, please get up," someone whispered.

"Tina?" I muttered hopefully.

"Please, Lance!" the quivering voice begged.

"Don't cry, Tina. Ungh … my … my head hurts. Go to school. I'll meet you there," I promised her, closing my eyes. I felt her hands trying to lift me up.

I heard distant voices for a second, followed by silence. I lay there shivering for what seemed like forever. I then felt someone grab me and lift me up, slinging my arm around the stranger's shoulder. I glanced over at the figure. "Help me … I'm so cold," I muttered as fear gripped me. I didn't know what was going on.

"You will be fine, Lance," the voice promised me.

I felt the warmth of the indoors hit my face and then I fell face first onto a mattress. "I'm … sleep …" I whispered—and that's the last thing I could remember.

I woke up with a start the next morning. I looked around the room nervously but was happy to find out that it was my house. I glanced over at Lara, who was sleeping beside me. "Thank God," I whispered as I stared at the fan slowly spinning overhead.

I was extremely hung over. The room was still spinning as I wiped the sleep out of my eyes, unhappily accompanied by the pounding headache of last night. "What the heck?" I muttered, looking at my hand—it was covered in purplish fiend blood. "Oh, my God! Lara! Lara, wake up!" I yelled in a panic. I jumped out of bed and ripped the blankets off, exposing her nude, curled-up body. I let out a sigh of relief as she opened up an eye. "What the hell happened?" I gasped, looking down at the bloodstained sheets.

"It was nothing. I just leaked a little last night when we slept. It's no big deal," she told me, uncurling herself.

"A *little*?" I mimicked her. "It looks like someone got murdered!" I was working myself up into a frenzy. "Is Rashellia okay?" I asked.

"Yes, she's sleeping. Calm down, buddy. You're starting to act like a girl." She tried to joke with me as she brought my hand down to her belly.

As a response to my touch, Rashellia kicked against Lara's stomach. I saw Lara wince as more blood came out. "You're not fine, you liar!" I shouted angrily. I clicked a button on our phone in a panic. She stared at me, embarrassed. "Why would you push yourself? You could have killed our daughter or yourself!" I yelled angrily. A voice on the automated machine asked me the name of the person I would like to contact. "Dr. Green," I muttered, holding up my hand as Lara started to protest.

The holographic image of Lara's doctor appeared out of the machine in front of me. "Hello, Lance," Dr. Green greeted me.

"Hello, Dr. Green."

"What seems to be the problem?" she asked me.

"I think Lara pushed herself too hard last night when we went out," I said, nodding toward Lara, who was lying there, humiliated.

The hologram of Dr. Green turned toward Lara. When she saw the blood, she quickly turned back to me. "I'll be right over." With a dull click, the image faded and the calling system shut off.

I dampened a rag to clean the blood off Lara's body as my anger was replaced with concern for her and the baby's well-being. I lifted her off the bed; she stared at me apologetically, trying to kiss me as I set her down on the floor. I recoiled, still angry with her. "Don't move," I ordered her.

Lara nodded obediently, sighing unhappily as she stared at the ceiling. I remade the bed with fresh sheets and then returned to Lara. I picked her up and laid her back on the bed, propping her head on a pile of pillows. "Why did you do this to yourself? God, sometimes you can be so stupid," I scolded her, half-mad and half-concerned. I sat down on the edge of the bed beside her, finally giving her a kiss. I wiped her hair away from her face as she looked up at me apologetically. A couple tears trickled down her face in embarrassment at what she had done. "So what happened last night?" I asked her.

She sniffled, wiping away a few tears. "I pushed myself," she admitted, but I could tell she wasn't being completely honest with me. "I tried to bring you back here, but I wasn't strong enough, and you passed out. Luckily, Tracy was there, and she helped me get home. Then she went back for you."

"Okay. It's okay now. You'll be fine. I'll take care of you," I promised her, stroking her hair and sniffling happily as a few tears sprang to my eyes.

She gave me a kiss. "I knew I kept you around for a reason," she giggled affectionately.

The doorbell rang, and I got up to answer it. "Hopefully, that's her," I said. I was ecstatic to see that it was Dr. Green. "Thank you for coming so quickly," I told her.

Dr. Green went right to Lara's side and examined her. I decided to stay out of the way—I leaned against the wall and watched anxiously, waiting for her to finish.

"Take these two pills," Dr. Green instructed Lara. "Your baby will be fine. You tore your uterus, which is what caused the bleeding. Those pills will repair it." I almost jumped for joy at the news that Rashellia would be all right. Dr. Green packed up her stuff to leave. "I'll be back in an hour. You can comfort her now, Lance. She is going to be in a lot of pain soon," Dr. Green warned us.

I nodded thankfully and was almost instantly by Lara's side, grabbing her hand, brushing back her hair, and smiling gently at her. Dr. Green quickly left, closing the door behind her. I knelt by the bedside. Lara and I made out, relieved by the news. "Painful?" Lara repeated to me questioningly, with a laugh.

I shrugged, leaning forward, giving her another kiss. "That's what she said," I told her, just as confused as she was. "I'm just glad you're both all right."

She nodded in agreement. "I love you so much, Lance. I don't know what I'd do without you." She winced and then smiled.

"I love you more," I whispered.

Lara lay in silence for a moment and then, without warning, she grabbed my hand, squeezing it gently as she flinched in pain. "Sorry," she whispered, seeing the shock on my face.

"Don't be," I muttered nervously, kind of getting scared.

"The … ungh … the pills are starting to work," she informed me.

I nodded understandingly as she took in a deep breath. "What's it feel like?" I asked.

She opened one eye and then winked at me. "I feel all tingly," she said. Suddenly, she screamed and curled up her body. "Ouch! Oh, geesh! Ouch!"

I was spooked by her sudden moaning as she recoiled in pain, while Rashellia unleashed a barrage of kicks inside her belly that I could see against her stomach. It looked like Rashellia was about to stand up and rip herself through Lara's stomach.

"I'll be all right," she said softly through clenched teeth, trying to divert my attention away from the pain. I brought my hand to her stomach so I could feel the constant kicks.

I felt so sorry for her, yet I was completely useless. I kissed her belly, and she tried to smile but was attacked by another surge of pain that caused her to curl back into a ball. After about half an hour, the pain started to go away—to our relief.

"You were so scared," she whispered, teasing me and giving me a playful punch, even as she winced as the light pains continued.

"Whatever. Sorry for being worried about you."

She laughed, trying to lighten the mood. "You're going to be a real mess when I have the baby," she teased.

I patted her shoulder reassuringly and then went to the kitchen to make her chicken soup. I fed it to her, as a mother would do for a sick child.

"You're going to be a great father, though," she said when I had finished feeding her.

"Thanks. You're not going to be a half-bad mother, either," I replied, rubbing her stomach gently.

"Yeah, right," she muttered unhappily.

"This is entirely my fault. I never should have taken you to that party." I stared down at the floor, ashamed.

"Hey, don't you dare blame yourself. I'm a grown women. I decided for myself to go, and believe me, it wasn't you. I mean, yes, after a couple hours of dancing, I was having a bit of bleeding, but it would have patched itself on its own, so don't you dare blame yourself." She paused for a moment as a wave of pain surged through her. "Besides, yesterday you actually made me feel like a normal teenage girl again—something I hadn't felt for a long time," she whispered gently, patting my hand affectionately.

"What happened to you, then, to make you bleed so much?" I asked.

"I don't know." She glanced away from me with a shrug, so I couldn't figure out if she was telling the truth.

Dr. Green arrived back at our place about twenty minutes later to examine Lara and listen to the baby's heartbeat. "Well, like I said before, your baby is going to be fine," she said.

"Thank God!" I exclaimed happily, hugging Lara. Lara patted my back happily, whispering she was sorry into my ear.

"You're lucky you have a husband who cares about you, because even though you didn't think there was anything to be worried about, you were wrong. If you would have gotten up, there was a chance that you could have punctured something and bled out internally, dying without warning. Now, I know you're a pure-blood, so you would be reborn, but do you really want to repeat nineteen years all over again and lose two good things going on in your life?" Dr. Green scolded Lara.

"Of course not," Lara told her.

"This wound wasn't inflicted by physically straining yourself either.

Your body can heal those types of injuries; this was definitely caused by another person pushing against your stomach. Tell me who it was, and I'll make sure he or she is sent to jail for jeopardizing the life of your child," Dr. Green told her.

"No one did it," Lara said, a stubborn expression spreading across her face.

"Fine, but if you change your mind, call me with the name." Dr. Green handed me her card and then told Lara, "Before I go, you're going to need to do a couple things for me. First, get up." Lara did so obediently. "Walk back and forth a couple times," Green told her, and again, Lara did so obediently. Next Dr. Green told Lara to bend down and touch her toes, then reach for the sky, and finally, to squat up and down five times. After Lara complied, Dr. Green nodded her head, satisfied, and allowed Lara to sit back down on the bed—Lara looked exhausted from the workout. "Okay, just take it easy for the rest of the day, and no sex tonight," she instructed Lara.

"Aw, poor Lance," Lara teased.

"Agh! Don't worry, Doc. I knew that her bending over was the most action I was going to see today anyway," I shot back.

Not even Dr. Green could help smiling as she gathered up all her stuff and left a few moments later. As Lara and I lay there that night, I thought about what the doctor had said, and Lara knew that I was thinking about it as well.

"Listen, Lance, the girl who did this to me could have just killed me and the baby, but she didn't. I had broken a law of Dracona by showing affection in public while pregnant, so in her mind, she was doing the right thing," Lara told me calmly.

I stared at her for a second. Revenge seemed to plague my mind. "She?" I repeated, my voice filled with bitterness. I stared blankly at the wall, resting my head on Lara's belly as she stroked my head in silence. I knew that she probably realized there was nothing she could do or say to stop me from plotting my revenge on this mystery girl.

Chapter 15

About two and a half months later, Lara had to quit her job—she had hit nine months, and being on her feet for the entire day was a bit too much for her. I knew she felt guilty, because she kept telling me she would find a job where she didn't have to move so much. But I convinced her that staying at home and relaxing for the last little bit of her pregnancy was a good idea. Anyway, I knew that no company would hire a pregnant chick who would be leaving them in a month or so.

In order to make up for her not working, I was forced to get another job, which I didn't mind since I had been working my entire life anyway. Tracy hooked me up with a day job at the city maintenance bureau, shoveling snow, making sure streetlights were working, and stuff like that. After work, Tracy and I would go play some indoor basketball to rack in roughly as much money as Lara and I used to make, so we could still live comfortably.

"Good games today, Tracy," I told her one night, splitting the money we had won between us.

"Yeah, those were some nice air balls you were throwing," she said, packing up her stuff to go home.

"At least I was throwing something," I teased.

She laughed, shouldering her gym bag. Lara came out of the stands and gave me a high-five and hugged Tracy. She was pretty big now, at nine and a half months pregnant, but she kept a good mood about it, especially after the incident with the mystery girl two months ago. "I'll see you guys tomorrow. Peace," Tracy called to us, waving good-bye.

"You came over to watch some games?" I asked Lara, giving her a kiss, along with one on her belly.

"Yeah, I got tired of tidying up the house, so I decided to come over and watch my professional superstar shoot some hoops." She snatched the ball from me and dribbled it playfully, trying to provoke me to play with her. I took a step forward with my hand out, pretending to block her. She shot the ball, missing the basket—the ball landed five feet short of the net and bounced to the sideline. I jogged over to it and dribbled it out to Lara so she could shoot a couple of times.

I stood by the net, teasing her as she missed and then chucking the ball back out to her. She jumped up excitedly as her last shot sailed through the air and hit nothing but net. "Nice shot!" I said. I dribbled out to center court and gave her a high-five. She cradled her belly, looking exhausted already.

"Phew, I have to take a break," she said. She leaned against my chest and placed my hand on her stomach—I could feel Rashellia kicking. "She missed her daddy," Lara told me in a babyish voice, causing me to blush. We sat down in the middle of the court, and I offered her some water. Lara seemed to be really excited that her pregnancy was coming to an end. She tried to stay active so Rashellia would come earlier, as opposed to dragging it out to a full year, which was normal for a fiend to have her baby. Lara was being smart about it, though. She took breaks whenever she got tired so she wouldn't push herself too hard and bleed.

"Have you had any contractions today?" I asked as we got up to leave.

"I had a couple after you left for work, but I think they were from that little present I gave you this morning," she told me with a giggle. She took my gym bag from me and grabbed my hand as we walked home together.

"Yeah, probably. Thanks again," I said, giving her a peck on the cheek.

"I hear it's better at night," she told me playfully.

When we got home, she set my bag down and kissed me while stripping down to a new pink bra and underwear. "Do you like it?" she asked hopefully.

"I love it," I replied with a nod of approval.

Now that she couldn't work, she was always eager to please me. I guess she was insecure about what I thought about her sitting at home all day. She ran her hand along my shirt, getting on her tiptoes to make out with me. "Whoa, whoa, slow down, girl," I said. "I'm all sweaty and stuff from work. I got to take a shower first."

She went into the bathroom and started the shower, returning a moment later, naked. "It's ready, sweetie," she told me, grabbing my hand and leading me into the shower with her.

I kissed her and wrapped my arms around her. I rubbed her back as she hugged me close, and the water gently sprayed off us. Her belly was resting against mine. I laughed when Rashellia started moving around, which I could feel against my stomach. "Are you scared about going into labor?" I asked her.

"A little bit nervous; that's all," she said, reaching for a bottle of shampoo and doing my hair. "I always have random contractions now, so I'm used to them. I'm even a little crampy right now, just from that walk home."

"Really?" I asked nervously.

She laughed. "Are you scared of my giving birth?" When I nodded, she said, "Don't be; we will be fine." She gave me another kiss, adding, "Whatever I do or say, just remember that I love you."

"I know but—"

"I still have up to two and a half months until it happens, so don't worry," she reassured me, taking my hand and running it along her belly.

"True, but you *could* give birth any day now," I reminded her.

She just laughed and shrugged away the possibility. "I'm going to at least make it to ten months. I feel fine."

"You think so? You look like you're going to explode."

"Gee, thanks. You're the one who did this to me." She gave me a light punch against my chest, pretending to be offended. "How about we dry off and have some fun in the bedroom?" she suggested, turning off the water.

We got out of the shower, and I dried myself off and then her. "Let's just relax tonight," I said, nodding toward her pink underwear on the floor.

She stared at me, confused, but I lovingly picked up her items and helped her put her bra on and then her pretty pink underwear. I kissed the back of her neck in her favorite spot, once I was done.

"Really? I'm fine now. The cramps are gone," she reassured me, looking disappointed that I was turning her down.

"I'm exhausted from work," I lied.

"Aw, come on. It'll be fun!" she promised me.

"I just want to spend some time with you tonight and chat a bit. We never do that anymore," I told her, going over to the bed and flicking on the TV. It illuminated the dark room as the holographic figures sprang to life in front of us.

She placed her hands on her hips, letting out a defeated sigh before coming over and snuggling with me in bed.

"Sorry," I whispered guiltily.

"It's cool; don't worry about it," she told me. I think she understood that I didn't want to push her into an early labor.

We lay there watching the news for a bit. I was about to flick it off when a headline caught my eye: *Mutiny against top leaders spreads.*

"Shhh," I told Lara as she was about to say something. "Let's listen to this report."

"In the recent days," the fiend broadcaster began, "there has been a power struggle as a radical group of fiends, those opposed to their leader's strategy for peace, has emerged, mysteriously deserting the bases all across the region. The group of dangerously well-trained fiends seems to be led by General McGrey, one of the first deserters. If you stumble across the hidden whereabouts of these radical fiends, please inform your local authorities, who will handle the situation." The fiend broadcaster then moved on to how the war was progressing in Dublin City.

"That's interesting," I said.

Lara nodded in agreement, taking the remote and flicking the television off. "You have work early tomorrow morning," she reminded me.

I sighed, realizing she was right. I had to get up an hour earlier to take care of some stupid, finicky streetlight.

She gently shook me awake the next morning, offering me a cup of coffee and a bagel for breakfast, which I accepted gratefully.

"How are you feeling today?" I asked as she sat down with me to eat her bagel.

"Fat," she joked.

I smiled, chugging the remainder of my coffee. I got dressed into my snow gear in preparation for work. "What's up?" I asked, noticing that Lara was putting on her jacket and boots.

"Nothing. I just want to walk with you to work."

"All right. Cool." I knew she was probably bored of sitting around the house all day.

She held out her hand to me, which I accepted as we went outside and headed to the city's maintenance bureau where I worked now. She leaned her head against my shoulder as we walked along the sidewalk. We were about five minutes from work when a group of fiends rounded a corner and walked drunkenly toward us.

"Damn, it's only, like, seven in the morning, and those fools are wasted already," I said. Lara stopped dead in her tracks, giving me an urgent tug on my arm. "What?" I asked. She seemed paralyzed with fear.

"That girl in the middle is the one who threatened me at the bar," she whispered.

"Go get help," I ordered her. The group of fiends stopped a couple of yards away as they spotted us. Lara waddled away, back to our house, as fast as she could. The group laughed at her and advanced a little closer to me. They flashed their fangs threateningly.

"What's up? You look a bit scared," a girl fiend said as her group surrounded me.

Finally, I was looking at the mystery girl I had dreamed so vividly of killing. "I don't want any trouble," I lied, clenching my fists and getting ready for the inevitable fight.

"Neither do we," she said. "What do you think we are? Monsters?" She offered me a sip of her beer.

Her entourage chuckled as she taunted me a bit more, trying to provoke me to throw a punch. "So you like banging fiends, hey?" she asked, sticking a finger in her mouth and sucking on it, toying with me. "You think he likes me, Rial?" she asked one of her friends. She smiled devilishly, turning to face me. "I bet you want to screw me, don't you," she said bluntly.

That set me off, and I swung my fist at her. She nimbly avoided it.

"Oh, we got a feisty one," a guy laughed.

The female fiend waved her finger at me playfully. "Tsk, tsk. That wasn't very nice," she taunted me, as her two fingers formed into a jagged blade.

I swung again, connecting with her this time, square against the side of her face. It knocked her back in surprise, and her nose cracked open, spilling her purplish fiend blood and staining the snow around her feet. Her friends piled on top of me, beating the shit out of me, and then one stabbed me in the chest. I let out a surprised gasp as he smiled victoriously, pulling his blade out of my chest. In shock, I clutched my chest, feeling my warm blood soak my shirt.

One of the fiends dragged me across the street and propped me up against a tree. Another guy pulled out a gun, but the girl grabbed it from him angrily. She wiped away the blood from her face and knelt down beside me, shoving the gun into my mouth. "You have until tonight to leave Monatello, or I'm going to strangle that bitch in front of you and personally rip that filthy half-blood human out of her stomach," she told me, clicking off the safety and flashing a deranged smile. "Bang," she whispered into my ear.

She pulled the gun out of my mouth, and they all laughed, scattering as they ran away. I fell over in the snow, watching it turn bright red as I helplessly felt my life slipping away. My body began convulsing uncontrollably as the shock set in.

"*Lance!*" David yelled, appearing beside me, followed soon after by Lara, Carana, and Tracy.

"Save him, Lara!" Tracy cried in a panic as I bled out.

"Hold him down," Lara ordered calmly, which Carana did obediently.

"Hold on, Lance. Everything is going to be okay," Carana said reassuringly.

Lara calmly started casting spells, which spread all over my body into my stab wound, healing it instantly. I struggled to breathe as she propped my head up, and then, after a minute of intense chest pains, I could finally breathe normally again.

"They told me that we have to leave or they're going to kill you and the baby," I told Lara, taking another deep breath as she had instructed me to do.

"Okay, it's okay now," Lara said. "They didn't puncture your heart, thankfully. Let's just forget about this place, and go find somewhere else to live." She held her stomach, breathing slowly, as the others helped me up.

"Are you all right?" I asked Lara as she rubbed her tummy, flinching uncomfortably.

"Yes, I'm just having cramps from that run. Let's go home and pack so we can get out of here," she begged me. I wrapped my arm around her, and we all headed down the street toward our house.

"I'm not leaving," I told her stubbornly. I glanced over at David, who returned the look in agreement, knowing what I was thinking.

"I got your back, man," he grunted, and Tracy and Carana nodded their agreement.

When we got to our house, Tracy helped Lara into bed, although Lara was objecting stubbornly that she wanted to fight them with us.

"What do we have for weapons?" I asked. Now that I knew who we were dealing with, we huddled by the door to hatch a plan for revenge.

"Well, my gun was destroyed by someone ... not saying any names out loud," David said pointedly, nodding over to Lara.

"Hey, leave the pregnant girl out of this," she objected, smiling innocently.

"I'll just morph into my fiend form," Carana told us. She wandered over to Lara and sat next to her on the bed, checking her over to make sure that she didn't push herself into an early labor.

"Here—I have a 9mm that I smuggled from the firing range in case something like this happened. It only has one clip, though," Tracy told me, handing me her pistol.

"The clip from David's 9mm is in the drawer," Lara called over to us. She shooed Carana away from her and got up to retrieve the clip. She loaded the loose bullets into it and tossed the loaded mag over to Carana. Lara winked at me, signaling she would be fine as she lay back down on the bed.

"Thanks," I told Carana, taking the gun from her. Then I asked her quietly, "Is Lara all right?"

"Yeah, they were just cramps, like she said, from the running. She waddles pretty fast for a nine-month-pregnant chick, though, huh?" Carana joked.

The four of us laughed, looking over at Lara, who gave us the middle finger.

"Okay, so here's the plan," I began, shifting their attention back to me. "David, the guy with the blue jacket has a 9mm on his left side. I'll take him out first, and then you run from behind them on the right side, grab the gun, and shoot at whoever is still standing. Carana, you charge from behind on the left side and maul the others. I'll stand out front as bait to attract their attention and shoot out the cameras. Leave the blonde girl for me." Any questions?"

"Yeah, where do I fit into all of this?" Tracy asked.

"You need to stay here with Lara and make sure she doesn't come after us," I explained to her.

"Aw, how come I'm the bench warmer?" she complained, glancing over at Lara, who was just as angry with me as Tracy was.

"Keeping her safe is the most important part of this entire plan. Tracy, you don't know how much this means to me." I patted her shoulder in gratitude.

"Fine, but you owe me," she muttered, giving me knuckles before taking a seat next to Lara.

David and I pulled out some clothes and tossed on black hoodies. Carana got naked and transformed into a fiend. "Hey, no looking!" David joked, putting his hand in front of my face.

Lara begged me to let her come with us so that she could save us if something went wrong, but I shook my head. Tracy guided Lara back to the bed, reassuring her that we would be fine.

It was eerily quiet as we walked down the empty street toward the bar. Once we got there, Carana and David both got into their positions, blending in with the shadows of the building. I leaned against the pole, casually lighting a smoke. I put my hood up and kept my head down, away from the surveillance camera. I was spotted by the group of fiends a couple of minutes later. They all glared out the window at me in disbelief.

"You just don't learn, do you?" the girl asked as the group of six emerged from the bar. They came to a halt a few yards away from me.

"I brought something as a peace offering," I called to them.

"Oh, how nice. So let me get this straight—you give me this gift, and we forgive and forget, right?" one of them responded. They all laughed, and the girl that hurt Lara sneered at me, showing me her fangs and spitting on the ground.

I smiled darkly. "I guess it's something like that."

"So what the hell do you have that's going to make us not want to kill your dumb ass?" the girl asked aggressively.

"I got this, bitch!" I yelled, pulling out the 9mm. They scrambled for their weapons. I shot the male in the forehead and neck. He fell lifelessly to the ground. I then swiftly turned to the girl, shooting her in the stomach. Carana blindsided them, knocking a male and female fiend to the ground and savagely killing them as they tried to morph into their fiend forms to defend themselves. David sprinted out from the shadows, sliding about twenty feet across the pavement in the snow. He took the handgun out of the dead fiend's belt and shot the other two as they ran away.

He marched over to them, cold-heartedly executing them with one shot each to the head, as they begged him for mercy. I walked over to the girl and put a foot on her stomach. As I shifted my weight, it caused blood to gush out. "Look at me! No one's coming to save your pathetic life," I spat into her face.

She yelled out in agony, screaming for help. She was in tears, crying as blood seeped out of her chest. "Look, I didn't kill your kid. Please let me go. I won't tell anyone you did this."

I continued to stare down, a blank expression in my eyes.

"What are you doing?" she cried as I bent down beside her. "No, no, please, no!"

I shoved the gun into her mouth. "Bang," I whispered into her ear.

She let out a muffled scream, and I squeezed the trigger, blasting her brains all over the sidewalk, peppering myself with purplish fiend blood. The three of us nodded to each other, satisfied by the completed mission. I glanced up at the security camera and shot it out. Then I took off my hood.

"You didn't shoot it out before we started?" David asked, shocked.

I shrugged, not really caring. "I wanted them to see this," I told him coldly, tucking the gun into the back of my pants.

David and Carana nodded in agreement, and then we split up, jogging in different directions to our homes. It only took a couple minutes for me to reach my house. I entered swiftly, closing the door behind me. Tracy glanced up at me, and I nodded to her with a faint smile. "Everyone's fine," I informed her.

She smiled and gave me a pat on my shoulder as she left to go to her place.

"Are you okay?" Lara asked, getting up awkwardly and waddling over to me.

I nodded, and she took my hand, leading me into the bathroom. "Take off your clothes," she ordered me. After I did, she burned them in the bathtub and washed away the remnants with steaming hot water. "You got them?" she asked softly.

"Yes, I got them."

"So it's done with?" she asked.

"Yes," I assured her, feeling relief wash over me. The realization of what I had just done hit me, along with powerful feelings of revenge. "You and Rashellia are safe now."

She slid her hand across my face, giving me a kiss. We went back into our room, where she flicked on the television to watch the news. Sure enough, a clip came on about ten minutes into the show, with the breaking news.

"Six fiends have been shot down at the Cavern Bar on Main Street. We have video footage of the incident, but we are also asking that anyone with information relating to this case please contact this station. It is believed that the perpetrators were two male humans and one fiend, whose gender is unknown. Again, if you have any information, you can call this station anonymously." The reporter then played the clip of our ambush.

"You didn't shoot out the camera?" Lara asked me, surprised.

"I wanted the public to see what happens when you fuck with me," I muttered darkly.

She patted my arm consolingly, giving me a gentle kiss on the cheek. "Don't worry; they won't ever find out it was you."

I smiled at her doubtfully. Sure enough, early the next morning there was a rough knock at the door. Lara opened it, and two police officers walked in, uninvited. I went to Lara's side, wrapping my arm around her waist nervously.

"We have reason to believe that your husband was part of the massacre last night," one said to Lara. "We've reviewed video footage over the past few months and saw your husband get in a scuffle yesterday with one of the dead girls at the scene, who had threatened to kill your baby."

"Well, it couldn't have been him because I picked him up from a basketball game the night before, and he was too tired to go to work the next day," Lara insisted. "I was feeling a bit crampy, so Lance stayed with me all night, and we watched some TV. We even saw the news broadcast. It truly is a shame what happened to those guys."

I had to admit, she was a pretty good liar. Even I would have believed that she was telling the truth.

"So you're okay with us searching your home for weapons?" the cop asked. She nodded confidently, and one searched me, while the other went through the small room, opening up drawers and looking under the bed and any other possible places to store a weapon. "Okay, you're clear. Sorry to bother you, ma'am, and good luck with the baby." Then, without another word, they left just as fast as they had come.

Lara smiled at me once they were gone. "See? Told you they wouldn't catch you," she said, pulling the 9mm from the back of her pants and handing it over to me.

I laughed and kissed her gratefully. "How did you know they wouldn't search you?"

"It's against the laws of Dracona for male fiends to touch a pregnant female fiend," she said with a devilish smile.

"I never thought I'd say this," I admitted, "but thank God for Lord Dracona."

Chapter 16

The next few weeks passed by uneventfully. Lara and I decided to redecorate our room before the arrival of Rashellia. "Sweet! Mission accomplished," Lara said happily.

I put down my roller, sharing her excitement at the completion of the freshly painted baby-blue walls. "Awesome job!" I agreed.

We gave each other a high-five and again admired our work. "Now we just need to put together her crib and playpen. Then we'll be golden," Lara told me, indicating the two items lying on the ground still in boxes.

"Sounds good. Is tomorrow after work all right?" I asked her with an affectionate kiss.

"Any time is fine with me." She wiped the paint from her hands onto her shirt. When I laughed, she said, "What? It's going to be garbage in less than a month anyway."

I laughed and wiped my hands on her shirt too. "You don't plan on having another one anytime soon?" I asked, nodding at her plump belly, which the shirt only half-covered now.

"Only if you want to," she said lovingly.

I hugged her close, wrapping my arm around her. We stood there, still celebrating the successful completion of the room. She was ten months and a couple days pregnant now and looking pretty huge. To this day, I can't figure out why she was so intent on having a baby so early in our lives, but I had two theories. The first one was that she thought that having a baby would seal the bond between us; the second one was that she was afraid one of us would be killed before we agreed to have a baby. Both of them seemed to make sense to me, but knowing Lara, she probably had a secret agenda in wanting a hybrid child.

"So would you like to fool around a bit tonight?" Lara asked me sincerely as we got undressed for bed.

"Huh?" I responded. We hadn't even had sex for probably close to a month now. To be honest, the thought hadn't even crossed my mind. I knew how tired she was as her pregnancy was coming to an end.

"Why not?" she said. "I got a little bit of energy, and besides, tonight might be our last chance for a while."

I knew she was right. Any day now, she would be in labor, and once Rashellia was born, we probably wouldn't have any free time to fool around anymore. "Sweet," I said excitedly. I quickly tore off my clothes and began to make out with her. I quickly realized, though, that her new size made it to awkward for me on top.

"I'll do it," she panted affectionately as I rolled over, letting her get on top of me. She only lasted about three or four minutes before becoming sluggish and lying down beside me, exhausted. "Sorry," she panted, trying to catch her breath.

"Don't worry about it; we tried," I told her affectionately.

I could tell she was unhappy with her performance. She slipped her underwear back on and gave me another kiss. I rested my head against her breasts, and she ran her hand down my chest, trying to please me in other ways.

When I awoke the next morning, Lara was not by my side. I sleepily got up, and stumbled to the bathroom. I knocked on the door and peered in, relieved that she was in there. "Hey, buddy, what's up? How did you sleep?" I asked, sitting on the tub.

She was sitting on the toilet, rubbing her stomach. "I didn't sleep. I think Rashellia was having a party all last night or something, because she wouldn't stop bumping into my bladder." She reached over to the sink where she had a glass of blood and sipped on it contentedly.

"Well, you're almost done," I reassured her, patting her plump belly. I felt Rashellia's kick in response to my touch.

"We are," she corrected me lovingly, giving me my good-morning kiss. She got up, finishing up her business and letting me do mine.

I couldn't help noticing that the baby had dropped in her belly in preparation for labor. "I don't think you going to be able to walk for much longer," I teased, washing off my hands.

"Shut up. I'm fine." She slid along the counter, using it as a crutch to keep her balance.

In our birthing class, we had learned that fiends usually had to crawl for the last bit of their pregnancy because they were too unbalanced to walk. At the time, Lara had said, "Yeah, right," but her words had come back to haunt her as she grew bigger and bigger. It was obvious she was going to have to stop being stubborn sooner or later.

"You have any big plans for the day?" I asked her when we'd finished in the bathroom.

"Nope. I'm going to try to catch a nap. Then I might hang out with Carana a bit while you're away." Following me into our room, she swayed back and forth as she struggled to keep her balance.

"I'm going to laugh when you fall," I told her playfully.

"Shut up," she giggled. Then she glanced down at her leg. "Damn it," she said. Her underwear was darkening as a liquid ran down her leg.

"Did your water just break?" I asked, surprise filling my face.

She laughed, shaking her head. "No. I just peed myself."

"Don't worry about it. It's nothing to be embarrassed about. Who's going to know, aside from me and you?" I quickly helped her to the bathroom—I was running late for work now—and then gave her a kiss good-bye and jogged out the door.

"Cutting it close today, hey?" my boss said as I ran through the door.

Out of breath, I checked in with about a minute to spare. "Sorry, Mr. Brodare. It won't happen again."

"Let's hope not," he said grumpily, disappearing into his office overlooking the workers below.

Tracy was waiting patiently for me at our lockers. "Hey, Lance? What's up?" Tracy said as I reached my locker beside hers.

"Not much. What's on the go for today?" I asked.

"Just got to go down to Thirty-Fourth and Seventy-Fourth streets to lay some salt down." She nodded toward the four bags of salt beside her.

"All right. Cool. I … um … got a kind of embarrassing question I need to ask you," I told her, as I felt an emotion from Lara run through me, reminding me of something.

"What's that?"

"Do you use pads for your periods?" I asked.

She laughed. "Yeah, why do you ask?"

"Would you mind hooking me up with a few?" I asked her awkwardly.

She laughed again, rummaging around in her locker and retrieving five of them. A playful smile was plastered to her face. I knew she'd never let me live this one down. "You on your period, Lance?" she teased.

"Shut up. It's for Lara," I shot back with a laugh. She nodded understandingly, offering me some more. "Thanks," I muttered, embarrassed as I took a handful.

"No problem. That's what friends are for. Maybe next time you should ask me for a condom," she joked.

"Oh, my God, I hate you, Tracy," I muttered, unable to hold back from laughing at her joke.

When I arrived home that night, Lara was on the floor, trying to figure out how to assemble Rashellia's crib. "I thought you were going to wait for me to do that," I said.

She glanced up at me; I could tell something was wrong from her smudged makeup—she'd been crying. "Oh, I'm sorry," she whispered.

"What's wrong, buddy?" I asked, quickly sitting down beside her and wrapping my arms around her.

"It's nothing. I'm just so glad you're home! I had some bad contractions today. They scared me really bad, Lance." She sniffled and buried her face in my chest as she began to cry.

"Aw, don't cry, baby. I'm here. Everything's going to be just fine," I promised her, reassuringly stroking her hair and placing an affectionate kiss on her forehead. I realized she had gone into labor while I was at work.

She happily cuddled with me on the floor, regaining control of her emotions. She began to purr affectionately.

"I got you a present while I was at work," I told her.

"What?" she asked, eyes lighting up.

I pulled the pads out from my bag, and she giggled, hitting my chest playfully. "Hey, you better appreciate these. Do you know how much teasing I had to endure from Tracy?" I asked.

We spent the rest of the day putting together the crib and playpen. That night, I ran my hand along her belly, watching Rashellia's paw follow mine against Lara's skin. She was having minor pains. I could see the discomfort in her face, but she pretended like everything was fine. I read a fairy tale to her belly as she lay there, purring softly and kissing me affectionately. I could tell she was proud of me as I tucked the book that she had taught me to read under our bed. Then I reached over, flicking off the light happily.

Four days later, things were starting to worsen a bit. Lara tried to hide it from me, but that night, I woke up to the sounds of her whimpering through a few contractions. She was covering her mouth with her hand in an attempt to not wake me. "Are you all right?" I asked.

She smiled, pretending nothing was wrong. "Of course I am. Don't worry about me." She purred and gave me a kiss before struggling to get out of bed, sliding weakly along the wall. "Go back to sleep. I'll join you in a bit," she whispered gently and then disappeared into the bathroom, where I heard her puke a few moments later.

I would have gone in to comfort her, but I knew she would just be embarrassed, so I pretended to sleep. After an hour or two, she returned to bed and fell asleep, exhausted from the worsening labor. I woke up the next morning to the smashing of glass. Lara had fallen while attempting to bring breakfast over to the table.

"What the hell, Lara?" I scolded her.

She looked at the food littered across the floor. "Breakfast is served!" she joked, rubbing her stomach as a contraction passed by. She tried unsuccessfully to get up. "Labor sucks," she muttered.

I got out of bed, helped her to her feet, and carried her to our bed. "It's okay," I told her as I swept away the broken dishes. "But no more walking unless I'm there to help you, okay?" She sighed, but nodded in agreement. "Maybe I should stay home for the day," I suggested, seeing her flinch in pain as another contraction hit her.

"I'll be fine," she told me confidently.

"I know. I want to spend the day with you anyway. We won't get a lot of time together once there's a little baby crying every five minutes."

She stared at me for a second, and I wondered if she noticed my insecurity with being a father. "Come here," she whispered, patting a spot beside her on the bed. "You're going to be a wonderful father, Lance. Stop worrying." She cuddled with me, comfortingly. "Want to know what would feel awesome?" she added hopefully.

"What?"

"A bath."

I laughed lazily, not wanting to get up.

"Pleeeeease?" she begged me.

I sighed but got up and ran her a warm bath. Just as I helped her into it, the phone rang. I answered it, and the holographic image of Tracy appeared in our room. "'Sup?" I asked.

"Nothing much. Did you sleep in or something?" she asked.

"Nah, Lara's had a rough night. I think she's going to have Rashellia soon," I told her, taking a seat and flicking on the television.

"Today?" Tracy's voice rang out excitedly.

"Nah, probably still a couple days to go."

"All right. Well, I'll talk to you later. Tell Lara I said hi!"

"For sure," I replied, and with that, the contacting system went dead as her image disappeared into thin air.

"Who was that?" Lara called to me.

I went back into the bathroom and took a seat on the toilet. "Just Tracy, wondering why I wasn't at work. She says hi, by the way."

Lara smiled and fiddled around with some bubbles.

"How are you feeling now?" I asked.

"Excellent. Thanks a lot for doing this for me." She gave me a thumbs-up, smiling warmly.

"Any time," I told her, returning the smile. "It's been a while since you had a contraction, hey?" I asked her.

She nodded. "They're gone for now. I'm just all crampy again."

When she was finished with the bath, I helped her out and gently guided her into our room. I stood by her, making sure she didn't fall over as she pulled out one of her maternity skirts and a black tank top. She proudly showed off her belly.

"You're so beautiful," I told her as we sat on the edge of the bed.

She smiled happily, giving me a peck on the cheek. "Had to dress up nice for my man," she giggled, rubbing her stomach gently. "I think this is the last day that we're not going to be parents."

I looked at her in shock. "Really?"

"Yeah, I think she's coming faster than normal because she's a half-breed."

"I thought your contractions stopped, though," I said in disbelief.

"They did for now," she replied. "They're going to come back, probably ten times stronger, though."

I laughed nervously as she reached into her drawer, pulling out a book written in Jural that she had been reading to me over the last month or so. We lay back against the bed, and she read to me for a little bit. I loved when she read to me, but suddenly, she moaned and stopped reading in mid-sentence. She looked at her belly, gasping in pain as a contraction hit her. I rubbed her back, trying to help, as she moaned again, cringing in pain. The book fell out of her hands.

"Damn random contraction," she said, once it had finished.

I looked at her worriedly. She messed up my hair, seeing my fright, before picking up the book to find the page where she'd stopped reading. Before she could find it, though, another contraction came, and she gave up, tossing the book aside. The contractions continued deep into the night. I was awakened around one in the morning by Lara's whimpering. She was rocking back and forth on her knees, clutching below her stomach, and occasionally letting out tiny groans. I silently sat up with her, rubbing her back gently.

"Lance, I think it's starting to happen," she whispered into the darkness.

"Yeah, it's okay. You're doing great." I comforted her.

She smiled, bringing my hand to her stomach so I could feel Rashellia—she was lower in Lara's stomach than before. Her stomach tightened, and then, moments later, untightened, followed by a tiny growl from inside Lara's belly. She lay down, and I put my head softly on her belly. I could hear Rashellia making baby noises, along with feeling an occasional kick.

I felt Lara's stomach tighten again, and she closed her eyes. Rashellia slid down farther, and then I felt her move a bit back up. "Wow, that's sucks," I said. "She went back up farther, and then she came down."

"She only comes down about this much," Lara told me, holding her fingers apart by about half an inch. "After that, my pelvis starts to widen so she can come out."

"Sounds fun," I joked. If I had it my way, we already would have been at the hospital, but Lara had insisted on having an unassisted birth.

"Yeah, it is so fun. Don't you wish you were a girl?" she asked with a laugh. "Go back to sleep. I didn't mean to wake you up." She petted my head, and I obediently went back to sleep.

When I woke up the next morning, Lara was still sleeping. I softly put my hand on her belly, waking her up. She smiled warmly, giving me a kiss before glancing at the clock sleepily.

I felt her side and noticed her hips were jutting out a bit more.

"Not long now," she told me, confirming my thoughts.

I glanced outside, sighing when I saw there was fresh snow from the night before that I would have to shovel. "How do you feel?" I asked as I got up and started breakfast.

She lay in bed, rubbing her back. "Like I'm going to have a baby."

"So you're making progress?" I asked.

She nodded. "I'm definitely starting to widen a bit."

"I'm going to take the day off again, I think."

"Hell, no," she told me. "I don't think I can handle another day of you freaking out every time something happens."

"Well, I'm not going to just leave you here for the day," I argued, coming over with two plates of breakfast.

"I'll get Carana to come over," she promised me.

I sighed unhappily but agreed. "Fine."

"It's not that I don't want you here," she reassured me. "I just don't want you to see me in pain when things get rough in a little bit." She flinched as her contractions began to start up again.

"Fine, but if anything happens, tell me through our private chat," I ordered her.

She laughed, handing me her plate, which I took over to the sink. *"Yes, Mom,"* Lara's voice broke into my head.

I helped her to her feet, and she kissed me. "Any day now, you're going to be a daddy," she told me, rubbing her hand down my chest.

"Today?" I asked.

"Not today." She handed me my coat and pushed me out the door before another contraction hit her.

I walked down the street toward the office of my street service building, entering and going to my locker. I pulled out the shovel and salt.

Tracy entered the room, already dressed and ready to go. "There you are! How's Lara?"

"I think she's going to have the baby today," I told her. I got dressed quickly, walking out the door with her.

"Oh, congratulations, man. That's great news. Shouldn't you be home with her?"

"She doesn't want me there," I replied unhappily.

"Don't worry, Lance. She's probably just scared and doesn't want you around to see her when she's vulnerable," Tracy assured me as we approached the street we had to clear.

"I may have to go early if things speed up," I told her before we split up.

"That's fine. I'll stay behind and finish whatever you don't," she called over her shoulder, trudging through the deep, freshly fallen snow toward her end of the street.

I smiled to myself grateful to have such an understanding friend. With a sigh I began shoveling my half of the street, trying to do it as fast as possible so I could get back to Lara. All of a sudden, out of nowhere,

I heard the familiar *thwock-thwock* of bullets cracking in the distance. I glanced over my shoulder in shock toward the tree line, about three hundred meters out. It had been so long since I'd heard those sounds that I almost thought I had imagined it.

Fighter jets appeared in the distance, streaking across the sky toward the city and dumping a barrage of ammunition onto it. It snapped me back into reality as I ran for cover. Muzzle flashes of concealed machine gunners in the woods soon followed, as the city was hammered by artillery. I tried to drop to the ground, but an artillery shell hit near me, throwing me against the wall of a building and creating a gash in my forehead. I momentarily lost my senses as my ears rang noisily. Tracy was lying in a gruesome position on the other end of the street. The once-white snow was now blood red all around her body. What was left of her arms was hanging by the flesh across her chest; her legs were completely gone.

I stumbled over to her, but it was too late. She lay there, dead, staring up blankly into the sky. Her eyes clouded over with the dull gaze of death. I tried to hold back my tears, but I couldn't.

Oblivious to the machine gunfire strafing around me, I crumpled to the ground, picking up Tracy's lifeless body in my arms. I propped her head up against my shoulder, cradling her like a mother would a newborn child. "No! Not her, damn it!" I yelled angrily to the sky, loosening my grip as her head dangled lifelessly off the side of my arm.

"Lance! Lance! *Lance!*" David sprinted around the corner toward me. Then he saw Tracy. "Oh, no …" he cried as he realized that she was dead.

"We need to do something," I sniffled.

"Get up, Lance! Pull yourself together," he told me firmly, holding back tears.

We both picked up her limp body and raced down the street. We were knocked down once by an RPG that flew by us from somewhere off in the distance. We continued as fast as we could. Once we reached my house, we both burst through the door, shouting hysterically for Lara to come help. Carana appeared and gasped, looking at Tracy's mangled body. She went into the bathroom and returned a split second later with Lara wrapped around her neck—she was moaning as a contraction tortured her body.

"What ... what happened?" Lara panted, clutching her stomach as she knelt on all fours, staring down at Tracy.

"Artillery," David and I answered simultaneously.

"She's dead. I can't do anything for her," Lara sobbed, recoiling in pain as another contraction came.

I felt rage boil over me as I slumped against the dresser, defeated. David plopped down beside me, sharing the same defeated look and cradling his head in his hands. The room was dead silent, except for the loud crying, sobbing, and whimpers as Lara went deeper and deeper into labor.

I couldn't bring myself to comfort her. I was too busy staring in disbelief at the dead figure of Tracy. An explosion outside the house snapped us all back into reality, as fire fights could be heard in the distance between the city's guards and whoever was attacking us. Lara struggled to her feet, holding her bulging belly, and waddling carefully over to the window.

She grunted as Rashellia caused another contraction. I noticed blood trickle down her leg as she tried to cross them while leaning against the windowsill. "There are fiends in the street with guns, dragging people out of their homes," she said. She suddenly flinched in surprise, her eyes widening as she heard the *bang, bang, bang* sounds of innocent civilians being executed. She swiftly closed the curtains. She tried to walk over to me, but her legs gave way as the relentless contractions continued.

I crawled over to her, putting my hand on her and kissing her gently on the forehead. She lay curled up on the ground, whimpering, but to my surprise, she wiggled a bit closer and kissed me on the lips. "Tell me what to do," I whispered, loyally vowing to myself that I would not let our daughter be killed without a fight.

Lara glanced at me, calmly panting. She spread out across the floor, and Carana checked her to see how far along she was.

"She's seven centimeters dilated, entering the transition phase. It's not going to be long, Lance," Carana told me as we looked over at the naked Lara, who had managed to flip herself over and was pulling out bags from under the bed.

"Can she still run?" I asked Carana. Lara motioned for David to come over, and they both busily began packing stuff into the bags, ignoring us.

"Not very fast or far. Her contractions are about a minute or less apart," Carana told me. "See? She's going to have one any second now."

Lara turned to face me, and she smiled, gesturing me over. Before I could reach her side, her expression changed to pain, and she clutched her stomach, moaning in pain and rocking back and forth. David got scared and gratefully let me take his spot as he shuffled over to Carana.

"Carana, David, go get us weapons from the armory," Lara panted as I rubbed her back.

They nodded and left to accomplish their task, leaving us alone. Her contraction soon passed, and I started my stopwatch. "One minute," I told her with a nervous laugh.

She let out a sigh, patting her belly, laughing with me nervously but avoiding eye contact. I kissed her and she returned it, getting rid of the tension in the air. "I guess it's going to be today after all," she told me with a faint smile.

"You could totally make it to tomorrow. Just cross your legs," I joked, packing one bag as she did the other.

She laughed, throwing a pile of clothes into her bag, along with papers and maps into one of her jackets beside us on the ground. My stopwatch went off, and I glanced over at Lara, who cursed under her breath. "Here it comes—don't fight it," I teased her.

She spread her legs wide apart while packing, trying to make it pass. Soon enough, she succumbed to it, leaning against me and screaming in pain as I rubbed her and soothed her. We packed in between contractions, and they began to slow down. I knew this was both good and bad—it meant that she was going to have a break, so we could attempt an escape, but it also meant that she was going to have Rashellia soon.

We got up with the bags as the back door burst open, and Carana and David burst through with a ton of weapons. "Help Lara get dressed," I told Carana, lifting Lara off the floor and bringing her over to the dresser.

"But the baby's coming. We can't escape yet," Lara objected angrily, having a sudden mood swing.

"We can't stay here," I told her calmly, nodding toward the window, through which we could hear the screams of people being executed.

"Well, I'm not leaving until the baby is here," Lara lashed out angrily, folding her arms across her chest.

I turned away from her, ignoring her moody rants, and started sorting through the weapons David had brought back. Carana comforted Lara as she continued to spit a barrage of insults in my direction. "It's like no one even cares about me," I heard her complain to Carana.

I slung a PSG sniper rifle around my shoulder and took a backpack, loading it with ammunition, a flare gun, grenades, and ration packs. David slung an M4 around his shoulder and packed his bag as well.

Carana already had her submachine gun slung around her shoulder. The only thing left from the pile was a 9mm handgun. I loaded it and went over to Lara, who was now dressed in her winter jacket but still on all fours, battling through another contraction.

"I'm sorry about arguing with you," she grunted apologetically, avoiding my stare.

I gave her the 9mm, which she tucked into the back of her pants as the contraction subsided. I was a bit worried, and she must have read it on my face, because she gently rubbed her hand through my hair, messing it up. "Don't we have to leave?" she asked me, giving me a light peck on the cheek.

"Is the baby already down in your pelvis?" I asked, thinking of a way we could all escape without getting killed. I knew that if she started giving birth once we were escaping, we would be screwed.

She nodded but stubbornly struggled to her wobbly feet and leaned against the dresser. "Let's go, before Rashellia decides she wants to come out and play," Lara urged me, holding the bottom of her bulging belly.

David took the dog tags off Tracy's neck, and we all said our good-byes to her, with tears in our eyes. Then we set out the door, stealthily walking along the sides of the houses. Lara leaned against my shoulder as we bustled along the back alley as fast as we could. I heard a gunshot at close range—and saw it was Lara, who was holding out her handgun. She had shot a fiend in the head behind us.

"Nice shot," Carana called out, and we started moving quickly again, finally reaching the fence. We rushed along it, looking for a hole that we could fit through. "Oh, no!" Lara gasped, clutching her stomach.

I covered her mouth as she was about to let out a scream. We were forced to stop as I rested Lara on the ground, and she thrashed around violently as the contraction shot through her belly. I heard the cracking of her pelvis as it expanded, getting ready to let the baby slide through.

"Is it crowning?" I asked her worriedly, kneeling down beside her. David and Carana looked over at us, fearfully.

"No, I'm fine," Lara replied a moment later, catching her breath once the pain had subsided. "Sorry; that was a big one," she muttered over the sound of gunfire that lit up the sky.

"It's fine you're so strong," I replied, helping her up as we set off along the fence again.

We had to move a lot slower. Lara was forced to waddle, and I assumed from the way she was struggling to walk that she had pushed Rashellia almost to the point where she was going to come out. Luckily, we found a hole in the fence a few yards away and helped Lara get through. Then we all wriggled through, lying down on the other side of it, camouflaged in the snow. "We have to wait for Lara to get a contraction," I told them as we stared at the two hundred meters of open field between us and the tree line. "If she gets one out there, we're screwed."

"You picked a hell of a time to have a baby," David teased.

"Shut up!" she shot back playfully as we waited patiently in the snow.

"Whatever you do, don't push, even if you have the urge to do it," Carana told Lara.

"Think you can run that distance?" I asked her, staring out into the snow-covered field to the woods.

"Try to keep up with me," she joked, giving me a playful nudge.

I nudged her back, and she smiled. She seemed about to say something when her face turned to pain as the contraction hit. She latched onto me, squeezing painfully as she sobbed silently.

"Don't push; just let it pass," I kept encouraging her. "Is it done?" I asked, once she had let out a sigh of relief.

She nodded. We all got up, running in a zigzag pattern, trudging through the deep snow, with Carana and David leading. Lara was slung around David's shoulder, and I was in the rear. Fiends quickly noticed we were escaping as we got near the tree line. I heard the cracking of gunshots as a machine gun opened up behind us, but it overshot and hit the snow in front of us.

I made the mistake of stopping as we were almost to the trees to glance through the scope of my sniper, hoping to take out the machine gunner. A round hit my right shoulder, knocking me down into the snow on my back. I gasped in pain and heard Lara's panicked cry as the gunfire started strafing around my body.

I shakily staggered to my feet and lunged deep through the tree line, out of range, as bullets hissed by me, narrowly missing. Carana helped me lower myself to the ground, as David kept watch around us.

"Don't move. You'll be fine. It's not that bad," Lara told me, crawling over to me, even while she was having a contraction. She clutched below her stomach, trying to fight off the wave of pain, as she dug out the bullet from my shoulder with a claw that emerged from her free hand. I covered my own mouth as I cried out in pain. Lara's contraction had gone away, and her concern for me quickly took over.

"Stop being a pussy," she joked with me as she operated on my wounded shoulder. She grabbed a handful of snow and cleaned out the wound. Then she cast a spell to heal it. I rotated the arm, testing it tentatively. It was a bit stiff, but Lara told me it would go away after I rested. "We have to find a hiding spot. They're going to be looking for escapees and—" She winced and breathed heavily.

I rubbed her back, and David and Carana watched nervously for any movement beyond the trees.

"You're going to be a father *really* soon," Lara said.

"Let's go," I told them, grabbing the bag and getting up.

We trudged through the snow, deeper into the woods, for several hundred yards. Suddenly, David shouted, "Wait—I found something!" David pulled open a door that led to an underground bunker. It was fairly big—Lara and I could fit comfortably in one corner; David and Carana plopped their stuff in the opposite corner. I came to the conclusion that it must be the abandoned den of resistance fighters, judging by the random sketches on the walls that indicated how long it would be until relief arrived, along with individual kill tallies and stuff like that.

I placed all our bags against the wall. Lara was constantly moaning now, making me nervous. I loaded the sniper rifle, trying to take my mind off Lara's screams. Carana and David both stood guard outside, wishing us luck as they stepped out.

I helped her get undressed, and she lay against me, trying to distract me with a kiss, whimpering as a contraction got too painful. She started to push, and I was no help at all, as I was scared stiff and wished I had a way out. I tried to hide my fright whenever she looked at me. I'd tell her what a great job she was doing, but she knew I was frightened.

"We … ugh … oh God … ugh … we … need firewood," she told me, squeezing my hand as she pushed.

I knew she was giving me a way out, and I took it, feeling like a complete jackass. I awkwardly freed myself from her and kissed her belly as I got ready to go out into the cold night air. I grabbed the sniper rifle, giving her another kiss and whispering that I was sorry.

She wrapped her arms around me, taking me by surprise as she kissed me gently. "It's not your fault. I wanted this baby and deceived you to get it," she whimpered, plunging her face into my winter jacket and sobbing uncontrollably—it was probably from the contractions and her emotions. I patted her back until she finally stopped. "I love you, Lance," she said through teary eyes.

"Me too," I replied.

We kissed again before another contraction hit, and then I went outside into the snow.

"What happened?" Carana asked me. The constant moans still came from the den, so when I ignored her question, she went into the den to comfort Lara.

I stared, as if in a trance, at the city in the distance—it was totally engulfed in flames. The constant roar of airplanes and gunfire ruined what could have been the best day of my life. Attacks like this made me realize that even if humans and fiends wanted peace, it would never be accepted. I guess we were natural enemies.

"Are you all right?" David asked.

"I have to go get firewood," I muttered.

"I can help," David offered, following me a few paces.

"No, stay here. Guard the entrance," I ordered him sharply, whirling around.

He lifted his hands up peacefully. "All right."

I stomped around in the woods and filled up the bag with the driest wood I could find. I deliberately took my time. When I returned, I knew that Lara had had the baby even before I stepped into the den. Carana was outside with David; they both were smiling. When they saw me emerge from the brush, they grabbed the bag of wood from me and bustled me inside the den.

Lara's eyes were filled with tears of joy as she looked up at me when I entered. She was holding Rashellia across her chest, breast-feeding her while softly humming. I sat beside Lara, silently watching Rashellia's feeding.

All my cares seemed to disappear as I looked at our little girl. She had blue eyes, just like her mother, causing me to smile. Rashellia looked like a normal human baby but after a minute, her eyes turned red, and she let out a tiny growl, sort of like a puppy would, and she bit into Lara's breast, sucking blood from her.

Lara motioned to me that it was okay, and she massaged the baby's jaw until she let go and resumed breast-feeding normally. Lara healed the bite marks. "Would you like to hold her, Daddy?" Lara finally asked me.

I held back tears and stroked Lara's hair affectionately. I nodded. Lara wrapped Rashellia up in a blanket and handed her to me. I felt a tear roll down my cheek as I cradled Rashellia in my arms and rocked her back and forth.

The small baby yawned, looking up at me and blinking sleepily. She nibbled on my arm a bit, penetrating the skin and sucking some blood from it. It didn't really hurt as much as I might have expected.

"She's going to be a daddy's girl; I can tell," Lara told me, putting her clothes on and then leaning her head against my shoulder as she sleepily watched our child.

"You did a good job. I'm sorry for … well … you know," I said.

She put her finger against my lips, whispering, "Shhhhhh," and then she just nodded, accepting my apology. She tickled Rashellia's belly, making her squirm around in my arms.

"Let's let Carana and David have a look at her," I whispered to Lara, who laughed groggily and nodded in agreement. We called them in, and the two of them pushed and shoved each other, trying to get in first to see the baby.

"She's so cute!" Carana said, taking her from me and cradling her in her arms.

David beamed over her shoulder. "Congrats, man. You're a father now!" David said happily. He reached down to pat Rashellia's head, but Lara suddenly snapped at him unexpectedly.

"Get your filthy hands away from her!" she growled menacingly, baring her fangs and growling as she bolted upright, snatching Rashellia back into her arms and humming to her protectively. "Whoops," she giggled, regaining control of herself. "Sorry. I guess my mother instincts sort of took over there."

"It's illegal for males to touch a newborn child for forty-eight hours—except, of course, the father," Carana explained to David, who nodded understandingly and then apologized. "Lara needs her rest now," Carana said, shooing David and me outside. "You two take first watch, and I'll take care of Rashellia."

I kissed both Lara and Rashellia on the head. Then I loaded my M4 before stepping out into the cold and taking a seat on a log a couple meters away from the entrance. David followed me, sitting down beside me.

"The sad thing is that the only place I've ever felt like I belonged was there," he muttered, staring through the trees at the burning city.

Occasional sounds of gunfire would crack through the night air—probably from the few remaining residents trapped inside the blazing inferno. I felt rage building toward the fiends as David and I talked about Tracy. "I'm going to miss her, man," I said.

"Same here," he told me. He took Tracy's dog tags from his jacket, dangling them in front of us. When I looked at him, he was crying silently. I placed a comforting hand on his shoulder.

And then, without warning, we both whirled around in shock as we heard the click of a safety being released and, seemingly out of nowhere, ten soldiers appeared through the tree line surrounding us.

I looked at the arm patch on one of them, as I pointed my M4 at the officer. They were resistance fighters.

"Whoa, whoa—don't shoot," the soldier beside him said, holding out his hand to the others. He took a step forward in the newly fallen snow, and the moonlight illuminated his face.

"Grant?" I whispered, not believing my eyes.

"*Lance!*" he yelled, throwing his AK59 to the ground and running over to me. We both hurled ourselves at each other, happily embracing for the first time in over a year.

"I thought you were dead!" I yelled happily, wrestling him to the ground.

"I thought *you* were dead!" he retorted, finally pinning me—he was always the stronger one.

Everyone lowered their weapons as Grant and I got up, brushing the snow off each other while laughing like two little kids. I signaled to David that it was okay, and he lowered his weapon as well.

"David, this is my friend Corporal Grant Benet from the PLF," I told him.

David extended his hand, shaking Grant's firmly. "Pleasure to meet you. I'm Private First Class David Legro, ex-NWO.

"You're NWO?" the officer asked uneasily as he walked forward, keeping a hand on the pistol strapped to his waist.

"Easy, Philip, any friend of Lance's is a friend of ours," Grant told the officer, who took his hand from his sidearm and shook our hands.

"Were you residents of Monatello?" Philip asked, gesturing toward the burning buildings in the distance.

I nodded and asked, "Who did this?"

"Apparently, a radicalized rebel faction of fiends decided to break from the original invaders. They are opposed to any negotiations of peace that the fiends have come up with, as you can tell." He nodded toward the burning buildings. "Is anyone else with you?"

"Yes, our wives," David spoke up. "They're both fiends, but they won't hurt you." He looked around at the uneasy stares the soldiers were giving each other.

"My daughter was born not even an hour ago," I told them, gesturing toward the den.

"Damn! You shacked up with a fiend?" Grant grunted, giving me a playful nudge.

"Well, that den is our sleeping quarters," a soldier muttered.

"Shut up, Luke," Grant shot back at the soldier, giving him a warning slap over the helmet.

"You may stay with us, if you wish," the officer told us, after thinking for a moment.

David and I both accepted his invitation, and then David went into the den to explain to Lara and Carana what had happened. He emerged a moment later, waving us in. As I lay down beside Lara, she watched protectively as the resistance fighters all noisily piled in, setting down their weapons and bags and joking with one another about a firefight from which they'd just escaped.

Once everyone was in and settled down, Carana and Lara became a little less tense. Lara cuddled closer to me, purring softly, as Rashellia slept safely between us.

"She's cute," Grant said quietly as people began to go to sleep.

"Thanks," Lara replied, seeming unsure whether to trust him or not.

"What's her name?" Grant asked, taking off his boots and resting against the wall of the den.

"Rashellia," Lara replied.

"Rashellia?"

I nodded, knowing that he was thinking of my old girlfriend Rachel.

"She was one of a kind, eh?" Grant said.

"Yes, she was," I replied.

"It's good to see that you made it, Lance. I thought I was the only one left from the good old Tenth Light Infantry," he told me.

I nodded, sifting through all the memories of friends that Grant and I shared who were now dead. I rested my head against Lara's, stroking Rashellia's head fondly. "Where are we going to go now?" I whispered to her, once everyone had fallen asleep.

"Brawklin City," she whispered back, toying with my hair. She pulled out a map from her jacket pocket, showing me roughly where we were located and then ran her finger along it to where Brawklin City was.

"How far away is that?" I asked her.

The fire in the middle of the den crackled, illuminating her face. "About a three- to four-day flight or a two-week walk," she told me. "I won't be able to fly for a couple days with all your weight until things settle down inside me from giving birth." She folded the map and placed it in my jacket pocket.

"Don't you need that?" I asked.

"Nah, I have a spare," she said, ruffling up my hair.

"You should go to sleep. You must be tired after pushing out this little trooper," I told her, bringing the blanket up to Rashellia's neck.

"I walked around with her inside me for almost a year. Believe me, I'm glad she's finally decided to come out," she replied, looking down at Rashellia.

"I really am sorry for leaving you. I just couldn't stand to see you in so much pain and not be able to do anything about it," I told her.

"I know. You don't need to keep apologizing. I know you love her. You were just scared; it's understandable. Besides, I accidently swiped Carana's cheek with my claw. If you'd been here, I might have hurt you badly."

I glanced over at Carana, who seemed fine, sleeping across David's lap.

"I healed it," Lara said, as if reading my mind.

"I love you," I told her, placing a kiss on her lips.

"Me too. Now get some sleep," she told me, returning the good-night kiss.

We hadn't slept long, however, when the silence in the den was broken by Rashellia's loud cries.

"What in the hell is that?" someone muttered angrily, followed by a wave of groans from the others.

I gave Lara a shake. Rashellia was having a fit.

"Shut that baby up!" someone yelled at us.

Lara took off her shirt to feed Rashellia, out of sight of the others. "Hush, hush," Lara coaxed Rashellia as she quieted down and began to feed.

"It's four fifteen in the morning," someone grumbled.

There was another barrage of insults, but then people started to settle down.

"Do you need help?" I asked Lara drowsily, sitting up beside her.

"Yeah, get out a cloth and wipe the milk from her face, please," Lara instructed me.

I pulled a white cloth from the baby bag we had hastily packed and then started cleaning up Rashellia, humming "Row, Row, Row Your Boat" to her as I did. Rashellia stopped sucking on Lara's breast and lay back in her arms, contentedly. Lara handed Rashellia to me, giving me a kiss. She laughed at me as I held her nervously. "She's not a bomb. Relax," Lara giggled, readjusting Rashellia in my arms.

"Here—you take her," I told Lara when the baby began to cry again.

Lara let out a frustrated sigh but took her back and rocked her to sleep. I knew she was mad at me, but she tried to hide it with a faint smile. "It's okay. You'll get the hang of it," she told me, placing Rashellia down beside us as we settled down to go to sleep.

"Is she a half-human, half-fiend?" I asked cautiously, wrapping the blanket around the small, curled-up body of Rashellia.

Lara nodded sleepily, rubbing her eyes.

"How can you tell?" I asked

"Well, yesterday she had fiend eyes. Plus, fiends don't grow human skin. We're shape-shifters. We have to first acquire a taste of the species we desire to be before we can transform into it. As you can see, she already has her full set of skin."

"Aren't you scared about how we're going to raise her? Teach her right from wrong? How to use her powers for good, not evil? She's going to be different from the others," I whispered nervously.

"Yes," Lara admitted, "but I know we can handle anything." She kissed me goodnight.

I reluctantly decided to drop the subject, returning the kiss and lying back, allowing sleep to overtake me. Little did I know, deep inside our little girl were powers begging to be unleashed that could one day change the tide of the war.

Chapter 17

We huddled in the den the next morning, eating what was left of the resistance fighters' rations, when a sudden crack of a gunshot rang outside. We all looked at each other in shock, and then all hell broke loose. A heavy firefight erupted outside, and the two sentries came under fire.

The resistance fighters all scrambled to their knees, loading their weapons, sending food flying everywhere. Then they raced outside to assist their comrades. I peeked out the den and saw that there were sixty to a hundred fiends, all firing at the logs, trees, and boulders that the PLF were taking shelter behind. "We're going to be overrun. Take Rashellia to Brawklin," I ordered Lara.

She slipped the diamond wedding ring I had given her into Rashellia's jumpsuit, preparing to transform. "I can try to carry you and her!" Lara pleaded, grabbing my hand.

I grabbed my sniper and shook my head, knowing that she was too weak from giving birth. Silently, I handed Lara and Carana the bags we had packed full of food and water. "You and I both know you can't carry me in your state," I told her.

"I can! Please don't stay! You'll die, just like the rest!" Lara begged. "I want our daughter to grow up to know her father, Lance." Her voice quivered through a sea of tears.

"I want to see her grow too, but these heartless monsters are going to destroy Brawklin after this. If I can kill at least one of them, then that's one less that you and Carana will have to deal with," I told her, trying to force myself to be brave.

"You will die," Lara sniffled, wrapping her arms around my neck.

"You all will die," Carana muttered from the corner of the den.

Carana's face was drenched with tears, which shocked me—she never really was an emotional fiend. There was nothing I could say. I unclipped the heart pendant necklace that my sister had given me and clipped it around Rashellia's neck before kissing Lara and whispering good-bye. "We will meet you in Brawklin," I told them, slinging the sniper rifle around my shoulder. I tapped the map in the pocket over my heart.

David whispered something in Carana's ear while cocking his assault rifle. She sniffled, nodding and wiping away a tear. She hugged him tightly as they both kissed.

"David?" I asked him, nodding toward the door.

"Let's do it," he said fearlessly.

The door slammed behind us as we plunged straight into the war we thought we had left so long ago. It felt so unfamiliar to me as I lay against the log, listening to the *thwock, thwock, thwock* of the bullets ricocheting off the side of it. My heart was racing and my hands were shaking as I cowered in fright, praying that I wouldn't be struck by one of the rounds.

Before, I hadn't really had a reason to live; now that I had Lara and Rashellia in my life, I was almost too scared to even peek over the log. We were in the kill zone of the fiends, with no escape, as they fired down on us from their vantage point up on the hilltop.

There were already two dead PLF fighters slumped against a tree stump, just in front of the log where I was taking cover. The air erupted with the familiar sounds of triumphant, lion-like roars, as Lara and Carana burst through the den, shooting up into sky and letting out another magnificent roar. Lara quickly made her escape, vanishing into the fog.

I perched my sniper against the log and shot down two fiends who attempted to pursue her. Carana stuck around, plunging twice to the ground and killing five or six fiends before yelping as a bullet ripped through her thigh. She let out an enraged roar, glancing over at David and me apologetically. Then she took off into the distance, killing a fiend who had flown up to kill her.

I shot one sniper perched in a tree. He fell to the ground with a loud thud. After that, I began to pick off fiends as they poked their heads over the ridge.

A resistance fighter set up a general-purpose machine gun on the rock to my left, lighting up the ridge by spraying bullets at anything that moved. We continued to fight but about fifteen minutes later, it was clear that we were going to lose the battle in no time. We only had five guys left; the rest were scattered along the ground, either dead, wounded, or playing dead.

"Our right flank!" I yelled to the guy on the machine gun, and then I realized that he was dead, lying against the rock with his finger on the trigger. "Grant!" I yelled, pointing to the unmanned machine gun.

Grant ran over to the rock and pushed aside the dead fighter. He aimed the machine gun back up at the ridge, while I picked off the fiends trying to flank us. "Hey, you! Call in artillery on that ridge!" David yelled at a kid who was trembling beside the PLF's radio.

The kid was about fifteen years old, curled up in fright, and shaking all over. "Ye … ye … yes, sir," the young boy stuttered, picking up the radio to transmit the message.

We were rewarded by the sound of artillery hitting its mark a moment later. It shook the ground, making us duck as shrapnel tore through the air in our direction. The fiends were only about thirty-five meters away from us now.

The young boy just looked at me in fright, calling in a suicide mission right on top of us, nodding his head toward me, and accepting his fate. Fully transformed fiends began flying at us, trying to dive-bomb us but to no avail—we shot them down. Others jumped over the logs, overrunning us.

Daid and I escaped to Grant's position. He was firing the machine gun at the log that David and I had taken shelter behind only seconds ago. As fiends jumped over the log, their dead bodies landed on the other side. "Run!" I yelled to David and Grant.

The three of us turned on our heels, sprinting away as artillery began to rain all around us. The deep winter snow bogged us down, making our escape impossible. The artillery pounded the area, and trees splintered as the ground shook. We were mowed down by debris. I fell to the ground, waiting for the artillery to finish me off—and was surprised when the barrage ended and I was still alive. An eerie silence was broken only by the chilling cries of the wounded, screaming for help. I felt my side, which was numb with pain, and gasped at the three-foot piece of wood lodged in my right side.

I shook my legs, realizing, to my relief, that I wasn't paralyzed.

"I … got hit," David and Grant both moaned simultaneously. Then David spotted me lying twenty feet or so from them. "Oh shit, Lance!" he gasped.

"I'm fine; it didn't hit anything major," I called out to them, holding up a hand.

Blood trickled from David's forehead, where a piece of debris—most likely a rock—had smacked him. Grant was lying about ten feet from us, covered in dirt, with a piece of wood through his left leg and right shoulder. We helped each other up, slowly making our way back to the den. As we stepped over the dead bodies of fiends and humans, we left behind a fresh trail of blood.

"Look for survivors," I told them through clenched teeth as I flopped onto the ground to catch my breath. I held on to the piece of wood that was lodged in my stomach so it wouldn't move and paralyze me. Grant limped over and sat down beside me, cringing in pain.

"So did you miss this shit at all while you were on vacation?" Grant muttered as we watched David flipping over the dead bodies of PLF fighters, checking for survivors.

"Not really," I shot back, flinching as a wave of pain shot through my body.

"Hey, the officer is alive!" David called to us, dragging Philip over.

Philip was worse than we were. He had three bullet wounds, and half his body was brutally peppered with shrapnel wounds. We all piled into the den, each taking care of our own wounds the best that we could. I couldn't help letting out a scream in pain as I pulled out the piece of wood. Blood squirted all over the place. I quickly took another piece of wood. Lighting it on fire, I shoved it into my wound, screaming as it burned the wound and stopped the bleeding. Gently, I sprinkled salt into the wound and cleaned it out with snow. I hoped I'd stopped it from getting infected.

I grabbed the first-aid kit from David, who had just finished bandaging his wound on his head. I took out the gauze and wrapped an entire roll around my stomach. My chest was still heaving from exhaustion after inflicting so much pain on myself. David and Grant had fixed their own wounds and were now operating on Philip, trying desperately to save his life.

I tossed over the first-aid kit to them with a defeated sigh, slumping to the ground and passing out a few moments later. I was the first to wake up the next morning. I looked at Philip's still body and thought at first that he'd died, but to my relief, I soon realized he was still breathing.

"Get up, guys," I said, prodding each of them separately with the butt of my weapon.

"Are we going to Brawklin?" Grant asked with a yawn, wiping the sleep from his eyes as he sat up.

I nodded, gathering two cans of tuna, three bags of bread, and fruit that was scattered around the floor of the den into a bag. Lara and Carana had left it behind in their hasty escape. I pulled out some machine gun and M4 ammunition from the bag, tossing it over to Grant and David.

"Just leave me behind," Philip muttered, opening up an eye. "I'm not going to make it."

"No, we will use that blanket as a stretcher and bring you with us, sir!" Grant objected instantly.

David and I nodded in agreement, even though we knew the officer was right. I attached a silencer to my sniper, and they slung their rifles over their shoulders. We picked up opposite ends of the blanket where Philip was lying and slowly made our treacherous journey to Brawklin City. It had snowed the night before, but the sky had cleared a little, allowing sunshine to peek through the dense pine canopy of the trees.

The snow was extremely deep, and it was difficult for us to wade through it, especially with our wounds. As we stopped to take breaks, David would backtrack to a random point off the track that led to a dead end in hopes of slowing down any fiends who might have picked up on our trail. Over the next week and a half, we didn't see many fiends or any sign of life, for that matter.

It seemed like we were stuck in a sick nightmare, going around in circles. The harsh winter environment seemed as if it would keep us trapped in the forest forever. The odd patrol of fiends would go by as we lay silently in the snow, praying for them not to spot us. I picked off about five stragglers throughout the week, as well as collecting rations and gear as our supplies became scarce.

A cold front came in that night, adding to our misery. My wounds had become infected, and I lost my gloves when I ducked in the middle of a contact between a lost fiend patrol and an NWO platoon the night before. I looked down at my hands, which were purplish-blue and so numb I could barely even feel them anymore. "This looks like a good place to set up camp," I told them as night soon enveloped us.

"Thank God," I heard Grant and David moan. They dropped Philip quickly to the ground, collapsing from exhaustion beside him.

We all began to succumb to our wounds as the days dragged on. David was starting to lose it, mentally—I think he had a concussion or something. Two nights ago, I woke up and saw him talking to a tree, debating whether to have eggs or bacon for breakfast.

Grant was holding up pretty well. He was limping a lot more now, though, and his leg was swollen from infection. Philip couldn't stop coughing, and he would go into occasional convulsions. I found that I was starting to become a lot sleepier. It was getting harder and harder for me to breathe as the days went on.

The other night, I had woken up gasping for air, and Grant had to literally pound on my chest so I could spit out the blood and mucus that had built up in my lungs while I slept. I was getting nosebleeds too. Now, I placed my hands in my armpits, trying to warm them up, as David re-bandaged Philip's crippled body.

Grant attempted to make a small campfire in the snow. I began to drift off, but suddenly I felt a warm surge of energy fill me—this wasn't the first time it had happened.

"Lara?" I asked hopefully in my mind, but my voice just echoed back, as if there was a sound barrier between us. I could soon hear the sounds of Grant's snoring. He had fallen asleep on the pile of wood he was using to

make the failed fire. Philip and David exchanged a few words, and then David settled down by a tree to go to sleep.

A strong wind blew over us, causing me to shiver again. I felt the wave of energy slowly dissolving from me, letting me slip back into reality.

David came over to sit beside me. He looked exhausted. "Do you feel these surges of energy rush through you whenever you feel like fainting?" he whispered, laying his M4 up against the tree. When I said that I did too, he said, "The angels must be looking after us or something."

"It's definitely something," I agreed, settling into the snow. Sleep overtook me as thoughts of Lara and my daughter began to flow through my head.

"It's so cold. We're going to freeze," David muttered. His morale seemed to drop as quickly as the night's temperature.

"Let's huddle together," I suggested.

He wrapped his arm around me in agreement. "Fine, but no homo."

We both laughed and then fell asleep almost instantly, comforted by our body heat. I had a dream—I was on a playground, pushing Rashellia on the swing. Lara was on a rock, reading a book and sprawled out in the summer sun. Rashellia got off the swing and enthusiastically ran to Lara, jumping into her arms. At that exact moment, Rashellia transformed into a baby in Lara's arms.

Lara suddenly was standing on the walls of a castle overlooking the forest as snow gently fell, covering her long blonde hair. "Keep going, Lance," she whispered into the wind as a single tear slipped down her cheek. She then vanished into the darkness.

I opened my eyes and stared up into the gray sky. There was a light drizzle pattering down on us. I rolled free from David, going into a coughing fit and spitting out a mouthful of blood, followed by my morning puke. Once I regained control of myself, I got up, slinging the sniper around my shoulder.

Philip was awake, staring at the sky.

"What's up, man?" I asked him. He didn't reply. "Philip?" I asked timidly, walking over to his still body.

He was dead, frozen to the blanket, with an awed expression plastered to his face. I put another blanket on top of his body and lay his pistol on his chest. I held back tears, knowing this was going to be our fate. I quickly woke up the other two before slumping to the ground and putting my head in my arms, defeated.

They both just stared solemnly at the blanket. "Philip's gone," I told them, dully confirming their thoughts. We just instinctively got up and left without saying another word.

David began marching around, singing as if reliving his boot-camp days, while waving to trees and calling up to squirrels and birds.

I was starting to realize that I wasn't going to make it. Every day, I felt my energy fading more and more, to the point that I was starting to cough up blood as I walked, every ten or fifteen minutes.

"Your boy's losing it. He's going to get us killed," Grant told me that night as I rested on a log, trying to clean my wound, which had started bleeding again.

David was playing fetch with his invisible dog, yelling at the top of his lungs for it to stop peeing on the neighbor's yard.

"What do you suggest I do about it? He's a good friend. He's saved me plenty of times, just like you have," I told him.

"I don't know. I don't think my leg can push me much farther anyway. I'm starting to get a tight feeling around my chest. I think the infection's spreading."

"You're telling me," I said, drowsily reaching into my jacket pocket and pulling out the map to Brawklin. I threw it on his lap.

"Why are you giving this to me?"

"I'm done. I quit. I can't go any farther," I said in resignation. "It's over for me."

"Don't talk that way, man," Grant said angrily. "You have a daughter and wife to get home to."

"Look at me, Grant. I'm whiter than a ghost. It hurts to even take a breath. I'm not even gonna last two more days. I'll be surprised if I wake up tomorrow." Grant remained silent; he seemed to refuse to accept the fact that I was dying. "I want you to keep heading west to Brawklin. Take David with you. It's only two or three more days of a hike."

"I'm not leaving you here, Lance. You're a hero. You may have forgotten about all the things you've done, but I haven't, and there's no way you're going to die here in the middle of the damn forest, alone. Rachel wouldn't allow you to give up, and I certainly won't either."

I knew there was nothing I could do or say to persuade him to listen to me, so I didn't try.

"I'll wake you up tomorrow when it's time to go," he said after a moment. He got up awkwardly, went over to David, and put him to bed—after reluctantly petting his invisible dog.

I woke up five times throughout the night, puking up blood, but Grant's passionate speech seemed to give me hope. I kept telling myself that I had to make it back to Lara and Rashellia. I woke up slowly the next morning as Grant shook me roughly.

"Time to get up, trooper," he said. He went to wake David, and I stood up groggily, bending down to grab my sniper. The world spun around me as I face-planted into the snow. That was the last thing I remembered.

When I came to, all I could see were blurs of people around me with masks over their mouths. One injected a needle into my arm. I lashed out with a grunt before passing out again, almost immediately.

I could occasionally hear people talking around me and feel the soft touch of a female. One day, the medicine wore off a bit, and I could make out a girl in a chair, sleeping at the foot of my bed. I realized excitedly that it was Lara.

I'd made it somehow; I was in Brawklin! I moved my hand painfully on top of hers, giving it a light squeeze, which seemed to take up all my energy. She woke up instantly, and I felt her gently squeeze my hand.

I tried to talk, but it came out completely incomprehensible. Lara's face was all a blur in my eyes, but I could make out her beautiful smile. She put a finger on my lips, whispering, "Shhh."

I squeezed her hand again, which she returned. She propped herself up beside me, casting a spell inside a bowl of soup on the counter, which instantly started steaming. I felt her loving stare burning through me as she fed me the soup. I could feel the warmth of it as it trickled down my throat.

She hummed to me softly while feeding me like a baby. I ended up coughing most of it out, but I managed to get some down before I drifted back off into my world of unconsciousness. When I woke up the next morning, I was ecstatic to realize that I could talk and move my right arm a bit.

The rest of my body was still numb from the medication. I knew Lara must have put some sort of healing remedy in my soup for my recovery to be so swift. The fiend doctor came in later that morning, surprised by my progress, telling me that he was happy with the healing of my frostbite and wounds.

I must have dozed off, because when I woke up, Lara was at my side, cradling Rashellia in her arms. "Good afternoon, sexy," she greeted me happily, putting Rashellia on my chest.

I slowly put my arm around the baby, patting her lovingly. "Hey, mini me," I said in a childish voice, as Rashellia looked up, staring at me with her sparkling blue eyes. "She has your eyes," I told Lara, trying to wipe off the silly grin plastered to my face. I played with Rashellia for a bit; she growled affectionately. I could tell Lara was deep in thought as she watched me playing with Rashellia.

"She has your face, though," Lara told me, purring softly as she closed the curtain around my bed. "Lance, I don't know if we can trust these people here. I told them about Rashellia, and they seemed very interested, wanting to do tests and blood samples," Lara whispered worriedly while glancing nervously around the room.

"Why'd you tell them?" I whispered back, trying to sit up as I stared at her in disbelief.

"I had to. They instantly noticed her difference from a regular fiend baby and wouldn't let me or Carana into the city until we explained to them about Rashellia."

"Well, let's just let it go. Maybe they were just curious," I told her, convincing myself that she was just being overly protective.

"Yeah, maybe you're right," she replied uneasily, trying to calm down a bit.

"How did I end up here? Are Grant and David all right?" I asked, finally getting a chance to ask the question that had been burning on my mind ever since I realized I was alive.

"Well, Grant popped a flare. I knew it had to be you guys. I saw it way off in the distance. I was so worried about you guys. I would sit on the wall every night, waiting for you to emerge through the tree line." A tear fought its way down her face as she spoke.

I wiped it away, comforting her. "I'm here now; don't cry," I told her gently.

"Anyway, the police sent out a chopper and picked you guys up before the enemy could kill you—that was after Carana and I screamed our lungs off at them to go rescue you." She wiped away another tear. "We flew with the chopper and killed some NWO fighters who were looting your bodies. All three of you were unconscious by the time we got there. I thought you might be dead already."

"Ouch! You little bugger!" I exclaimed, interrupting Lara as I glanced down at Rashellia, who was happily sucking blood from my arm. She let go a minute later and let out a tiny burp, purring affectionately. We both laughed at our daughter. I passed her over to Lara, who started breast-feeding her. She laughed at me as I turned my head away, giving her privacy.

"What's wrong, Lance? You had no problem staring at my two friends here before she was born."

"I don't want to get turned on by you feeding our little girl," I said with a smirk. She gave me a playful punch. "So how are David and Grant?" I asked, now that the mood had been lightened, thanks to Rashellia.

"David's fine. He just had a serious concussion, but he's already out of the hospital wing and in Carana's assigned room. Grant is getting an operation on his leg tomorrow to have shrapnel removed, and then he will be released tomorrow, and you, hopefully, will be released the day after." She happily leaned over and gave me a kiss after Rashellia was done eating. "She's cranky today," Lara added, as Rashellia began to cry. Lara slung the baby over her shoulder, attempting to burp her. "So how did you get that wound in your stomach?" she asked curiously.

"Artillery," I replied simply, with a shrug.

"So there were no survivors?" she asked me gently.

"Philip survived, but he didn't make it here. He needed a real doctor, not some useless infantry. There was nothing we could do."

"Hey, don't say that. He knew he would die one day for his freedom. Don't take away his pride like that. He died doing what he loved," she said, trying to reassure me.

As if on cue, my doctor came in, glanced over my medical chart, and showed me places that were recovering from the frostbite. He informed Lara and me that I would be able to leave the hospital wing in two or three days. He then gave me some pills to knock me out and left to attend to another soldier.

"I love you. Have a good night's sleep, buddy," Lara whispered gently, giving me a peck on my cheek. "Bye-bye, Daddy," she called to me in a babyish voice, waving Rashellia's little fiend paw, which was sprouting claws.

"Bye-bye," I replied, waving to them enthusiastically.

To my relief, the pills kicked in a few moments later, leaving me in the comfort of my dreams.

Chapter 18

"'**S**up?" Grant called over to us. He and Ellie sauntered toward us, happily holding hands.

"Nothing much," I said, greeting him with our usual handshake as they sat down next to us on the bleachers.

I pulled out the envelope of money I had received from Captain Murphy for our last mission, splitting it between the four of us. "So Murphy put us on bivouac duties for three days as a reward for our hard work," I told them, leaning back on the railing of the bleachers as the sun beamed down on me.

"Awesome. So we basically just get to keep the generators running, collect resources, and stuff like that?" Ellie asked.

I nodded lazily. "I'm going to go hunting in a bit, if anyone wants to come," I offered, them already knowing the answer as I saw Grant and Ellie share a disinterested look.

"I'll come!" Rachel volunteered quickly.

I smiled thankfully. She returned it with a playful wink, as I mouthed the words "thank you" to her. "So you guys are going to hold things down around here while we're gone?" I asked Ellie and Grant.

They nodded lazily, basking in the sun. "You guys want to do something tonight?" Ellie asked Rachel and me as we got up to leave.

"Sure," we both agreed as we left.

Rachel and I made our way up the path to our squad's shelter, where I grabbed my loyal Timberwolf sniper rifle, putting a sling on it while patiently *waiting for Rachel to get her hunting kit prepared, departing a short time later. As we walked along the woods, we would occasionally stop as she set up a few snares in some good escape routes for rabbits. After about twenty minutes of walking, we found a nice place on a mountaintop, overlooking a valley below us, about eight hundred meters away.*

I set up my Timberwolf, glancing through the sight down at the valley below.

"This is a beautiful spot," Rachel commented, pulling out her binoculars and glancing around at the layout of the ground. "I'd say that's about eight hundred meters to a kilometer, by the way, Lance."

I nodded, having already finished the calculations for my shot in my head. A few minutes passed by as I stared through the sight, patiently surveying the land below.

"Geeze, it's going be a long day if you plan on doing that," Rachel joked.

I smirked, setting the butt of the sniper rifle down on the ground. I knew something was on her mind and that she wanted to talk about it. A silence passed between us for a moment until Rachel finally said, "Do you remember what life was like before the war?"

"Not really," I told her honestly.

"Yeah, me neither," she muttered, pausing for a second to look at me and then tearing her eyes away from me and back to the field. "I was trying to go through my memories of my life before the war the other day, and nothing was coming up. I can't even see my parents' faces anymore."

I didn't say anything, knowing if I did, it would just upset her even more.

"I suppose it's not all bad, though. If it wasn't for this war, I would have never met you, Lance," she told me, smiling faintly. I gave her a pat on the back, which she returned with a peck on the cheek. Her attention diverted back to the field below us. "I wish the fiends would just hurry up and lose this war." She took her hair band out to let her long blonde hair drape down her back as we lay there motionless for a while. "Do you think we're going to win this war?" she asked.

"Honestly?" I asked. "I don't think we are going to be around to find that out, Rachel." Her smile faded away in disappointment. "Besides, there are no

winners in war anyway. Wars are just fought to pave the road to a political solution—in this case, who gets which parts of the world when all is said and done."

She remained silent; I knew that was not the answer she was looking for. "Well, that's cheery, Lance," she finally said.

"It's realistic; look around. It's been three years now, and I've still seen no progress by the PLF."

"What's wrong with you?" she asked quietly after a few minutes.

"Huh?" I said, confused.

"You've been so distant over the past few days," she told me, inching a little closer to me in an attempt to cuddle.

"I'm sorry; I'm just tired of this," I said, feeling emotionless.

"Help me—somebody help me!" A wounded soldier was screaming at the top of his lungs in his sleep.

I glanced around the military hospital wing I was sharing with nine other guys. At first confused, the sad reality of where I was slowly began to sink in, and I realized, unhappily, that I was only dreaming of my past. Most people here were wounded fiends and humans, deeply scared with post-traumatic stress and an endless list of other issues caused by the war. Don't get me wrong—most of them were awesome to hang around with, but by nightfall, the memories of our fallen comrades would always come back to haunt us, making grown men cry themselves to sleep.

Some were even too scared to close their eyes—they knew they would see their dead loved ones in their dreams. I was the lucky one; I had a family to go back to now, and I could finally leave this stupid war behind me, unlike them. I painfully sat up, resting on the side of my bed for a moment, while sleepily rubbing the crud from my eyes.

I struggled out of my bed and into my wheelchair opening the door and wheeling myself down the hall to the wing where Grant was being held. "Yo, man, you up?" I whispered to Grant.

"I am now," he grunted sleepily. "Oh hey, Lance, what's up?" He looked surprised to see me.

"Nothing much; can't sleep," I muttered unhappily, glancing two beds down at a soldier who was crying to himself.

"Yeah, there seems to be a lot of that going on around here," Grant said, nodding his head toward the soldier. "I can't wait to get out of here."

"Same here," I agreed, thinking of being reunited with Lara and Rashellia again.

"Ha-ha, man, I'll be living the life once I'm back up on my feet, hitting the gym again, so I can get back out on that court," he told me excitedly, referring to basketball.

"I know what you mean. It's been forever. There was a court in Monatello that I use to play on. I hope there's one here."

"You playing basketball? What a joke. I'm pretty sure a fifth-grade girl could beat you," he joked.

"Laugh it up, man. I actually had a pretty pro female partner in Monatello," I said, and the fond memories of Tracy began to come back to me.

"Really? Where is she now? I'll kick her ass any day of the week."

"She's dead," I said quietly. "Killed in that fiends' assault on the city." I turned my head so that he couldn't see the emotion that was gripping me, making it hard to breathe.

"That's too bad, man. What was her name?" he asked.

"Tracy. She was a pretty switched-on girl, kind of like Ellie. You would have liked her," I told him.

He nodded understandingly. "We had the two best girls in the world, man. Screw this war. If I could go back in time, I would say the four of us should have just bailed on the resistance and gone to live somewhere deep in the forest, where no one could find us."

I laughed in agreement. "I have Lara now, though."

His expression kind of changed when I reminded him of my situation. "Aw, yeah. I almost forgot about that. You love her, right?" I nodded. "Well, then, good for you. At least one of us found someone who's right for him."

"Really? You're not weirded-out by her being a fiend?" I asked, surprised.

He shrugged carelessly. "You never did do the dirty deed with Rachel, did you?"

I shook my head, kind of embarrassed.

"Ha-ha, that's hilarious. I never would have thought I'd see you anywhere near a fiend, let alone lose your virginity to one."

"Shut up, man!" I shot back, straightening up and giving him a playful punch on the shoulder. "So how did you escape Dublin City?"

"Luck, I guess," Grant said. "I saw them surround you. I thought you were dead. I was low on ammo, so I fought my way out of the city and rejoined the new camp—the one that your sisters and the others had set up once we left." He kind of looked ashamed that he hadn't stuck it out in the city until the bitter end.

"It's all good. You did the right thing," I reassured him. "So were Tina and Kate there?" I was dying for information about my sisters' haven, not having spoken to them in over a year.

"They were there," he told me hesitantly.

I knew something was wrong. He avoided my eyes for a second. "What's up, man?" I asked nervously, not wanting to hear whatever it was he was about to tell me.

"They got it stuck in their heads that you were still alive. I kept telling them I saw you get overrun, but they wouldn't let it go. One night, they snuck out to go to Dublin City to rescue you … and they never came back," he informed me. "I'm really sorry, man. I tried to keep an eye on them for you, but they just wouldn't listen."

I tried to hold back the tears that were fighting their way to my eyes. "It's all right, man. I already had a feeling something like that had happened to them," I muttered gloomily. "I thought about them all the time in prison. They were what kept me going."

He nodded understandingly. "I loved them like my own sisters too, man. Remember Tina?" he asked me with a snicker.

"Yeah, she was always such a pest. Anywhere I went, she always had my back." I smiled as my mind wandered off to the three of us before the war. "Kate had it rough. She basically had to be a parent for us at the age of fourteen, when Mom died, but she somehow kept the three of us together as a family," I told him, visualizing her chilling in the kitchen, making Tina and me her famous grilled cheese sandwiches. "What about you, bro? You never really told me much about your family in the resistance."

Grant hesitated and then said, "I lost them on the night of the invasion. Captain Murphy took me under his wing, though, and then I met you a week later." He seemed to accept his past.

"I almost forgot about Murphy!" I exclaimed with a laugh.

"He was a straight-up baller," Grant said, and we both laughed, remembering the man that basically was our father in the resistance.

"Remember that cane he used to always walk around with, telling us it was his beating stick?" I asked him.

Grant nodded and laughed.

"I remember that time he caught us stealing cookies from the mess on my birthday," I said fondly.

"I thought he was going to kill us, man, but he was like, 'You boys better have saved me one of those.'" Grant sat up and impersonated Murphy on the side of his bed.

"Good times," I said.

"Can you believe that there's a chance we might actually survive this war?" Grant asked me.

I shook my head in disbelief, realizing it was coming to an end for us. "If you would have told me two years ago that I was going to live to be nineteen, I would have laughed straight in your face," I told him.

He nodded in agreement. "What do you think we're going to do once this whole thing is said and done?"

"I don't know, I've never really thought about it before now," I told him truthfully. "Hopefully, I'll settle down somewhere, get myself a cottage by the lake or something, and live the dream with Lara and Rashellia." He stared at me, seeming thoughtful, so I asked him, "What about you?"

"I was thinking about being a carpenter or something trade-related like that," he said, settling back down into his bed.

I yawned, relaxing in my chair, and we sat there for a moment, just listening to the eerie silence of the infirmary. "Well, I hope it works out for you," I said.

He nodded his thanks. "Same to you, brother." He leaned over, and we did our secret handshake that we had been doing ever since we were little kids.

"All right, man. I'm out. I'll see you tomorrow," I said as I unlocked my wheelchair with a playful salute.

"All right, buddy. Peace!" he called back.

I wheeled away happily to my wing of the hospital and got a nice night's rest for the first time in a long time.

Chapter 19

I was in an exceptionally good mood the next morning. I don't know why; I guess it was the thought that I was nearing the end of my stay in the infirmary, not to mention that I had a feeling that today was going to be a good day. My physiotherapy doctor came by early in the morning. He made me do an array of exercises and allowed me to practice walking on my own.

He gave me a thumbs-up when I discovered I could make it short distances on my own now. My session ended an hour later, and the doctor wheeled me to my section of the hospital wing, where I watched television for a bit and played a game of chess with Keith, a wounded ex-PLF soldier. I wasn't really paying attention and stared blankly at the board, realizing I was in checkmate.

"Maybe next time, buddy," Keith said.

"Hopefully, I won't be around here for a next time," I laughed.

"You're getting out of this hellhole?" he asked enviously.

I nodded happily.

"All right, well, best of luck to you in the real world. It was nice meeting you." He shook my hand as we got up to go back to our beds.

"Thanks a lot, man. Same to you. Hope the leg gets better," I told him, nodding at his legs—one was badly scarred with shrapnel; the other had been amputated and replaced with a mechanical leg.

The rest of the morning went by pretty quickly. I was thrilled to see

Lara come in as soon as the visiting hours opened in the afternoon. "Ta-da!" I called to her. I got up out of bed to show her that I could walk on my own again.

"Wow, that's impressive! I learned how to do that when I was, like, a year old," she joked with me, giving me a kiss.

"Oh really, smart ass?" I shot back with a laugh.

She helped me back down into my wheelchair. "So I talked to your doctor this morning, and he told me that you're good to go. I already signed all your release papers, along with all that other stuff, so let's go pick up Grant and then go to our new home!" Lara said happily as she wheeled me down the hall to Grant's wing.

"All right. Sweet! We were accepted for housing in Brawklin?" I asked.

"Yeah, it's a pretty decent place. I think you'll like it," she said.

"So what's up?" I asked her suspiciously as she messed up my hair.

"Nothing. I'm just glad to see you," she replied mysteriously.

"Yeah, right."

She giggled. "What? I can't be happy?"

"It's not that. I'm just not used to seeing you so loose. I'm loving this side of you," I told her.

She smiled, kneeling down to kiss me as we approached Grant's bed. Grant had a wrap around his leg and was using crutches to get around now, but it didn't look like he was seriously wounded anymore. "Hey, man, what's up!" he called as he spotted me.

"Not much," I said, standing up and giving him our secret handshake.

"Oh, I see how it is. I get no hello?" Lara said playfully.

He smiled at her and wobbled over to give her a light hug. I could see the uncomfortable look in her eyes, but she returned his hug with a pat on the back. In her culture, a man wasn't supposed to touch a woman after she was married, but I had explained to her that in the human culture, it was polite to give a hug to someone you knew.

It was good to see that she was at least trying to accept some of our ways. I sat down in the wheelchair as Grant rummaged around under his bed, retrieving his backpack. Then the three of us made our way through the door and toward the housing section of Brawklin City.

"I have a surprise for both of you," Lara said happily.

"I knew you were hiding something!" I exclaimed.

"It better be strippers," Grant teased, making the three of us laugh.

"Did we win the lottery?" I asked hopefully.

She shook her head. "I wish," she laughed.

Grant and I looked at each other for a second, trying to figure out what the surprise could be. "So what is it?" we both asked simultaneously.

"You'll see," she told us. "Be patient."

As we stopped in front of our door a moment later, she fumbled around in her pocket for a second and then pulled out our house key. She gave me a spare and then unlocked the door.

"Welcome home!" David and Carana called to us happily as we entered the room.

"Hey, guys, thanks a lot," I said, happy that the five of us were reunited. Carana had a cake with "Welcome Home" written on it. Grant looked at the cake and joked, "Really? That's it? This surprise sucks."

"Shut up," Lara giggled, glancing over at me excitedly. "You can come out now!" she called out.

As my attention shifted to our bedroom door, a girl about my age emerged from behind it. "*Tina?*" I cried out happily, realizing who it was.

She nodded, tears running down her face as she ran into my arms, giving me a hug. We stared at each other in disbelief. "I can't believe it really is you!" she whispered, giving me a light peck on my cheek. "I thought you were dead, Lance." She still seemed flabbergasted, and she took a step back to look me over, as if seeing me for the first time in her life.

"I've seen better days," I joked, indicating my bandaged stomach.

When Tina didn't notice Grant, he cleared his throat in her direction and gave her a devilish grin.

"Grant! Hey! How are you, buddy?" she asked, helping him sit down on the recliner across from us.

"Could be better," he told her, lying back in the chair.

Lara was about to sit down when Rashellia's crying came from the other room.

"Whoops, sounds like someone wants to come join the party," Carana told us.

Lara disappeared for a moment and returned with Rashellia in her arms. She took a seat on the couch with Grant, David, and Carana, who playfully comforted Rashellia with funny noises.

I'd noticed that Tina's arm looked stiff, so I asked her, "So what happened to your arm?"

Her smile faded as she lifted her sleeve, revealing to me that it was a mechanical arm. "I lost it defusing a land mine," she said.

"And Kate?" I asked quietly.

Tina just shook her head, staring away gloomily as the memories seemed to come back to haunt her.

"Was it quick?" I asked hopefully.

She nodded reassuringly. "I'm pretty sure she was dead before she even hit the ground," Tina whispered.

"I'm sorry," Lara whispered to me in my head.

"It's fine," I responded, but I wiped away a single tear that had run down my cheek.

David, Tina, Grant, and I chatted for a little while about the resistance and our memories, as Carana and Lara politely and patiently listened to our stories.

"So who wants to dig into the cake?" Lara asked finally, getting up to cut each of us a piece.

"Thanks a lot!" we all told her gratefully a moment later as she served it to us.

I felt kind of bad for Lara. Just as she sat down to relax again, Rashellia woke up and began squirming in Lara's arms at the sight of me eating cake.

"Good morning, sleepyhead. Want a piece of cake?" I asked her, bringing the fork up to her mouth.

"No, Lance," Lara told me firmly, batting the fork away gently with her hand.

"Aw, why not?" I asked, feeling bad that I had just teased my own daughter, who was now staring at my piece disappointedly.

"She's too young. It will just make her sick," she told me in her firm motherly tone.

"Sorry, buddy. Mommy has spoken," I told Rashellia, who of course couldn't understand me.

"Hey, that little tyke has a full set of teeth already? I thought she was only, like, two months old," Grant said.

"Of course she does," Lara assured him. "She's a half-blood. She grows her teeth before birth. She's a real sweetheart, though. She's so much less aggressive than a baby fiend, and that's because she's half human." Lara leaned over and gave me an affectionate kiss.

"Yeah, right. I tried to play with her yesterday, and she nearly ripped my other arm off," Tina told us with a laugh.

"Those were only warning bites. If Rashellia wanted to rip it off, she would have," Lara told my sister cold-heartedly. "Besides, the only human she really likes is her father." With that, she happily handed Rashellia over to me, and I held her nervously against my chest.

Rashellia stared up at me for a moment with her sparkly blue eyes and gurgled contentedly, which turned into her gentle baby purr as she snuggled into my chest, absorbing the warmth.

"Can she crawl already?" Carana asked me.

I shrugged, embarrassed because I hadn't seen her in a while.

"Yes, she can," Lara told her, jumping into the conversation to save me. "That's the great thing about half-bloods—they learn quickly." Lara gazed at Rashellia proudly.

"Hey, man, she's drooling all over you," David told me with a laugh.

I instinctively recoiled at the sight of the greenish saliva dripping down my white T-shirt. "Here you go, Mommy," I called to Lara, handing Rashellia back.

Everyone laughed except Lara, who stared at me unhappily. She cradled Rashellia gently as the baby began to cry and squirm in her arms, being a pest. "I have to go settle her down. If you guys could keep it down in here, that would be awesome," Lara said before disappearing into our room.

"Uh-oh. Someone's in trouble," Grant teased.

I laughed, and a couple minutes later everyone got up, taking Lara's hint that it was time to leave. Tina remained after the others left, and we talked for a little bit longer, catching up.

"How is she treating you, Lance?" Tina whispered as we stood at the door.

"She's awesome, Tina. I love her," I told her truthfully, but she looked worried.

"You loved Rachel, too," she debated with me.

"Tina …" I said, wishing she hadn't brought that up. "She's gone. I have to move on."

Tina sighed. "Are you sure you're moving on? Lara looks and acts like Rachel in so many ways."

I sighed, knowing she was right, but I truly did love Lara for Lara, despite what Tina thought.

"Are you sure she's even right for you? She seems very emotionally demanding," Tina warned me quietly.

"She doesn't mean a lot of things she says when she's angry. Fiends have a hard time controlling their emotions, unlike us," I explained. It was clear that Tina wasn't very fond of Lara.

"All right. Well, I just wanted to make sure that you weren't forced into this," Tina told me with a gentle pat on my shoulder.

"Don't worry. I'll be fine," I reassured her happily with a hug. "It was nice to see you again."

She returned the hug and gave me a soft kiss on my cheek. "You too, Lance. I love you," she whispered.

I nodded in agreement as she walked out into the hall. "Hey, do you want to do something tomorrow?" I called after her.

She turned around, nodding happily. "Sweet. I'll see you tomorrow then," Tina called back to me.

As I closed the door behind me, I could hear the faint sounds of Rashellia in the other room as Lara sang gently to her. I wasn't in any rush to go in and deal with Lara. I knew she was angry, so I deliberately took my time. I poured both of us a glass of orange juice, giving her a chance to cool off.

When I finally entered her room, she was sitting there on the edge of the bed, softly humming to Rashellia, who was sucking blood sleepily from Lara's arm. "Come here," Lara whispered calmly, trying not to get Rashellia excited. She patted a place on the bed beside her. I obediently went over to her, taking a seat and placing our drinks on the bedside table. "Do you still love me, Lance?" she asked nervously.

I responded instantly with a nod, giving her a kiss. I knew she was feeling insecure about our relationship. "Of course I do!" I told her firmly.

"Let me hear you say it," she begged, resting her head against my shoulder as we looked down at Rashellia.

"I love you, Lara," I whispered into her ear.

She smiled happily, knowing I wasn't just saying it. "Do you love her?" she asked, nodding at Rashellia.

"You know I do," I replied. "She means the world to me."

Lara smiled contentedly, slipping the now-sleeping Rashellia into my arms and observing me as I held her cautiously. "She's not a bomb," Lara whispered patiently, rearranging my hands to support her body and head. "This is how you hold her, okay?"

I nodded nervously. "I'm sorry; I'm terrible at this," I admitted unhappily as I rocked Rashellia back and forth. She purred contentedly in her sleep.

"Don't be sorry. You'll get the hang of it. It just takes time, that's all," she whispered supportively. She snuggled closer to me as we stared down at our child.

"She's so tiny that I'm afraid I'll drop her or something," I whispered a few moments later, breaking the tranquil silence surrounding us.

"You're doing fine," she whispered encouragingly.

"Lies. I'm a horrible father, aren't I?"

"Hey, I don't ever want to hear you say that again!" Lara said softly, taking her hand and turning my head to look me in the eyes for the first time in a long time. "You're not a horrible father, Lance. A horrible father would have left me and Rashellia and never come back." She gave me a light kiss.

"But I did leave you," I whispered guiltily, returning her kiss with a soft peck on her neck.

"No, you went to get firewood to keep me and the baby warm, silly," she whispered in an attempt to ease my guilt.

"Yeah, right. You and I both know that I got scared and bailed on you when you needed me the most," I muttered, embarrassed.

"I don't care, Lance. I love you, you love me, and we both love Rashellia. That's all that matters." Lara gave me another reassuring kiss. "Why don't you tuck her in so we can spend some quality Lance-and-Lara time?" she whispered playfully, beginning to take off her shirt.

I nodded happily, and we both gave her a kiss on the forehead, being careful not to wake her up. We tucked her into her crib, gently bringing the blanket to her neck while placing one of her teddy bears next to her. Lara's eyes flashed yellow for a second, as she turned off the lights. She smiled at me and took off the rest of her clothes. Then she gave me a kiss and led me to the bed, where we cuddled with one another affectionately.

The moonlight gently floated in, partially illuminating Lara's face, as I softly slid my hand along her waist and wrapped my arms around her. She giggled, rubbing her nose against mine, lovingly. "I don't want you to feel guilty anymore for what happened, Lance. I'm just as responsible as you are. I knew you weren't ready, but I took the pills anyway and got myself pregnant, without even talking to you about it," she whispered softly.

"But—" I began.

She placed her finger against my lips with a gentle smile. "Who sat up every night rubbing lotion on my body so that I wouldn't get stretch marks?" she asked.

"Me," I replied.

"Who would gently sing to the baby and read to her every night while I was pregnant?" she asked.

"Me," I answered again.

"Who almost died trying to save her?" she asked.

"Me," I replied with a smile.

Lara got a bit choked up, and a single tear gently slid down her cheek. "That's right. It was you," she whispered, stroking my hair. I could see that she knew I was on the verge of tears as well, as she smiled joyfully. "You're the best father … husband … friend that a fiend like me could ever ask for."

I gently stroked her back while slowly working my hand along her body, down past her waist. She giggled softly, giving me a playful slap. "Same old Lance," she joked, kissing my chest affectionately.

"Same saggy Lara," I retorted with a laugh.

"Hey! That's it—no sex for you tonight," she threatened playfully.

I laughed, kind of relieved, not wanting to do it while I had my child in the same room anyway. I stroked her gently for an hour or so as we chatted casually to one another, which was rare. There were usually so many things about each other that we hid, resulting in our never actually having many heart-to-heart conversations in our relationship.

"So what did you want to be before the war?" she asked me, while propping herself up on my chest, making sure not to put pressure on my wound.

"Um, I don't know," I lied, looking away sheepishly.

"Come on, Lance. I won't laugh," she promised.

"An astronaut," I told her, and I wondered if my silly grin covered my entire face.

She burst out laughing, burying her face in my chest. She continued laughing so hard that tears began streaming down her beautiful face.

"Hey, you promised you wouldn't laugh!" I objected, giving her a playful shove.

"So why … ha-ha … why did you want to be an astronaut?" she asked me, trying to stifle her laughter as she composed herself.

I shrugged in embarrassment, thinking about the question. "I was always fascinated as a kid by the stars and the different planets. I wanted to one day go into space and just see for myself the other worlds. I heard that scientists were landing on plants like Mars and Venus and getting closer and closer to finding life on another planet." I paused for a moment with a smirk and then said, "I didn't know at that time that the creatures would end up coming to me."

The same smirk spread across her face, and I gave her a kiss. She lay on top of me, purring contentedly to herself. "Well, is this what you expected?" she asked, holding her hands out on either side, allowing her claws to rip through her fingertips. She flashed her eyes red with a smile that was sort of transformed by her razor-sharp teeth and gave me a playful wink.

"Not really," I told her with a laugh.

She turned back to her normal self, saying, "I find it funny how you're no longer scared of my transforming." She giggled, pausing to stroke my hair lovingly. "When we first met, you used to be so nervous around me. Now it doesn't even seem to faze you."

I laughed. "I know you would never hurt me."

She smiled and kissed me. "Always remember that, Lance," she whispered as the silence of the night surrounded us.

We lay there staring at the ceiling as the light of the moon spilled through the window. The dull sound of gunfire was mysteriously absent from the night air.

Chapter 20

Lara and I only got a few hours sleep that night. Rashellia's whimpering woke us periodically throughout the night, and Lara would get up to attend to her. Rashellia hated being alone, so this apparently was her way of getting our attention.

Sleepily, I got up to join Lara, glancing in the crib where Rashellia was on all fours, ripping apart her pillow with her tiny teeth. She had sprouted her little wings, which protruded from her back. Her attitude strengthened more aggressively as she bit deeper into the pillow, thrashing it all around and sending feathers flying all over the place.

I couldn't help giggling, which diverted Rashellia's attention from the poor pillow to us. She glanced up at me, growling playfully. I saw the bones in Lara's hand shifting, accompanied with the dull cracking noises as she carefully placed her fiend paw in play-fighting with Rashellia.

Rashellia rolled over onto her back in a defensive position, beginning to flail her little paws wildly, protecting her tummy as Lara tried to tickle it. Rashellia soon got tired, and her human skin reformed over the scaly, hard skin as she settled down into her new pillow, tuckered out from the play-fight with Lara. Lara placed my hand against Rashellia's chest, gently feeling her heart.

There was no heartbeat. "Aw, you're an immortal, just like your mommy," I told her.

Lara changed her hand back, gently tickling Rashellia under her chin.

The baby responded with a sleepy yawn as she fought to stay awake, her head bobbing uncontrollably. Lara and I giggled, staring down at her.

"Good night, sweetie," we both whispered, kissing her head affectionately as she drifted off, giving us a few more hours of sleep.

I heard Lara get up a few hours later and silently get dressed. A moment later, I heard her bustling around in the kitchen, probably getting breakfast on-the-go for me. She really was a great wife; I don't think I could have ever asked for anyone better. I lay in bed lazily for another ten or twenty minutes, until the delicious smells of breakfast slowly drifted into our room.

I got up and went over to Rashellia's crib—she was snoozing contentedly. "Rashellia," I whispered cautiously, giving her a light shake. I didn't want to spook her and have her rip apart my arm or something. She opened her little eyes a second later, yawning and wiping at her eyes with her tiny paw.

"Hey, sweetie, how's my little buddy doing today?" I asked her.

She purred happily, squirming around in her crib and begging for me to pick her up.

"Hey, Daddy," Lara called to me as I emerged through the bedroom door a moment later, cradling Rashellia. The baby's arms instantly shot out toward her mommy, excitedly.

"Hey, Mommy. I think someone's hungry," I told her in a babyish voice, handing Rashellia over to her. I sat down at the table, where Lara had already served us breakfast. I glanced up from my food to see Lara taking off her shirt and bra to feed Rashellia. "Do you have to do that here, buddy?" I asked her with a nervous laugh.

Lara glanced over at me with one of her warning glares. "She needs to eat, Lance."

"Yeah, but why not just do it after breakfast, in our room or something?" I asked her cautiously, knowing this conversation would probably lead to a fight.

"Fine! God forbid I disturb you from your busy schedule," she snarled, getting up from the table and storming away with Rashellia. She slammed the door to our room behind her.

I sighed unhappily. I had a feeling that Lara was on her tricnoses, as I heard her muttering profanity to herself in the other room while she fed Rashellia. The rustling of a crib a few moments later indicated Rashellia being tucked in, soon accompanied by profanity. The door swung open violently as Lara stormed through the living room and over to the sink, where I was washing our dishes nervously.

She seemed about to say something, but instead, she sat down at the table and angrily began to eat. I knew she was in the mood for a fight, and I think she knew that too, but I was determined not to give it to her. I walked over to the table, buttered two pieces of toast, and poured her a glass of bag blood and then set it all down beside her plate of eggs. She glared at me, but I just avoided her stare and walked back to the kitchen.

"*Bon appétit,*" I called cheerfully over my shoulder.

"So you're just going to ignore the fact that I'm mad? Huh, Lance? Is that the game we're going to play today?" She teleported to my side and her eyes flashed, turning blood red, to show me she wasn't playing around.

"You're not mad," I whispered gently.

She grabbed me by the collar of my shirt and pinned me up against the counter with her fiend strength. "*Don't tell me how I feel!*" she screamed at me, angrily grabbing the plate I had just washed and smashing it against the counter.

"This isn't you; it's your tricnoses," I reminded her, turning my back to her to finish off the remaining dishes. I pretended that I wasn't scared of what she could do to me, but inside, I was frozen solid by the grip of fear. "You're not going to attack your husband while he has his back turned to you, are you, Lara?" I called over my shoulder.

I heard her angrily breathing behind me, trying to calm herself down. "Turn around then," she grunted threateningly.

I ignored her, knowing if I challenged her, it would be the end of me. I almost jumped out of my skin in fright as I felt her hands wrap around my waist. To my surprise, she gripped me in a hug, standing there a moment in silence.

"I'm sorry, Lance. You're right. This isn't me. I'm acting so foolishly," she whispered apologetically, having a brief, clear moment as she seemed to realize what was going on. Tears trickled down her face for no reason as she left my side and sat down to eat.

I finished the dishes and then carefully pulled a chair up beside her. "What's wrong?" I asked comfortingly, patting her shoulders.

"Nothing. Just the usually tricnoses stuff. I hate it," she whispered to me, rubbing her stomach unhappily as she gloomily ate her eggs. "Great, now my eggs are wet," she muttered unhappily, sniffling with a hiccup in between every few words.

"You're a real mess today, eh?" I asked her with a laugh.

She looked up from her food and began to giggle to herself, even as she sobbed uncontrollably. She nodded her head in embarrassment as she buried her face in my T-shirt, getting it sopping wet. "I hate tricnoses so much," she whispered unhappily in between sniffles.

"Don't worry; you're not the only one," I muttered while patting her reassuringly.

"You could always get me pregnant again. Then we won't have to deal with it for another ten months or so," she joked.

"Yeah, I think I'll take a rain check on that idea," I snickered. "Time to pull yourself together. We have a baby to look after," I reminded her, leaning my head against hers affectionately as she purred softly.

Lara nodded in agreement, wiping away a tear. She finished eating and then helped me with her dishes. "I'll cancel our day with the others. We can do it some other time," I told her as we dried the last plate and placed it in the cupboard.

"No, that's nonsense. You go have fun with them. I'll stay here and do some work around the house. I need to clean up this pigsty anyway. Bring them by tonight," she proposed, "and we'll all eat supper together." She gave me a hug before heading toward our room to lie down.

"Are you sure, buddy?" I asked, following her to the bedroom.

"Of course. Go have fun," she replied firmly.

I tucked her in, momentarily leaving her side to give Rashellia a light peck on her forehead. "All right. Well, I hope you and Rashellia have a good time together. Eating popcorn and chilling at the movies is no fun anyway," I teased her.

She laughed, throwing her pillow at me as I left. "You're sleeping on the floor tonight!" she called after me.

I laughed, quickly making my escape into the hall. I glanced up and down, wondering where to go. I had never been in this city before; all I knew was that I was supposed to meet everyone at the movie theater. It took me about half an hour to finally find it. I showed up just in time. "Eh! Better late than never, huh?" Grant called to me as the group spotted me.

"Ha-ha. Shut up. I've never been here before," I told him, giving him a playful punch.

"I got your ticket already," Tina told me, welcoming me with a hug.

"Perfect, thanks. Sorry, guys, for being late," I told them. "David, where's Carana?"

"She's sick," he told me and then winked.

I nodded knowingly. "So is Lara."

He laughed sympathetically, as Grant and Tina wondered what the secret joke was. The movie was brutally bad, so we ended up leaving early and heading down to the pool hall. We played a few games—Grant and I destroyed Tina and David.

"Nice games," Grant said, gloating over our three victories in a row.

"I was just warming up. We'll get you next time," David responded, and Tina nodded in agreement.

We walked along the hall, passing right by my place by accident. "Geesh, the poor guy doesn't even know where he lives," Grant joked.

"You sure you didn't get a permanent concussion from that artillery?" David asked me playfully.

"You're about to get a permanent concussion if you don't stop talking," I threatened him with a smirk.

We all laughed as we entered my place. We must have spooked Lara, because she dropped her glass as we came in. It shattered into a million pieces and spilled its contents all over. I glanced in surprise at Carana, who was staring at the six of us.

"Is that blood?" Tina asked nervously. She and Grant backed up to the door cautiously, thinking Lara and Carana were going to attack us or something.

Lara smiled awkwardly. "Oh, hey guys. We didn't expect you here so early. Sorry about the mess. Don't worry about it."

Carana got up to stand at Lara's side with the same friendly smile.

"Don't worry, guys," I said. "They're safe. I'll explain it to you later."

Grant and Tina relaxed a bit and stood next to David and me. Lara flicked her wrist, and her eyes flashed green, which instantly cleaned the blood and glass off the floor—it seemed to vanish into thin air. She smiled, quickly turning on her heels and bustling away with Carana into our room.

"I'm so sorry. I didn't think you would be coming home this early!" Lara explained to me, embarrassed.

"It's fine. Grant and Tina were just a little spooked, that's all. Are you okay? It looked like you bled a lot."

"Yes, I'm fine. Carana and I will be out in a minute," she told me, going silent in my head.

The rest of the gang and I sat down around the television. David and I explained to the other two what tricnoses was. Lara and Carana came out of the bedroom a moment later, just as we were wrapping up the awkward conversation. Lara flopped down onto the recliner on top of me, cuddling affectionately. Carana did the same to David, who looked at her in surprise.

"Someone's in a good mood today," Grant said to David.

"Leave them alone," Lara warned him gently. She purred softly, giving me a light nip on my neck.

"What's up?" I asked her.

"Nothing. I just want to cuddle with my man. I missed you today," she whispered, casting a spell to warm up my cold hands.

"Same here. I've just never seen you so happy during your tricnoses," I laughed.

"Well, there's a first for everything." She giggled happily.

"You've gotten a lot better at pool since the last time we played," Grant told me, interrupting the little conversation Lara and I were having.

"I had a pro to practice with," I told him, nodding at Lara.

"You guys played pool today?" she asked, patting my shoulder.

"Who won?" Carana asked.

"Lance and Grant cleaned our clocks, three games in a row," Tina complained.

David let out a defeated sigh, his arms crossed in front of his chest. "We will get them next time," he promised Tina.

"We went to a movie as well," I added.

"Was it any good?" Lara asked.

"Nah, why do you think we're here so early?" I joked.

The rest laughed in agreement.

"So what's for supper?" Tina asked impatiently as we moved from the living room to the dinner table. She unfolded her napkin and placed it on her lap, glancing around hungrily.

"Turkey," Lara replied, using her powers to make the oven door swing open and bring the turkey floating across the room to our table.

All in all, we ended up having a pretty good evening. Lara and I destroyed them at a board game called Ramoli. It felt so good to be playing with her again, like a little kid.

Ever since we had Rashellia, our relationship had kind of been up in the air. We hadn't really had the freedom to do whatever we wanted to do. As a matter of fact, we barely had fun doing activities together anymore, so it was nice to see a smile on her face that was genuine. She sat on my lap, purring, while the others packed up the board game and got ready to leave. Tina and Grant were tired and departed together a short time later.

"I think your sister is getting a little crush on Grant," David said with a sly grin.

"Shut up," I laughed, having already noticed the developing connection between the two of them.

"Hey, would you two mind taking care of Rashellia tonight?" Lara asked David and Carana. Carana nodded instantly, winking to Lara. David and I glanced at each other, confused. "Is that okay with you, David?" Lara asked.

"Yeah, sure," he replied with a dumbfounded look on his face.

"It's good for Rashellia to spend some time with her guardian parents," Lara said as she retrieved Rashellia and brought her out to the living room.

She gently placed the baby in David's nervous hands, laughing as he held her nervously. Rashellia yawned sleepily as she woke up and looked around, soaking in the sights of the room.

"Are guys always nervous when it comes to holding babies?" Carana asked, showing David how to hold Rashellia the proper way.

"Yes," we both replied in agreement.

The girls laughed. "She's in a good mood today," I told David, tickling Rashellia's belly, who responded with her happy-baby gurgles and squirmed around energetically in David's arms.

"We should probably give Lance and Lara some time alone," Carana told David after we chatted for ten minutes or so.

David nodded, carefully handing the baby to Carana as he got up.

Once Carana and David left to go back to their place, I asked Lara, "So what's up? Why did you ask them to take care of Rashellia?"

"I wanted to spend some time together. I have a surprise for you." She kissed my cheek and grabbed my hand, leading me into the hall and locking the door behind us. We headed down the abandoned hallway toward the main gate. "I heard you and David explaining to Grant and Tina about tricnoses, by the way," Lara told me, giggling playfully.

I was kind of embarrassed. "Well, they didn't know what it was," I said bashfully.

"Don't be embarrassed. You guys sounded like professionals." She paused and then added with a laugh, "It was kind of cute."

"So where are we going?" I asked as we jogged along the silent corridor, with the echo of our footsteps chasing behind us.

"Hurry up, silly, or were going to miss it!" she told me, ignoring my question. We came to an abrupt halt at the gate and shuffled through our wallets to show the guards our identification cards. They nodded us through, and we trudged through the snow into the woods.

"I don't even have a jacket," I complained.

She ignored me as we waded deeper and deeper into the woods. "Aw, suck it up, muffin." She started to take off her clothes, throwing them over to me.

"I'm not having sex with you in a snowbank!" I told her.

She laughed, beginning to transform into her fiend form. I saw the muscles in her body changing and bones growing and shrinking as she slowly transformed. With a sickening crack of her backbone, it was complete. She allowed the sheer power of her fiend's wild side to briefly take over. She let out a ferocious roar, standing on her hind legs, before slamming back down to the ground and sending snow flying everywhere. I backed up a couple paces, and she took a step toward me, peacefully bowing her head to me. *"Why are you so scared, buddy?"* she asked me, lying down in the snowbank and watching me with her beady eyes.

"I'm not scared," I lied to her, speaking out loud with a nervous laugh.

She playfully gave me a gentle tap with her enormous paw, sending me tumbling face first into the freshly fallen snow. I retaliated with a perfectly aimed snowball straight to her muzzle, realizing as it sailed through the air how bad of an idea it was. I saw the fiend anger rise up in her, wanting to kill me, as she jumped to her feet, but she quickly doused the fiend's instincts and sat back down on the ground, letting me climb onto her back.

"Sorry about that, Lance. Keep in mind I'm still on my tricnoses, so let's take it easy, okay?" she suggested.

"Sounds good," I replied, relieved that she didn't lose it on me.

Once I got my tiny little hands wrapped around her enormous neck, she leapt into the air and took off into the starless sky. The cold air felt so good against my face as she flew along the tree line at a gentle pace. She caught a thermal and glided toward the shoreline, searching for a suitable place for us to spend the night. Slowly, she descended along the side of the cliff and landed in a small cave overlooking the ocean below.

As we settled down inside the cave, the sky began to light up with red, blue, and green lights. Streaks of them exploded up from all around us, exiting the earth's atmosphere. As if on command, the stars suddenly came to life above us, seemingly dancing in the air. I propped myself up on Lara's shoulders, staring at the sky, transfixed by the flashing lights, which reminded me of a fireworks display.

Occasionally, a rumbling sound would erupt around us, which sounded similar to thunder. *"It's beautiful, isn't it?"* Lara asked. She lay down on the floor of the cave and let her fur absorb the dampness of the wet ground, while heating me up with her body warmth.

"Yes, it is. Thank you for taking me out here." The awe in my voice seemed to surprise her. *"What is this?"*

"Draphila."

"What's Draphila?" I asked, confused.

"When a fiend dies, its soul wanders the earth, lost in constant sorrow until Lord Dracona comes to collect all the lost souls to guide them to my homeland, Fraturna. It's basically a repatriation for all the fiends that were killed in the war, which happens once a month," she explained.

I gently slid off her back and sat down in between her paws, watching the sky as if in a trance. It was weird how once she explained this to me, I actually felt kind of sorry for the fiends that lost their lives here on earth, even though they were my enemies. I glanced down at the ocean, where slowly flashing blue light started to appear around the surface of the water.

"What's that?" I asked, pointing toward the sea, as the creatures emitting the light shadows could be faintly seen in the depths.

"Those are shellians. They are aquatic creatures who are at war with us. We once lived in peace with them on Fraturna, but once the war against the reliks began, they saw the opportunity to become stronger and declared their allegiance to them, leaving us to be slaughtered."

"Why would they come to the surface, then, and make themselves a target?" I asked, confused as I watched the creatures swim around in the depths below.

"They do that to taunt Lord Dracona. They're basically laughing at all the dead fiends." A hint of bitterness was noticeably present in her voice.

A few moments later, the area around us returned to normal, as the last of the souls escaped the earth's surface. Lara shook the water off her fur like a dog would, and she glanced apologetically at my now-drenched body. She cast a spell, instantly melting all the snow around us, drying it off and trapping the heat inside the cave, while lighting a small fire that flickered happily.

She then transformed to normal, motioning for me to lie down beside her. "So Lord Dracona is like your God?" I asked as I snuggled beside Lara's naked body, keeping her warm.

She nodded and allowed me to ask a few more questions, which was rare for her. She usually didn't talk about her culture unless I broke some rule.

"Do you ever miss your home planet?" I asked a bit more seriously.

She lay her head against my chest, listening to the dull thumping of my heart. "Not really."

"Why not?" I was taken by surprise to her response.

"Feel my heart." She took my hand and placed it against her chest.

"You have no pulse," I responded after a minute or two of silence.

"Immortals have no pulse because they can't die, Lance," she told me dully. "I've been alive for hundreds of years, and you're the first good thing that's ever come around in my life. I'm a monster, and I hate it. I wish I could just be normal like you humans and not have these constant urges to kill and drink blood." She stared gloomily at the ceiling of the cave.

"You're not a monster," I whispered, stroking her hair and giving her an affectionate peck on her cheek.

"I have a question for you, Lance," she muttered, abruptly cutting me off as I was about to speak.

"I have an answer," I replied, making her laugh. "So what is it?"

"When you look through the scope of your sniper and see the faces of your enemies, what would flash through your mind?" She cuddled a little more closely, staring into my eyes to see if I was lying. "No bullshit, either. I want the straight-up truth." She'd spotted that I was scrambling to think of an answer that would please her. "I promise I won't be mad." She assured me.

"Well …" I began, grinding my teeth nervously as my mind raced for an answer. "I guess right before I pulled the trigger I would tell myself that if I was on the other end of the stick, they would do the same thing to me." Then I turned the tables on her unexpectedly, asking, "What about you?"

"Huh?" She looked shocked.

"How did you justify to yourself that what you were doing here was right?" I asked impatiently.

"That's kind of personal," she shot back, ignoring my hopeful stare.

"That's basically the question that you just made me answer!" I protested.

She tossed me a warning glare to shut up. I let out an irritated sigh and removed my hand from her waist—I wanted her to feel guilty, knowing she had betrayed my trust by making me answer a question that she couldn't.

"Lance?" she said gently.

"Hmm?"

"Want to know the difference between a coward and a soldier?" she asked.

"What?"

"Before I would rip their hearts out, one would scream for help, while the other one would just accept his fate in silence." She looked away from me in shame.

"There's no right or wrong in war," I replied slowly. I began to comfort her by stroking her gently.

Lightning streaked across the sky as a heavy rain poured down outside against the cliff where we were taking shelter. "Should we go take Rashellia off Carana and David's hands?" I asked, trying to lighten the mood.

She sniffed and wiped her eyes. "Yeah, we should probably go spend some time with the little rascal." She got herself back into her happy, energetic, teenage-girl mood.

"So what's next, if this city is attacked?" I asked as we lazily dangled our feet off the edge of the cliff.

She shrugged. "I don't know. This is the last city open to the public."

"So basically, we're screwed?" I asked with a laugh.

She nodded.

"We could probably get shelter by the resistance," I reassured her after a moment of silence.

She didn't look too pleased with my idea, but she pretended she was to satisfy me. "Yeah, I suppose, if that's our final option." She stood up, starting to transform again. "Are you ready to go?"

I nodded as her rib cage expanded, ripping through her human skin. A moment later, the transformation was complete. I shuffled onto her back as she waited patiently, and then she let out her triumphant roar as we sped away from our shelter and soared into the sky.

Chapter 21

L ara flew along the coastline slower than usual, letting me absorb the sights of the towering cliffs. I took my hands from around her neck and spread my arms out, as if I was flying. I could hear her purring happily as we flew through the gentle night breeze. The soft pounding of the rain against our bodies was ever present as we began our ascent to Brawklin City.

It really was too good to be true, though, and like all good things, it had to come to a crashing end. It all happened so fast—a shot rang out and I felt it whiz by my head. Before I could get a grip on Lara, she let out a ferocious roar and took off toward the cliff's edge. A lone soldier standing at the top of the cliff was armed with a rifle, and he took aim at us. "*Stop!*" I yelled in a panic, but it was too late.

I was thrown off Lara's back and smashed through the surface of the ocean below. It was freezing cold. I struggled to the surface, yelling for help. Lara swooped down. I felt her claws dig into my arm as I started to succumb to the water's icy grasp. I felt my body momentarily lifted from the surface as she struggled to fly away, and then, with a sick plop, I fell back in, sinking deeper into the depths of the sea.

"Lance, swim! You need to come to me!" she begged me in my head.

I tried to move my arms, but I had no more energy left. I felt myself drifting off into unconsciousness from the lack of oxygen. My scar burned bright red, bringing me briefly back into consciousness. It was like a dream as I slowly sank to the ocean floor. A creature looking like a cross between a shark, eel, and dragon slowly swam toward my body. I sucked in my final gasp for air but filled my lungs with water. The creature's beady eyes watched me as I slowly died, twisting violently for air.

The next thing I knew, it transformed into a human-like creature, with webbed feet and hands, elf-like ears, sparkling green eyes, and ghostly pale skin. It was so beautiful; it had long, silverish-white hair that gently swayed back and forth with the current. It sang gently as it swam toward me. Its voice seemed to echo around me, and I stopped struggling. I fell into a trance from the creature's beauty.

She kissed me suddenly, allowing me to breathe underwater, cheating death by a fraction of a second.

"Lance … Lance, please!" I heard Lara's cry in my head.

I tried to respond, but it just came out in a mess of sound. As I heard it in my own head, it made me grab my ears in pain—it erupted into a mixed scream that echoed all around. The creature grabbed me roughly, dragging me to the depths, as I struggled against it, trying to fight my way back up to the surface. I looked above as Lara's elegant fiend body dove into the water. She spotted the two of us as the creature clamped steel shoes onto my feet.

"Thank God you're alive," her relieved voice rang out inside my head. *"It's a shellian. It won't hurt you. You're not at war with it,"* Lara reassured me. *"But it must be blocking your thoughts from reaching me. Don't worry; I'll figure something out, Lance."*

I looked up as she spread her elegant wings in the water and then broke through the surface, flying away. The shellian's smile seemed to comfort me momentarily, as she pointed at my feet. "Does that hurt?" she asked, speaking to me for the first time.

I shook my head. She smiled again. I realized that the shoes were to prevent me from swimming away by anchoring me to the ocean floor, where I could walk around freely.

The shellian cast what appeared to be a spell on my shivering body, making the cold water seem warm to me. "You do not need to be afraid of me, human. I'm your friend." She comforted me, motioning for me to follow her.

I really did not have a choice in the matter. "Thanks for saving me," I told her, surprised that I could talk under the water.

"No problem," she replied as we walked along the bumpy ocean floor's terrain.

I looked around in amazement as schools of fish peacefully swam by, along with other aquatic creatures poking in and out of a coral reef we were passing. "If you could just swim me up to the surface, my friend can take me home," I told her hopefully.

She let out a laugh, crushing what little hope I had of a painless escape from my underwater prison. "Once you're in shellian territory, you're not allowed to leave," she explained to me, ignoring my protests of displeasure. "The first shellian to find you automatically earns rights to keep you as his or her own."

I unhappily went silent for a few minutes. We continued walking along the ocean's floor for what seemed like hours. "I fell—I didn't mean to invade your territory. I would never purposely invade your territory. I was attacked," I objected.

She ignored my plea. "I saw you with that fiend. Stuff like that should never be tolerated between a fiend and a human," she told me passionately.

I didn't say anything, so she flicked her fingers, and the soldier that was on the cliff appeared beside her, smiling over to me. I realized it was a hologram. It then vanished, and the shellian glanced over to me with a devilish grin. "You set me up to fall!" I blurted out angrily, as the realization of what just happened hit me.

"You should be thanking me; I saved you from getting killed by that fiend," she told me. We appeared to be in what looked like a shellian's version of a city, which was clumps of mud, forming igloo-like shapes beside one another.

"She loves me! She wouldn't hurt me!" I told the shellian angrily.

"Sure, she loves you now, but believe me, one day she will snap, and that will be the end of you," she debated convincingly. "Don't worry; you and I will have a swell time together." She broke out laughing at her own joke. I looked at her, unamused. "Get it?" she asked. "A swell time." She continuing to laugh. "As in an ocean swell?" I looked at her, a blank expression on my face. "I guess you're not in the joking mood today, hey," she muttered.

We walked up a rocky hill, stopping at the foot of a rocky cave. "Home sweet home," she told me fondly, staring at it. I glanced from the hill down to the little Shellian village below, realizing she had a pretty mint piece of real estate compared to the others.

"Nice view," I muttered, following her into the cave.

"It comes with being the daughter of a king," she said snobbishly. She cast a spell, and all the water rushed out of the underwater cave, forming a wall of water at the foot of the cave, kind of like a window that I could see through into the ocean. "What's your name?" she asked, sitting me down on a rock by what appeared to be a stone table.

"Lance."

"I'm Fiona, daughter of Lord Olaf, commander in this region of the Atlantic Ocean." She extended her webbed hand for me to shake.

I shook her hand, debating with myself whether this shellian was my enemy or a very valuable ally. I stared into her bright green eyes for a second. She smiled, so I decided to give her a light smile back.

"Well, since you're my guest, I'll let you decide what we eat tonight—fish and seaweed or shark and seaweed?"

"Hmm, it's a hard decision. Can I have a second to think about it?" I muttered, leaning against the table in thought.

"Fine. Fish and seaweed it is, smart-ass," she shot back. Her temper flared up a bit as she leaned over and kissed me and then pushed me away aggressively. "I just took away your ability to breathe underwater, so good luck escaping while I'm gone," she told me angrily before diving into the wall of water, transforming into her dragonish-eel form and swiftly swimming away.

I looked around the small rocky enclosure that she called home. It was damp and wet. The rocky surface was rough, and the sound of my steel shoes sliding along the floor was sickening, almost to the point of being unbearable. Fiona returned about twenty minutes later with a huge blue marlin in her mouth. She spat it out onto the floor of the cave, transforming to her elfish form before stepping inside the cave.

"Do you have a fishing permit for that?" I asked, trying to make a joke.

She smiled as she transformed her right arm into a huge blade, ignoring me as she began slashing through the giant fish, squirting blood all over both of us and the rest of the cave. Once Fiona had finished, she threw a slab of meat onto one side of the stone table. She lit a small fire on the floor with a snap of her fingers, which she used to cook mine, handing it across the table to me once it was done. "Eat," she ordered me, sitting down on her end of the table and devouring the large chunk of raw meat she had cut for herself.

"We shellians are the superior race," she said to her food, startling me. She looked at me for a second and then began ranting on about how the shellians would one day take over the world. "Sure, right now we are letting the fiends demolish the humans, but once they have gained control of the humans, we will strike and wipe out anyone who opposes us, gaining control of both races and finally having our own world order."

"What do you need us for?" I asked.

"Breeding, of course," she said, as if I had just asked the world's dumbest question. "For every male shellian, there are twenty females. Since only one female can be bound to him, the population grows at a very slow rate. With humans mixed into our culture, we would be able to stay out in the sun, becoming both an aquatic and land animal, while our population would also grow at an alarming rate, compared to the fiends." Pure passion filled her voice.

"So what do fiends gain from controlling the world?" I asked casually as I finished off the rest of the marlin on the table. I couldn't help being a little bit interested by what Fiona was telling me.

She glanced over at me, I guess a bit surprised that I was actually freely asking questions. "Well, um ..." She thought for a moment and then said, "They would be able to easily harvest human blood, which is the purest form of blood you can get. It helps normal fiends live past their average life span. If they were to successfully breed with a human, then the offspring would be immune to all diseases, be able to suppress the mood swings fiends suffer from, and would be calmer and more effective in combat."

She paused for a moment again and then adopted a more serious tone. "Basically, a half-blood would be the superior fighting machine. Legend has it that all fiends are born with hidden powers that they can't access, but a half-blood can grow up and unleash these devastating powers, which are basically equivalent to what you humans would call a nuclear bomb. That will never happen, though. We will take over before they figure out how to breed."

"You're too late."

"Huh?" she said, confused.

"I said, you're too late. I had a baby with Lara. She was born about two months ago," I told her with a chuckle.

Silence enveloped the room as she stared at me in disbelief. "You're lying!" She got up and paced back and forth.

"Special pills were made for us, and Lara got pregnant a year ago," I continued, ignoring her accusation.

"That's impossible!" she yelled at me, with a flustered look on her face. "Go to bed," she told me quietly.

For the first time, I could see fear in her eyes. I lay down on the hard, damp, rocky surface of the cave, obediently falling asleep a couple moments later, exhausted from the day. Fiona rudely awakened me a short time later. She was on top of me, with her hand against my forehead.

"What the heck!" I exclaimed. I tried to get up but was forcefully pushed back down.

"So it's true," she whispered, staring at me in disbelief.

"Yes," I replied, simply trying to match her tone.

"Why would you have a baby with another species?" she asked.

I shrugged. "She raped me," I told her after a moment.

"Yes, but you're still with her?" she asked, keeping me pinned to the ground.

I nodded, trying to shift her weight to one side of my body. "I love her very much."

"Where do you live?" she asked, maintaining eye contact with me—I suppose it was to see if I was lying or not.

"Brawklin City."

"That's one of those mixed experimental cities the fiends have built, right?"

I nodded.

"I've decided to let you go. You're no threat to me or my species," Fiona told me.

I nearly jumped with joy as excitement spread across my face.

"On one condition," she added.

"What?" I asked her skeptically.

"You come to visit me," she said sincerely. "I won't hurt you. I just want to talk. It gets lonely down here."

"I will," I lied to her. I kind of felt guilty, but I quickly wiped the guilt away as she kissed me, giving me the power to breathe underwater, before she walked me outside. An hour later, we were standing on the beach, waiting for Lara to come.

"Is your girlfriend an aggressive fiend?" she asked nervously, shifting around on her webbed feet and looking around anxiously.

"Not really, but you had me as a prisoner, so she might not be in the greatest mood." After a while, I could hear the whooshing sounds of a fiend's wings in the distance, which slowly got louder and louder as Lara approached us. I heard the roar of rage as she spotted us on the beach below. "Did you unblock my thoughts to her?" I asked Fiona.

She nodded.

"Lance! Hold on! I'll save you!" Lara's happy voice sounded in my head.

"Oh shit!" Fiona grunted, sprinting to the water as Lara swooped into a death-dive, aiming at her.

"No! Don't hurt her!" I yelled in my head.

To my relief, Lara obediently pulled out of the dive about twenty feet from Fiona's head and swooped around, landing by my side. Fiona picked herself up off the ground, trying to save some dignity as she casually walked over to us, wiping off the sand as she advanced. "What's your girlfriend's name?" she asked, stopping about ten feet away from us.

"Lara," I told her simply

"Girlfriend?" Lara asked in my head, letting out a low, threatening growl.

"She's my wife." I corrected Fiona quickly, before Lara decided to give me a smack over the head with one of her paws.

"I'm Fiona," she told Lara, bowing politely.

"Tell her that I'm grateful for her saving you," Lara told me.

"Lara says thanks for saving me," I said to Fiona. I left out the part to Lara about how Fiona had orchestrated it all, figuring it was for the best.

"Okay, well, it was nice meeting you guys. Good-bye," Fiona called, waving to me.

Lara took off, purposely covering Fiona with the beach sand just as she'd finished dusting off the last of it. I heard her chuckle as we soared up into the air. We looked down at Fiona before speeding off into the night sky toward Brawklin.

"Are you okay?" Lara asked me worriedly. As soon as we entered our small apartment in Brawklin she checked me thoroughly for any spells Fiona may have left on me.

"I'm fine. She wasn't violent at all. As a matter of fact, she was kind of nice, in her own way," I reassured Lara.

"Did she try to have sex with you?" Lara demanded forcefully.

"No. She had to kiss me, though, to let me breathe underwater," I told her truthfully.

"*What?*" Lara screamed, her eyes blazing red as she angrily knocked over a bookshelf. The noise woke Rashellia in the other room, who started bawling.

"It was that or death," I told her, trying to calm her down.

Lara angrily went to the door, as if she was going back out to find and kill Fiona. She paused, looking at me for a second, letting my words sink in. The sound of Rashellia's crying in the background seemed to trigger her motherly instincts, which washed away her rage. "Shhhh! Mommy's sorry for yelling," she called to Rashellia. She bustled over to her crib and picked her up, rocking her back and forth gently.

Lara and I took turns tickling Rashellia, and she made happy baby gurgles. "Want to say hi to Daddy?" Lara asked her in a babyish voice, handing her over to me.

I sat down on the edge of the bed, cradling her and supporting her the way Lara had taught me. Rashellia occasionally would cry and then start sucking her thumb a moment later as she calmed herself down. I glanced over at Lara, who was watching me affectionately.

"I don't get why she won't stop crying. I'm doing everything right," I told her, confused.

"I think she needs some personal Mommy time," Lara told me. She took off her T-shirt and motioned for me to hand over Rashellia.

Rashellia sucked on Lara's breasts happily, making a mess all over her chin, which I wiped off, noticing that some kind of yellowish fluid was dripping down her. "Ew, you're not feeding her milk?" I asked disgustedly, looking at the yellowish liquid that had stained the cloth.

"Of course not. I'm a fiend, not a human," Lara told me, as if I just asked a stupid question. "Don't worry; this stuff will help her to become a big, strong half-blood," she reassured me, realizing that she had snapped at me a bit roughly.

Rashellia fell asleep with a loud yawn almost instantly after she was finished eating. Lara gently placed her in the crib, and I tucked her in, while Lara put her stuffed bear close to her to play with in case she woke up. Lara and I both sat on the edge of the bed, exhausted from the long day.

She kept glancing over at my arm. I could tell she wanted to ask me something but was too embarrassed. "What?" I finally asked her.

She glanced at me and then tore her eyes away for the fifth time. "I'm thirsty," she told me timidly.

"Then go get a drink." I laughed.

She shook her head, seeming a little bit embarrassed. "Not that kind of thirsty, Lance."

"Oh …" I replied, looking down at my arm.

I glanced over at Lara, who was quivering like a crack addict as she stared at my arm. "Sure. Just be gentle," I told her, closing my eyes and holding out my left arm. I cringed in pain as I felt her fangs sink through my skin.

She began to suck blood from it, and to my relief, she cast a spell, numbing the pain, allowing me to relax as she sucked greedily on my arm. "All done, buddy. Thanks a lot," she said a minute or two later.

I opened one eye, timidly looking down at my arm, which was healed up to the point that I couldn't even tell it had been torn apart a second ago. Lara was quickly wiping the blood from her face. I watched as she cast a spell, taking the stain of blood instantly off our blankets.

"Sorry. I hate when I get those cravings," she told me.

"Don't worry about it. I never donated blood as a kid, so this is basically karma catching up with me," I joked.

She laughed, stripping down to her underwear, while I did the same, getting ready for bed. She flicked off the lights, and her eyes glowed in the dark. She checked my stomach wound to make sure it wasn't opening up or becoming infected. "I was worried about you when you were out there," she told me after she finished her checkup and sprawled herself across me to cuddle.

I felt her chest heave in and out as she slowly breathed. I gently rubbed her back, making her purr affectionately like a cat. "Something weird happened to me today," I told her.

"What?" she asked, toying with my hair.

"When I was drowning and I was about to die, my scar burned so badly that it felt like it was trying to rip out of my chest or something. It brought me back into consciousness for that split second. If it wasn't for that, I think I probably would have died," I said. "I should have been dead before Fiona reached me, but it was almost like that scar kept me alive just long enough for her to save me."

"Well, that scar connects us, so when I was freaking out, my emotions were probably so intense that I somehow transferred adrenaline to you, which the scar used slowly to try to keep you from dying." She toyed with my hair as if we were talking about a hockey game or something.

"Lara?" I asked.

"Lance?" she asked mockingly.

"Ha-ha, very funny, smart-ass," I muttered as she burst out laughing.

"What do you want?" she asked repositioning herself on top of me so she could stare down into my eyes.

"Is Rashellia the first half-blood ever born?" I asked.

Lara nodded cautiously, trying to figure out where this conversation was heading.

"Fiona warned me of Rashellia's growing up with these super-powers that could potentially be used in a negative way, instead of a positive way," I said, trying to avoid looking at her.

Lara burst out laughing. "That's only a myth made up by some old lady, probably. If anything, she will be less powerful than a fiend because she has a human as her father," Lara reassured me with a laugh, messing up my hair.

"Okay. I just wanted to make sure we weren't raising a mini Hitler," I replied with a laugh as we kissed goodnight.

Chapter 22

Life had been going well for the last three months. It was a beautiful day out. Lara and Tina were in the living room, cutting up some vegetables, as they watched me play-fight with Rashellia. I gave her a gentle push, and she plopped down on her butt with a surprised look at my unprovoked attack. She snarled at me, showing me her little dagger teeth in retaliation.

"What are you gonna do about it?" I taunted her. Her little wings expanded, and she stood up three feet off the ground on her hind legs. I poked her belly, and she fell back over onto her side with a surprised squeak.

"Play nice, Daddy," Lara scolded me, glancing up from the vegetables she was slicing.

"Hear that? Mom doesn't want me to beat you up too badly," I told Rashellia, who let out a tiny growl, attempting to bite my arm.

Lara said something in Jural to Rashellia, who obediently morphed from her fiend body back into her baby form. I diapered her and then got up to sit at the table with Lara and Tina. I helped to peel the vegetables while Rashellia explored the room. Occasionally, she would get into something she wasn't supposed to, making her happy baby noises.

We would all laugh, and Lara would retrieve her, scolding her gently in Jural. Things had become so calm that we were basically in a daily routine now, just doing normal day-to-day activities. I hadn't had to worry about fighting for months now, and I actually had a family, something I would have never thought possible in my life.

Lara had been in an unprecedented good mood for the past few months, even on her tricnoses days. Plus, she was letting me have sex with her again, now that everything was calm around the house. We weren't even having our tiny arguments that we used to have over silly nonsense.

I gave her my peeled vegetables, and she smiled thankfully, giving me a kiss, and then she followed Tina into the kitchen to get supper started. I grabbed Rashellia out of her box of teddy bears, where she had managed to crawl. She looked up at me with her innocent, sparkling blue eyes. I smiled, kissing her on the forehead.

"You ready to eat, buddy?" I asked her, even though I knew she didn't understand what I was saying. I strapped her to her high chair as Tina served us all vegetable soup. I ate it gratefully, occasionally dunking in a slice of bread. I glanced over at Lara, who was feeding Rashellia, occasionally cleaning up any soup spilling down her chin.

I wasn't able to feed her—my hand shook too much. Lara had told me it was just shell shock from the years of war, reassuring me that it would go away with time. Tina offered to look after Rashellia that night, which Lara and I gratefully accepted. We headed down to the pool, where we played some water volleyball against another couple, destroying them three games to zero.

"The last couple of months have been awesome, hey?" Lara asked, reaching for my hand as we walked across the busy street.

"Yeah, I actually feel like a teenager again," I told her with a laugh.

"Rashellia really likes you. You're doing a great job with her," Lara complimented me happily.

"How can you tell?"

"For a baby to play-fight, it's a sign of affection, and you and she are always play-fighting and spending time together, which is why you have such a great bond."

We entered the hall leading to our apartment. When we finally reached our room, we were pleased to see Tina relaxing on the couch, reading, having already put Rashellia to sleep. "Did you guys have fun?" Tina asked, grabbing her stuff.

Lara and I nodded, throwing our towels in a heap in the corner and flopping down on the couch. "We beat a group at water volleyball, three to zero," I told her with a smile.

"Awesome. Well, I'll see you guys tomorrow," she told us, reaching for the door as we said our good-byes.

I listened to Lara purr as she slept that night. I didn't know why; I wasn't trying to be a creeper or anything. It just felt so good to have someone that cared so much about me by my side. I just hadn't ever thought it would be someone like her.

The faint rumbles of artillery could be heard in the distance, constantly sending the reminder that there was a war still going on—a war between two species that maybe, if they got to know one another, could one day set aside their differences, just as Lara and I had done.

The last three months during the cease-fire between the fiends and humans had been the best days of my life, but tonight, the barrage of artillery fire sprang back to life once more as the cease-fire drew to an end. I got out of bed, cleaning my sniper carefully, inspecting every detail of it. I had killed so many fiends with it, and I knew I would kill so many more to protect the three most important girls in my life.

It made me sick to my stomach to know I would have to keep on killing to survive, which was really my only goal in the past year and a half. I let out a cry of rage, pushing the weapon away.

Lara had quietly gotten up out of bed and now sat down beside me. She took my shaky hands, placing them in her lap before pressing my head against her chest as she gently stroked my hair. "I thought we said no more fighting?" Lara whispered, slowly sliding the sniper along the carpet into the closet.

"When I die ... can you make sure Rashellia knows that I was a good father?" I asked her.

"I won't have to, because she's going to grow up to see it with her own two eyes," Lara replied gently. "You need to stop being so obsessed with this idea that you're not going to live. You're with me now. I would never let you die."

"I'm a soldier," I told her with a sense of passion in my voice.

"Yes, you are. No one can ever take that away from you," she told me gently.

"Soldiers were born to fight, and fighters were born to die," I whispered.

Silence enveloped the room. "Go to sleep, Lance. You'll feel better in the morning," she finally whispered.

I felt her stare pierce through me as my tears slowly stained her shirt. "Promise?" I sniffled, looking up at her.

"Promise," she repeated. Then I felt myself slowly drifting off as I finally succumbed to the warmth of her body.

I woke up the next morning in our bed. Lara must have moved me last night. She came into the room, smiling when she saw I was awake. I could smell bacon in the background as she stripped down to her underwear and bra and wordlessly flopped down on top of me.

"How's my man feeling?" she asked, cuddling against my chest as I stroked her hair.

"Good. I'm sorry about last night," I muttered, giving her a kiss.

"There's no need for you to be embarrassed about it. I know you males feel the need to hide your emotions, but I will never think any less of you for sharing your feelings with me, Lance. I'm your wife; you're supposed to let me in a little bit every now and then, silly." Lara paused as she readjusted herself, getting up on her knees and looking down at me.

"Okay, I'll try to be more open with you about stuff like that," I promised her.

"Thank you," she told me, lying back down and looking satisfied by my response.

As we lay there cuddling, I felt her stomach, which was growling unhappily. "Tricnoses?" I asked as I put my hand against her belly.

"Don't worry about it. I'll tell you later," she told me, kissing my neck and trying to shift my attention away from it.

"You just had your tricnoses, like, five days ago, and you've been having them every couple of days. What's up?" I asked.

She let out a sigh but ignored me as she got out of bed, attending to our breakfast in the kitchen without answering me. "Do you want them scrambled or over easy?" she called out.

"Scrambled," I answered.

She let out a groan, bending over the counter in pain, watching the eggs cook.

"So what's wrong? Are you sick?" I finally asked.

"Sit down, Lance," she ordered me moodily, pointing to my chair at the table.

"I can help you, buddy," I offered reassuringly, grabbing two plates out of the cabinet beside me.

"*Sit down!*" she screamed at me, unleashing one of her powers by accident.

The sound wave seemed to erupt all around me. It shattered the plates in my hands, knocking me to the ground. My ears were ringing, and Lara was instantly over to my side, quickly lifting my head. I could see her lips moving, but I couldn't hear anything.

I groaned, letting myself fall back down. Blood trickled from my ears, but Lara slid her hands gently along both my ears, healing them. "Can you hear me?" she asked worriedly, propping me up against the wall.

I nodded, stunned from the sound. After a minute or so of getting my senses back, I struggled to my feet and sat down at the table with my head in my arms, trying to block out the ringing in my ears. I felt a plate nudged against my elbow as Lara came with the food.

"Eat up, buddy. Your ears will feel better in a couple minutes," she reassured me. I felt her powers lift my head up, and then she let me take over. I straightened up in my chair, eating my eggs. "I'm sorry," she finally told me, leaning over to kiss my cheek, but I recoiled from her. "That's really mature, Lance."

I threw out the rest of my eggs and stormed into the bathroom, slamming the door behind me. A moment later, there was a timid knock. "Listen, Lance, I didn't do that on purpose. It just came out," she told me. There was a pause and then her voice crept through the door again. "Lance, I was reading in a book about how you humans like to camp, and I was thinking that you and Rashellia and I should go camping together.

It sounds fun, hey?" she asked, hoping I would talk to her. After another moment, she let out a frustrated sigh. "Lance, open this damn door!" she finally cried out, pounding on it viciously.

"It's unlocked, genius," I called out to her.

There was a pause and then the handle turned, and she opened the door. "I knew that," she giggled, pretending to be serious.

I tried to keep a straight face but couldn't; I burst out laughing. We apologized to each other for fighting and then agreed to take a little vacation. I slung the M4 over my shoulder, along with two bags for the camping trip.

Lara strapped Rashellia to her belly, carrying the backpack of ammunition and my faithful Timberwolf sniper rifle. I grabbed the backpack with the tent and food in it, and the three of us left our room and walked down the hall.

"Where are you guys going?" Tina asked, opening her door as we passed by her and Grant's room.

"Were heading out on a camping trip," I told her excitedly.

"Want us to take Rashellia?" Grant asked, poking his head around the corner.

"We figured we would give you guys a break from babysitting and just take her with us," Lara told them, leaning against the door frame.

"I'd go with you, but if I break this hand, I'm screwed," Tina told us with a laugh, holding up her mechanical hand.

"Come on, man. The least we can do is take care of Rashellia and let you guys have a little bit of personal time," Grant offered.

"I guess if you guys want her that badly, you can," Lara told them. She glanced at me with a shrug as she unstrapped Rashellia from her belly and handed her to Tina, who had her arms outstretched.

"When do you guys plan on coming back?" Tina asked, cradling Rashellia, who was staring up at her sleepily.

"Three days, tops," I told her. "See you later, buddy," I added, poking Rashellia, who responded with a smile after Lara kissed her forehead good-bye.

I gave Tina a hug and then gave Grant knuckles, and then Lara and I left. We passed David and Carana in the hall, who decided to walk with us to the gate. "Where are you guys going?" David asked.

"Camping," Lara replied, beating me to the punch.

"So your sister's taking care of Rashellia?" Carana asked me.

I nodded.

"She and Grant may need help, though, so if anything comes up, can you give them a hand?" Lara asked them.

They both nodded. "So where you guys going camping?" David asked.

I shrugged. Lara smirked and whispered to Carana, whose face slowly spread into a smile. "Have a nice trip," they both called to us as we approached the entrance where the guard's desk was.

"I feel bad leaving Rashellia with Tina," I told Lara as we showed the guards our IDs.

"This trip is for you and me to relax. Plus, Rashellia gets into her little fits, and that's not relaxing for you, is it?" Lara replied with a smirk as we scanned our fingers and eyes at the gate before the guards let us through.

"You have little fits too, but I don't leave you at my sister's place," I said, laughing. She punched me playfully as we turned off onto a path leading into the woods. "So where are we going anyway?" I asked her, kicking a rock along the ground as we walked down a gravel road in the forest.

"I can't tell you," Lara giggled, grabbing my hand.

We turned off the gravel road onto a tiny dirt path. About ten minutes later, we finally made it to where Lara wanted us to set up camp. It was an open field, with flowers growing all over and a pond in the middle of the field.

"It's beautiful, isn't it?" Lara asked, looking dreamily into the sky as the sun sparkled off her. I nodded in approval, absorbing the scenery around me. She sat me down on a rock near the pond and then looked back up into the sky, as if in a distant land.

"What's up? You're acting weird," I told her, looking up at the sky, trying to find what she was looking at.

"I think it's time … I've been holding it back for a while now, but now is the time," she said dreamily. I looked at her, confused, as she patted my shoulder, and then she got up, taking a step back from me. "I'm sorry, Lance, but it's time," she repeated, taking another step back.

I watched, confused, as she transformed, but it wasn't her usual fiend battle form. Clouds started to form overhead as white wings sprouted from her back, elegantly unfolding. She closed her eyes, tilting her head back, and recited a prayer in a sing-song voice that put me in a trance, as everything seemed to come to a halt around us.

The bees stopped buzzing, the leaves stopped shaking, and even the birds stopped chirping. Everything fell into slow motion. Her voice had me transfixed as I stared at her beautiful body. A beam of red, green, and blue light shot down from the sky.

She began to float off the ground, spinning around slowly. With a loud crack of thunder that seemed to boom from the heavens above, a blinding flash occurred, making me gasp as I shut my eyes. The wind picked up, seeming to twirl around me, as if I was in a hurricane.

I could hear the prayer being recited but not by Lara; instead, it was what seemed like a thousand voices mixed into one as the wind swirled around us. Then, with a sudden gush of air and a blinding white flash of light, it was over, leaving us in silence.

Chapter 23

The sound of trickling water slowly brought me back to consciousness a few hours later. I felt a hand slowly stroking my hair as water lapped against my feet. I opened my eyes; the dazzling light was gone. Lara was exceptionally beautiful. Her wings fluttered gently in the breeze.

She had cat-like ears and a whip-like tale that swayed back and forth in the wind. She glanced down at me, smiling gently, as she cradled me in her arms. We were lying in the shallows of the pond. She gently wrapped her wings around me, hugging me closely. I could feel her calmly breathing in and out.

She closed her eyes without saying a word and began purring and softly kissing my neck. I closed my eyes, silently returning the kisses. We clumsily rolled deeper into the pond, both laughing like little children as we splashed around in the shallows, still making out.

I ended up on top of her. She stared up at me, and for the first time in a long time, we stared into each other's eyes unblinkingly, as if reading each other's minds. We filled in the gaps that had distanced us over the past few months, falling in love with each other all over again.

"I love you," she whispered into my ear as the water lapped against us.

"Me too. You're the best thing that's ever happened to me," I whispered, remembering back to what seemed like so long ago, when we had first fallen in love.

As night began to set around us, we built a campfire. Lara snuggled next to me in the sleeping bag beside the tent. "Did you camp a lot before the invasion?" Lara asked.

I stared at the fire in silence for a second before replying. "Yeah. Kate, Tina, and I basically lived in the woods, twenty-four/seven, growing up," I told her.

"What are those sounds?" Lara asked, still snuggling next to me.

"Crickets and frogs," I told her.

"They sound so nice at night," she replied. "You told me that you grew up without your parents, so who looked after you?"

I let out a sigh, but I decided to open up to her a bit. After a silent pause passed between us, I said, "Kate was seven years older than me and Tina. Mom died when I was about eight, and Kate started taking care of us. Our father had walked out on our mom, apparently when he found out she was pregnant with me and Tina."

"You and Tina are twins?" Lara asked, nudging me to turn over, which I did. I nodded, and she smiled, resting her head against mine. "Why would he leave?" Lara asked.

I shrugged. "He was young and not ready for a family, I guess. Kate always told me that when he was around, he was always bitter about being stuck at home with her and mom. He liked to travel, and I guess he felt we would tie him down," I told her bitterly.

"I know I've said this before, but you're nothing like your father, Lance," she reminded me, giving me a kiss on the forehead.

We silently watched the fire swaying side to side in the wind. Lara purred, and I stroked her back, occasionally kissing her. "So what happened today?" I asked her as she rolled over to face me.

"I ascended, which basically is just something that happens when a pure-blood fiend goes from childhood to adulthood. I told you a little bit about it in Monatello, if you remember."

I nodded, remembering her mentioning something about it. "So you're more powerful?" I asked.

"Yeah, I can cast spells for longer periods of time, and I won't have tricnoses anymore; plus, I can gain more powers."

"How?" I asked.

"By killing other magical creatures," she replied. I went silent—this didn't sound good at all to me. She must have caught my sense of unease, because she smiled reassuringly. "You know I'll always be the same, though, Lance. Right?" she said, softly rubbing her nose against mine.

I nodded. "Are you always going to look like this now?" I asked. "With the cat-like ears, and fur in random places, and the long whip tail, and the set of angel-like wings?"

"Yes. When a pure-blood ascends, he or she loses the shape-shifting abilities."

"Okay, it doesn't matter to me. I'll always love you for you, Lara," I promised her.

She smiled, and just as she seemed about to say something, a military helicopter flew overhead toward Brawklin and disappeared behind the tree line. Not even seven minutes later, it reappeared, quickly flying back overhead in a northeast direction.

"That was weird. I thought Brawklin was a no-fly zone," I whispered to Lara.

She nodded in agreement as we stared up at the now-clear sky. We lay in silence for a couple minutes, occasionally calling out an idea of what the helicopter was doing. And then the cracking of gunfire erupted from off in the distance, causing us to jump up. I looked in the sky, and the figure of a fiend streaked through it, crash-landing in the field close to us.

"Carana!" Lara cried out as we neared the panting fiend, whose wings were peppered with bullet holes. "Don't move," Lara urged her. Carana quickly transformed to her human form as she lay on the ground, drenched in a pool of her own blood.

"Is she going to make it?" I asked Lara, who was speedily digging through Carana, pulling out bullets and healing the wounds. She looked at me and nodded comfortingly.

"What happened?" I asked Carana, who was fighting to stay conscious.

"All dead … Dracona … back … Rashellia …" she whispered into my ear. Then, with a shudder, her eyes fluttered shut as she went unconscious.

"Heal her!" I yelled in a panic to Lara.

"Calm down; she's fine. She's just unconscious from the loss of blood. Everything is healed. She will live."

I quickly grabbed my assault rifle, slinging my sniper over my shoulder and ignoring Lara's yells as I sprinted across the field into the woods toward Brawklin. As soon as I reached the opening to the gate, the guards opened fire on me. I could see humans being thrown from top floors of buildings to their death below. I crouched behind cover in fear.

The all-too-familiar roar of rage erupted from the tree line behind me, and Lara streaked through the sky, crashing headlong into the entrance, which exploded from the force of the brutal impact. I raced to the door, shooting a fiend that was aiming a fifty-caliber machine gun at her. Bullets seemed to bounce off her as she regained her senses and took me under her enormous wings—bullets ricocheted off them.

Once inside Brawklin, she transformed to her new fiendish form, and I quickly handed her my handgun. We slowly crept through the halls. I killed a fiend as we rounded a corner, spotting him eating a dead human.

The lights were off, flashing red, with a loud siren echoing through the halls. When we finally reached the door to our room, fear clenched my chest. We entered, staring in disbelief at the demolished room. The whole place was trashed. They had obviously been looking for something.

"Rashellia!" Lara screamed at the top of her lungs, exploding out of the room into the hall.

I realized immediately that they must have been searching for our daughter. Drawing my gun, I burst into the hall, chasing after Lara. All the video cameras swiveled, locking onto us and following us as we ran, jumping over all the dead bodies that littered the hall. I was first to burst through the door into Tina's room, and I stopped dead in my tracks. David lay face down, dead, sprawled out across the coffee table, with a smoke still burning in his hand.

"She's gone!" Lara cried out, looking at the empty crib where Rashellia would have been sleeping.

I wasn't paying any attention to her, though. My rifle dropped with a dull thud as I walked to the center of the room, my arms outstretched and my face stained with tears. Tina was hanging by her neck. A sign around her read "*Death to the vermin*," spelled out in her own blood.

I cut her down, collapsing to the floor with her in a heap of tears. "Tina! *No!* Tina …" I cradled her lifeless body in my arms and kept whispering into her ear. "Come on, get up … not you. You can't die. Get up."

"She's dead, Lance," Lara whispered softly, taking her fingers and closing Tina's eyes, which had fogged over with the gaze of death.

"Bring her back. Please. She's my sister," I begged and pleaded with Lara, holding onto Tina. I latched onto Lara's leg, not letting her leave.

She dragged me away from Tina with her fiend strength. "I can't. I'm not a shellian. She's been dead for too long, Lance. There's nothing I can do. I'm so, so, so sorry." Lara tried to comfort me as tears stained her face.

I sat in the corner, crying, while Lara began to frantically search under the rubble for Rashellia. Not caring what happened to me, I walked over to David, reached into his pocket, and pulled out his 9mm. "This one's for you, brother," I muttered to him. I was deranged, driven by anger.

I walked into the bathroom and threw aside the shower curtain. A guard was lying in the bathtub, with a pistol pointed at my chest. Shots rang out—it was like something you would see in a movie. I shot and the bullet sailed through the air, going through his head.

His bullet sailed into my chest, just below my heart. I tried to breathe, but blood seemed to squirt out of my chest every time I let out a breath. I covered my chest with my hand, looking at the blood in shock, as I felt all my strength drain from my body.

"They killed me," I muttered as Lara looked over at me, stunned.

I put a hand on the shelf to balance myself but collapsed to the floor, bringing all the stuff on it piling down on top of me. "*Lance!*" Lara screamed, sliding across the floor to cradle me in her arms.

I gurgled, trying to respond, but I couldn't. Spitting out blood, I raised my pistol to the door as three fiends burst through. I unloaded the whole clip into them, killing them and letting the empty handgun go as my hand dropped limply to the ground.

"Hold on, Lance. We're getting out of here!" she reassured me.

I felt Lara pick me up and hurl herself through the window of the building. Everything kind of went by in a blur. There were fiends on machine guns shooting at us. Lara tightly held my lifeless body in her claws. She landed on the beach, frantically ripping off my shirt to examine the wound. I wasn't sure who was crying more—her or me—as I quickly felt myself fading away.

I brought my hand up, patting her, which seemed to take up all of my strength. I tried to signal that it was okay, knowing there was nothing she could do to save me. In a way, I wasn't scared. I knew one day I would die in this war. I had lived past my nineteenth birthday, which I never would have thought I'd do, not in my wildest dreams.

The thought of leaving and letting Lara down was the only concern I had left as I struggled for my last breath. Lara was bawling, trying to stop the bleeding with her powers, but we both knew it was hopeless.

* * * *

Lance looked up at Lara, who was staring down at him with pleading eyes. "Don't you die on me, Lance!" she pleaded, trying frantically to open his airway.

His face tightened in pain as he raised his hand, grasping onto her shirt and summoning all his strength as he pulled her down to him. "They went northeast," he whispered vengefully, committing his last act in the war.

Tears streamed down her face as she nodded understandingly. "Don't you worry. They won't get away with this," she whispered lovingly as rage boiled in her eyes.

Lance smiled to himself, coughing up more blood, which trickled down his mouth as his grip loosened. His body convulsed violently, and he let out his final breath, closing his eyes peacefully, knowing that he had died a free man.

Chapter 24

"It's time for you to go to bed," 159 told 2-5, giving her a light kiss on the forehead. She briskly got up, walking over to the door.

"Wait, Aunty 159! What happened to Grant?" she asked the young fiend, whose eyes were aged over with many years of pain.

"He managed to make it out and rejoined the resistance," 159 told her solemnly. "There's a note under your pillow. Maybe one day you will be able to piece together the full story of Lance," she told the little girl. She took off her white gloves and lab coat, pulling out a loaded handgun, cocking it, revealing the scar across the top of her left hand.

The little girl's voice was quivering as she called out her final question to 159, who had opened the door to 2-5's room in an attempt to make her escape. Warning sirens came flooding through, filling up the room.

"159! Why would you tell me this story?" she called nervously to the shadowy figure in the doorway.

"Because Lance was your father, Rashellia."